DEADLY WHISPERS

DEADLY WHISPERS

TED SCHWARZ

ST. MARTIN'S PAPERBACKS

Disclaimer

Every effort has been made to assure the accuracy of this book. However, many of the facts came from interviews with Tom Bonney conducted by law enforcement officers, psychologists, and members of the press. Most of these were recorded on audio or videotape which was reviewed and admitted into evidence during his trial. This means that allegations, statements of fact, and statements of personal history that came from Tom Bonney came from a man who has been called a liar, mentally ill, and a multiple personality. That he is guilty has been established by a jury of his peers. That he confessed to the murder has been established through his own recorded statements. Yet he has also professed his innocence at other times, and even claimed that his daughter was alive despite the fact that her corpse was buried. Thus if there are any mistakes made, they have been made unintentionally and with no intention of doing harm to anyone, living or dead. This book is accurate to the best of my knowledge, and the caveat concerning Tom's statements is made to assure there is no misunderstanding given the unusual nature of this case. Although efforts were made to talk with Tom Bonney, he refused all requests for interviews for this book.

In only one instance has a re-creation been made. This is the scene where Tom Bonney is leaving his home and heading to Florida. It has been based on Bonney's interviews with psychologists, psychiatrists, and law enforcement officers. It is believed to be an accurate representation of what occurred, though at no time did Bonney provide a continuous narrative of this period following his daughter's murder.

DEADLY WHISPERS

Prologue

"THEY tell of a young man, who lost his mind upon the death of a girl he loved, and who, suddenly disappearing from his friends, was never afterward heard of. As he had frequently said in his ravings, that the girl was not dead, but gone to the Dismal Swamp, it is supposed he had wandered into that dreary wilderness, and had died of hunger, or been lost in some of its dreadful morasses."—Anon.

"La Poesie à ses monstres comme la nature."
D'Alembert.

"They made her a grave, too cold and damp
    For a soul so warm and true;
And she's gone to the Lake of the Dismal
      Swamp,
Where, all night long, by a firefly lamp,
    She paddles her white canoe.

"And her firefly lamp I soon shall see,
    And her paddle I soon shall hear;

Long and loving our life shall be,
And I'll hide the maid in a cypress tree,
    When the footstep of death is near."

Away to the Dismal Swamp he speeds—
    His path was rugged and sore,
Through tangled juniper, beds of reeds,
Through many a fen, where the serpent feeds,
    And man never trod before.

And, when on the earth he sunk to sleep,
    If slumber his eyelids knew,
He lay, where the deadly vine doth weep
Its venomous tear and nightly steep
    The flesh with blistering dew!

And near him the she-wolf stirred the brake,
    And the copper-snake breathed in his ear,
Till he starting cried, from his dream awake,
"Oh! when shall I see the dusky Lake,
    And the white canoe of my dear?"

He saw the Lake, and a meteor bright
    Quick over its surface played—
"Welcome," he said, "my dear one's light!"
And the dim shore echoed, for many a night,
    The name of the death-cold maid.

Till he hollowed a boat of the birchen bark,
    Which carried him off from shore;
Far, far he followed the meteor spark,
The wind was high and the clouds were dark,
    And the boat returned no more.

But oft, from the Indian hunter's camp
    This lover and maid so true

Are seen at the hour of midnight damp
To cross the Lake by a firefly lamp,
And paddle their white canoe!

—From Irish poet Thomas Moore's work "The Lake of the Dismal Swamp," as it appeared in Moore's collected works following his visit to the Virginia/North Carolina area in 1803.

CHAPTER 1

The Disappearance

HAD the murder victim been someone else, Kathy Bonney would have delighted in the circumstances surrounding her death. There was the mysterious young man, seemingly harmless, who drove off with her under the normally watchful eyes of her father. There was a second stranger, deeply religious, allegedly divinely inspired, who claimed to have let God guide him to the death site. And there was the bullet-riddled body, naked in the water of the Great Dismal Swamp, the nudity hinting at sexual perversion, the truth proving more shocking than the originally suspected rape and murder. For a young woman who longed to write mystery and suspense novels, Kathy would have applauded the way she had been unknowingly stalked for a week by her deadly assailant, the televised trauma of her grieving parents, the baffled police detectives, and the killer so brilliant that he was able to hide in plain sight, invisible even to those who saw him.

It was a story Kathy had to miss, of course. The victim of a murder always becomes the center of attention only after it is too late to appreciate all the particulars of the story in which he or she has the leading role.

Saturday, November 21, Late Afternoon

It was a good time for Tom and Kathy Bonney, a happy time, a period of growing closeness between father and daughter. They had always shared a special relationship, a love more intense than he showed his other children, though he worked hard to prove he had no favorites.

Kathy was the rebellious daughter, yet Tom knew that her rebellion had purpose, direction. It wasn't just the conflict of the generations that caused her to leave the parochial high school where he thought the intensity of the Christian education might teach her to conform. Kathy wanted to be a writer, but more than that, she wanted to explore the sensual side of life. She wanted to be independent, to have her own apartment, to feel responsible for whatever triumphs and failures might come her way.

She had already taken a lover, a seemingly risky situation given that she lived at home and he was married to another woman. Her friends did not think the relationship would last. The intensity of Kathy's passion was fueled more by the newness of the experience than by a deep, abiding love. The friends thought Kathy would outgrow the tawdriness of the man who was cheating on his wife. Kathy would break off with him, then utilize the knowledge of the emotions he had touched in her when creating backgrounds for the characters who peopled the novels she was trying to write.

Tom Bonney had mixed emotions about his daughter. He was saddened by the fact that she dropped out of school, though he recognized that there was a purpose to her actions. Kathy, despite her youth, had a better understanding of what she wanted for her future than her father had. She was a serious-minded young woman, working for him in his business, writing when she had a free moment. She was floundering a bit, occasionally following a path he believed was wrong, yet he felt she was a better person than most nineteen-year-olds. He decided to show her his love. When a man named John called his company, A-1 Salvage, to ask about selling a black 1979 Chevrolet Blazer 4x4 for four hundred dollars, Tom realized it would be the perfect vehicle for Kathy.

The Blazer was in good shape, the man assured Tom. Nothing wrong with the engine or the brakes. You could drive through a rainstorm and the roof wouldn't leak. But it was old, had seen a lot of miles, and the man needed the cash more than he needed the vehicle. He figured Tom could cut it up for parts, making more money selling it in pieces than he would have to pay for the whole thing.

Tom wanted the car if it was as good as the caller said it was, though not to sell it for profit at his scrap business. A-1 Salvage was so successful that Tom often netted a thousand dollars per week. One car, more or less, wouldn't change that. This purchase would be a personal one. It would be a gift for Kathy, showing her how much he cared, how happy he was that her rebellious days seemed to be behind her. He would have John bring the Blazer by the house. If Tom felt it was as good as the man said, and if Kathy liked it, he would buy it for her.

John was unfamiliar with the area where Tom Bonney lived, so the two men discussed possible meeting places, finally settling on a 7-Eleven convenience store at Route 168 and Old Drive. It was not only a place they both knew, it happened to be across from Earl's Supermarket, where Kathy and her mother, Carol Bonney, liked to shop. Knowing that the women would be home shortly, Tom arranged for a late afternoon meeting so that he and Kathy could evaluate the car.

Kathy was quieter than Tom expected as they drove to the 7-Eleven in the family's Chevrolet. She seemed stunned by her father's actions, becoming excited only when she saw the car. As Tom had hoped, it was perfect, at least from the outside, and he suspected the engine and brakes had been well cared for.

"Hello, John," Kathy said, happily walking to the Blazer. The man shifted to the passenger side, letting Kathy get behind the wheel for a test drive.

The man sat close to the passenger side door. He was young, no less than Kathy's age; though no older than around twenty-three, Tom later said. He seemed slightly taller than average, perhaps five feet ten inches and 160 to 170 pounds in weight. He had dark hair, a mustache, and was wearing a baseball cap and windbreaker jacket. The way he was talking, it was obvious to Tom Bonney that the youth was only interested in selling the Blazer. He seemed oblivious to Kathy's attractiveness, a fact that made Tom comfortable with not joining the two of them for the test drive. Besides, Tom thought, Kathy would be pleased with the trust and respect he was giving her.

Tom said he would wait in the lot of the convenience store. He watched the Blazer as John and Kathy drove down the road, looking for signs of unnatural exhaust smoke, a loose muffler, or a damaged undercarriage. Everything looked fine, the Blazer soon out of sight down the highway. Tom returned to his car to sit and wait for John and his daughter to return.

Saturday, November 21, Night

Tom was partially annoyed, partially worried when Kathy did not return to the convenience store as he expected. Perhaps she had gone home to show her mother the Blazer, he thought. Or perhaps the young man asked her to go for a burger and fries to celebrate. Whatever the case, she could call him from the 7-Eleven when she returned. He was going home.

Such a lapse in good judgment was just like a teenager, of course. They were mature one minute, thoroughly irresponsible the next. He was mad. He'd probably threaten to not buy the car after all, or to buy it and cut it up for parts. But in the end he'd give it to her. However, he wasn't going to wait around half the night while she was out joyriding. He went home to his wife Carol and the other children.

Sunday, November 22, Late Morning

Wes Lindquist was troubled that Sunday morning as he sat in the White Harvest Assembly of God Church in Chesapeake, Virginia. It should have been a time of great joy for him. He was employed at the church, handling maintenance and other chores while also going to school. And he was recently engaged to be married to a young woman whom he felt was the answer to his prayers.

But Wes Lindquist had what he felt was an embarrassing past. By his own estimation, he had been a wild youth, chasing after girls in pursuit of casual relationships. His actions and desires were no different from those of hundreds of thousands of other young men, except for the fact that after living such a life, Wes had come to the Lord. He had embraced Christianity, started regularly attending church, reading the Bible, and taking spiritual counseling from Paster Kevin Turner. Many of his desires had not diminished, but they were now focused on the young woman who had become his fiancée after his conversion. Sexual desire was healthy in marriage, he believed, where a man and a woman rightfully give fully and completely of each other, but to have felt such desire before marriage filled him with guilt. He made no attempt to violate his newfound moral standards with the woman he loved, yet he felt that thoughts were as bad as deeds in the eyes of the Lord.

Lindquist was wrestling with such thoughts during the service that Sunday when Pastor Kevin began talking about men who abuse women. His words were meant for those men of the congregation who physically or emotionally abused the women they married. "The pastor started to operate in gifts of the Holy Spirit," Wes later explained. "It moved him to the point where he was weeping, and he asked for an altar call."

The pastor wanted any men who were hurting their wives to publicly admit their actions and seek the forgiveness of God by coming to the altar and kneeling in the midst of the congregation. Then other church members would gather around, laying their hands on the man seeking forgiveness, lending their physical and spiritual support to his desire to change.

"There was one fellow that went forward. Myself, at the time, I wasn't even married. I went forward also," said Lindquist. He had decided that his past actions were disrespectful to women. The fact that the past young women in Wes's life had been willing participants in the relationship did not change his newfound feelings. He was emotionally upset and thought that walking to the altar would be a way to heal himself.

"I wanted to be right with the Lord," he said.

The congregation was shocked to see Wes walking prayerfully up the aisle. They knew he was single, knew his fiancée, knew their relationship together. Wes Lindquist had never been physically or verbally abusive to the young woman. He was a gentle man, always friendly, always helpful around the church.

The other man who came forward was different. That man and his wife had been having marital problems which they were determined to resolve. It was for such a man that the pastor had announced the altar call, and it was to this man that the pastor first addressed his prayers. Then the pastor and the other members of the congregation turned their attention to the troubled Wes Lindquist. "The pastor prayed for me, and nothing really happened," he explained.

Wes, unsure what to do next, left the church without listening to the sermon. He climbed inside his 1982 Chevrolet pickup truck and began driving without thought or purpose. Mile after mile he drove, heading toward the North Carolina border. It was an area that was unfamiliar to him, an area where he had never driven before, yet he was convinced that something was leading him in that direction.

Wes's truck crossed the border, the narrow two lanes of Virginia's highway becoming four lanes as he traveled along Interstate 17 going south beside the area known as the Great Dismal Swamp Canal. The land was beautiful at that time of year, even though the trees had lost most of their foliage and winter weather was approaching. Yet he did not notice the scenery, thinking more about his fiancée, his past, his determination to change and become a better person in his heart, not just his actions.

He drove his truck to the outskirts of Elizabeth City, then turned around and came back, parking on a small turnoff approximately a hundred yards from the Virginia line. He had crossed the median line, the truck stopping so that the driver's side was by the canal. It was one of several areas where you could pull off the highway, enjoying the view, resting, even having a picnic if you felt like staying in your car or sitting on the ground. There was a sign warning people to not dump, though the water's edge held the usual array of paper, disposable diapers, beer cans, broken bottles, and other trash that indicated how frequently people ignored the notice.

Wes took his Bible from the seat beside him and began reading. He wanted to make himself open to the Lord. He felt that God would give him a sign to show that He understood his troubles and would help change his heart.

Hour after hour he read from the Bible, concentrating so intensely that he lost all sense of time. Yet like his experience in church that day, nothing seemed to be happening in his life. Finally, certain that whatever divine guidance he thought he was supposed to receive was not going to strike him as he sat in the truck reading the Psalms, he stepped from the cab.

The area was quite narrow, just wide enough for him to walk between his truck and the canal bank. He looked around, then glanced down toward the trash at the water's edge. That was when he saw the doll.

It was a large doll, he realized. One of those life-size blow-up plastic adult toys that were sold in the back of magazines devoted to sex. You inflated the doll, added a wig and some clothing, and you had a device that was meant to serve as an aid to masturbation. The idea that some men desired such

an item cheapened the sex act far more than anything Wes had ever experienced, a fact that seemed
to indicate to him this might be the sign he was
seeking. He thought he would go down the bank,
pick up the doll, and fling it as far away as he could,
signifying to the Lord his intention to change.

Wes carefully made his way down the side of
the bank. The doll was naked, though it had what
appeared to be a slightly askew wig on top of its
head.

He approached the doll, reached down and
touched its heels and the bottom of its leg. Suddenly, a small amount of blood trickled down what
he was horrified to realize was skin, not plastic. It
wasn't a doll that was naked, it was the body of an
attractive young woman. Her hair was floating on the
water, and her knees were bent up toward her chest,
her head positioned away from him. Her skin looked
slightly mottled, the result of what would prove to be
twenty-seven small-caliber bullet wounds.

Terrified, Wes ran back to his truck, looking about
Route 17 for someone to help him. There was no one
there, and though he could have driven the short dis-
tance to Elizabeth City to call the police, he no longer
could think clearly about what was happening. He
headed back to Chesapeake, desperately searching
for a pay telephone.

Finally a phone loomed up ahead, but Wes realized he had only fifteen cents to make the quarter
telephone call.

Pray. He was certain that God had brought him
to the site of the girl's corpse. God would bring him
a dime.

He pulled his truck near the roadside telephone booth, beseeching God to help him find the extra dime he desperately needed. The image of the dead girl's body seemed indelibly etched on his mind, as though it was crying out for his help.

Looking around, Wes spotted a ten-cent piece on the floor of the booth. To him, it was another sign from God that he was doing the right thing.

He dialed the police, telling them what he found, then returned to where he had discovered the corpse. Within fifteen minutes the first of the police officers had arrived.

Wes Lindquist showed the officer where the corpse was located. He asked the officer to help him move the victim, to cover her. He wanted to protect her modesty, to help her retain whatever dignity might be possible in so brutal a death.

The police officer humored Wes, taking him back up the water bank to his patrol car. The corpse would be covered, her body moved to a more dignified location. It was the least the two men could do, the officer agreed. But first Wes should sit in the back of the patrol car for a moment.

Wes complied, realizing only after the doors were closed that he had been locked in the cagelike compartment used for transporting prisoners. The car's back doors could not be opened from the inside. The officer felt that there was a good chance Wes was the killer, yet he had no probable cause for an arrest. He would keep Wes locked in the car, away from any evidence he might otherwise move or destroy, until the investigators arrived and could make more sense of the murder site.

Sunday, November 22, Late Afternoon

The telephone call came in to the Chesapeake Police Department, Dispatcher Rogers answering. The caller was trying to reach a patrolman who had been working the day shift, an officer who had talked with the caller about filing a Missing Persons report. The officer had explained to the caller that a person had to be missing a full day before the report could be made official.

DISPATCHER: Is it twenty-four hours?
CALLER: Yeah.
DISPATCHER: So in other words, you want to make the Missing Persons report.
CALLER: Yes, ma'am.
DISPATCHER: Where do you live?
CALLER: Four twelve Briarfield. Right down the street from ya'll.
DISPATCHER: Who is missing?
CALLER: My daughter.
DISPATCHER: Okay. How old is your daughter?
CALLER: Nineteen.
DISPATCHER: Okay. And what is your name?
CALLER: Mr. Bonney.
DISPATCHER: Mr. Bonney. Okay. And your phone number?
CALLER: [*Gives number.*]
DISPATCHER: Are you at home now?
CALLER: Yes. Yes, ma'am.
DISPATCHER: Okay. And you have not heard from your daughter, right?

CALLER: No. There is something suspicious about the whole thing.

DISPATCHER: We'll get someone on the way.

CALLER: Can you send an unmarked car, because the neighbors over here, they look out the windows and—

DISPATCHER: To tell you the truth, the unmarked units that we have working today, which is Sunday, they are on another call at this time.

CALLER: Well, when he gets here, just tell him to drive up in the driveway.

DISPATCHER: Okay. Four twelve Briarfield. Okay. Thank you. Bye-Bye.

Sunday, November 22, 7:05 P.M.

Officer Anthony T. Perkins had been a uniformed patrol officer with the Chesapeake Police Department for a little over two years when the dispatcher asked him to go to the home of a man named Bonney. It was a nice home in a good, middle-class neighborhood, the type of suburban dwelling where families feel safe from the violence and horror stories occurring in nearby Norfolk. Crime isn't supposed to touch such people; certainly not the agony of experiencing a missing child.

There were many possibilities, of course. A nineteen-year-old girl was vulnerable to all sorts of pressures. She might have stayed out past her curfew, then been afraid to come home. She might have spent the night with a boyfriend, perhaps even run off to get married. She also might have been a victim of a mugging or rape. Girls that age were often too trusting, paying unexpected consequences for their naive openness to strangers. There were many possibilities, and the investigating officer had enough experience to make no assumptions when he met the man who identified himself as Tom Bonney.

The facts were simple. Kathy Bonney had been born August 26, 1968. She was five feet, two inches tall, and weighed around 110 pounds. She was an attractive girl, according to the photograph on the driver's license her mother gave the officer. And while she had been known to be somewhat rebellious, neither parent thought she had run away of her own free will. She was working as a secretary for A-1 Salvage, just off Military Highway, they explained, and had been in good spirits when her parents had last seen her.

The more Tom Bonney talked, the more obvious it became that he thought his daughter might have met with foul play. He explained that at twenty minutes to seven the previous evening, Kathy and her mother, Dorothy Carol Bonney, known as Carol to her friends, had gone shopping at Earl's Supermarket on Route 168. He told of the call from John about selling the Chevrolet Blazer for four hundred dollars. He told of his decision to buy the vehicle for Kathy, of their going to the 7-Eleven to meet the young man, of her driving off with him.

Tom was extremely upset, though he seemed to calm a bit as he explained about his business. He said he never knew when a call might come, so he had both his home and office number printed on his business card. It was not unusual for someone from the Navy base to decide he needed money at an odd hour of the day or night. The customer would drive what was left of the family car, often a rusted-out body with shattered windshield and torn interior upholstery, to the salvage yard, a friend following in a second car to take him home. Tom would meet him there, perhaps after having been awakened in the early hours of the morning, and they would negotiate a price such as seventy-five dollars, assuming the engine still ran. Then, in the days that followed, Tom would remove whatever parts could be resold to low budget, do-it-yourself car repair buffs. His sales would ultimately bring in ten, twenty, or more times what he paid for the car.

John seemed like just another customer. The only difference was that Tom Bonney wanted John's Blazer for his daughter, not his business. Had he only known what would occur, his daughter missing, perhaps kidnapped, raped, or worse . . . If anything happened that he could have prevented, he didn't know how he could live with himself.

The officer interviewing the Bonneys was not particularly concerned with the Missing Persons report. A nineteen-year-old girl was more likely to be voluntarily shacking up with some guy, perhaps drunk or stoned, than she was to be hurt. The police saw too many of these reports that turned out to be nothing more than a situation where casual partying got out of hand. Sometimes the girl passes out, returning after she has slept off whatever she has consumed, smoked, or otherwise ingested. Sometimes the girl stays out just enough past curfew that she is frightened about returning home, prolonging the inevitable confrontation with her parents until they are so worried that they're satisfied with just having her safe with them, no longer wanting to punish her.

The police officer was finishing with his report when he received a call from the dispatcher. The officer was then linked with the officers at the site where the corpse of a young woman had been found. The body had not been identified, nor was there any reason to think that the missing girl might be the victim. There was also no reason to exclude her. The officer was asked to get a photograph of Kathy Bonney without alerting the family to what was happening. He was to make it sound like a routine procedure, borrowing Kathy's driver's license so her photograph could be compared with the face of the dead woman. It was still too soon to alarm the parents.

Sunday, November 22, 10:15 P.M.

Detective Martin Williams of the Chesapeake Police Department had been at the crime scene since approximately four P.M. He had gone into the ambulance containing the corpse after Officer Perkins brought the driver's license to the canal bank, hoping to make an identification of the victim. The woman had multiple bullet wounds to her head, blood matted in her hair. There were twigs and leaves further concealing the identity, though nothing could be removed for more careful observation. Everything surrounding the corpse that had been recovered from the crime scene might prove important. To handle anything more than was necessary in the process of taking the victim from the water could ultimately affect the outcome of the case. Even transporting her to the medical examiner was a slight risk, though the girl and the surrounding scene had been carefully examined and photographed before the men at the scene carried her into the ambulance.

The Camden County Sheriff felt certain that the victim was Kathy Bonney. This was not an area where young women routinely disappeared. A Missing Persons report and a female corpse coming in the same twenty-four-hour period had to be connected. There were drug problems in the county, rapes, burglaries, and robberies. But the area was not known for transients and hitchhikers. The murdered woman was likely to be local, and the only people reporting someone missing were the Bonneys.

When Detective Williams was back in Chesapeake, three blocks from the Bonney home, he called to see if he could stop by. As he later testified: "When the phone rang, a gentleman answered that sounded like I had woken him up. I advised him who I was and I was investigating the case of his missing daughter. I told him I wanted to come by his house and talk with him about the incident. He told me it was too late at night, for me to come back by.

"I told him it would only take a few minutes and it was very important that I speak with him tonight, being that Sunday night. He once again said it was too late for me to come by.

"I told him I wanted to get a better photo of his daughter, that I only had the driver's license photo. He told me he would leave a copy of a picture in the mailbox the following morning.

"I asked him what she was wearing when he last saw her on that Saturday evening. He said he had already told the officer that. He told me I'd have to wait until tomorrow to get more information from him."

Bonney was exhausted, Williams frustrated. The detective knew that he could not press the issue. There was no way to tell the girl's father that he wanted to try and match her picture to that of a corpse. If he was wrong, the man would needlessly go through hell. And if he was right, waiting twenty-four hours would not really matter. If anything, the family could have a decent night's sleep and be better prepared to handle the shock. Yet Williams wanted to resolve the matter. The sooner the corpse was positively identified, the greater the chance of finding the killer.

The detective knew that Bonney was undoubtedly doing what many parents do in similar circumstances. First there would be anger because the daughter had not returned when expected. Next would come fear. Had she been kidnapped? Raped? Was she lying unconscious somewhere, battered by an assailant? That was usually when the parents called the police.

But once the police made contact without showing undue concern, the parents frequently returned to their earlier feelings of anger. Unless the police mentioned a "Jane Doe" in the hospital or the morgue, the parents reassured themselves by deciding their child was simply acting irresponsibly, perhaps having a tryst with a boyfriend. Usually they knew better. Usually they understood that something very wrong was happening. Yet knowing they could not protect their daughter, wherever she might be, it was easier to accept the fantasy. Anything that forced them to face the probable truth, such as making an extra effort to cooperate with the police that night, was more than they could handle. Tom Bonney's reaction was hindering the murder investigation, but since no one had told him that a murder had occurred, since there was only a Missing Persons report, his reaction was a normal one the detectives had seen frequently in the past.

The identification of the murder victim and the search for the killer appeared to be problems that would be shared by law enforcement officers from two states. Chesapeake police, Camden County Sheriff's deputies, and North Carolina State Bureau of Investigation officers had all been called to the location because of the unusual nature of the crime. The Bonney girl, if that was who the corpse turned out to be, had probably been kidnapped from Virginia, then murdered in North Carolina, dividing the jurisdiction and requiring all law enforcement officers involved to work together.

Such cooperation concerning felonies was not unusual. The area was rural, Elizabeth City's 17,000 population forming the largest North Carolina community in the area. But Elizabeth City was home to both a branch of the North Carolina State University system and the College of the Albermarles. And Route 17 was a major pipeline for drug dealers traveling from New York to cities throughout the South. Murder was relatively rare, but felony crimes involving narcotics, weapons, prostitution, and assault were all too common, and investigators from both states frequently worked together.

The Great Dismal Swamp that runs through parts of Virginia and North Carolina has always been an area that invites extreme reactions from those who pass through. In 1728, Colonel William Byrd II of Westover, Virginia, led a surveying crew along the waterfront. He described the area as a "horrible desart," adding that "the foul damps ascend without ceasing, corrupt the Air, and render it unfit for Respiration . . . Nor indeed do any birds fly over it for fear of the noisome exhalations that rise from this vast body of dirt and nastiness." His party took ten days to travel just fifteen miles, sleeping on the ground, constantly chilled, and forever battling flies that abounded on the land.

By contrast, George Washington saw the swamp as a "glorious paradise" where there was endless wild game and beautiful plant life. The waterway had long been used by travelers, including numerous pirates who found the area an ideal place to escape their enemies.

The pirates were known as privateers by the English, indicating their favored status by Queen Elizabeth I. Often based in the West Indies, these men delighted in stealing from any ship they encountered, not just those that were Spanish.

The North Carolina coastline made an ideal refuge for pirate ships. There were tidal rivers, inlets from the sea, and many sounds. The ships could flee pursuers, or use the waterways for their attacks.

Edward Teach made his home in Elizabeth City when he wasn't terrorizing the high seas as "Blackbeard, the pirate." And there were Peter Michaux, Gentleman Stede Bonnet, and Calico Jack Rackham, among others.

The name Bonney was a familiar one in the Great Dismal Swamp. Almost three centuries before Kathy's body was found along the shore, Anne Bonney, another willful daughter, was leading a life that would give her the notoriety Kathy only found in death.

It was the early part of the eighteenth century when Anne Bonney, tall, attractive, though with a preference for wearing men's clothing, fell in love with a young sailor and ran off with him to the West Indies. No one knows if they were married. All that is certain is that Anne soon learned the man wanted a traditional lifestyle with home and family, while she craved excitement. She found that excitement with Calico Jack Rackham and his band of pirates.

Calico Jack was a man of limited personal hygiene whose life was devoted to fighting, drinking, and plundering the cargo of ships traveling the high seas. He delighted in torturing and maiming the crews of the vessels he captured, regardless of whether or not his victims offered resistance. And it was this ruthlessness that excited Anne, who joined him on his ship.

Soon Anne realized that a mutual thirst for blood

and delight in the screams of one's victims was not an adequate substitute for regular bathing. She abandoned Calico Jack in order to have a love affair with Stede Bonnet, a member of the pirate Blackbeard's trusted crew. Bonnet was apparently as vicious as Calico Jack, but he had the decency to keep his body pleasant-smelling as he dispatched his captives. Bonnet was also a former major in the military, whose background included family wealth and a good education. Since Anne was the daughter of a successful plantation owner, she and Stede had far more in common than sex and violence.

Anne Bonney saw Calico Jack only once after separating from him. He had been captured and sentenced to death, something she felt he richly deserved. She told Jack that a courageous man would have fought until he could fight no more, something Bonnet soon had to do when he, too, was captured. Bonnet escaped once, then tried to use his family's wealth and political influence to buy his freedom. That effort failed and he was hanged on December 10, 1718, in Charleston, South Carolina.

Anne was upset, but recognized that hanging was simply a risk of the business they were all in. She aligned herself with Mary Reed, another woman pirate, and the two of them were quickly captured and taken to England in chains.

Neither woman met the fate decreed for them— hanging by the neck until dead. Mary Reed died from a fever contracted in prison. Anne, on the other hand, declared herself to be pregnant, a guaranteed way to achieve her freedom. Neither pregnant women nor nursing mothers could be killed. She was released without anyone trying to learn if she truly was going to have a baby. She was believed to have returned to America, probably living a far more quiet life in the Carolinas.

Despite its name, the Dismal Swamp was not always so bleak nor limited in use to the perpetrators and victims of violence. By the 1770s it was an important route for the shipping of goods, especially lumber. In November of 1772 land was donated to turn the area into a canal, the construction eventually completed in 1830. The change was so dramatic that the area was considered a paradise for tourists. In fact, on November 22, 1830, the Virginia *Herald* published a glowing description of the land, including the area where, more than 150 years later, Kathy Bonney's corpse would be found:

The scenery on the canal is unique rather than romantic; it is delightful to drive along its banks, or skim its surface, in the morning or evening of a summer's day, when the sun is just above the horizon; the mirror-like surface below reflecting the trees, whose limbs embrace above, forming umbrageous vistas, beyond which the eye now and then catches a view of an opening to the blue firmament and the gliding of the sun beams, relieved by the lengthened shadows of the object upon which they rest, and then, to inhale the delicious fragrance of the jessamine, the laurel, the eglantine and the wild rose, and various other aromatic shrubs and flowers with which the swamp abounds—not even the spicy gales of Arabia can exceed it, and no effort of the pictorial art can do it justice.

There was beauty and there was also a reputation for violence along the Great Dismal Swamp. Many men reported their fear of the area both before and after the construction of the canal. For example, a few years earlier, in February of 1817, a recent Yale graduate named Samuel Huntington Perkins was hired to spend a year as tutor for Dr. Hugh Jones in Hyde County, North Carolina. He had to travel from Norfolk to Elizabeth City along the canal in a horse and gig. Frightened, he wrote in his diary:

"Travelling here without pistols is considered very dangerous owing to the great number of runaway negroes. They conceal themselves in the woods & swamps by day and frequently plunder by night." Resting at Elizabeth City, the relieved young man wrote: " . . . at length arrived thus far without the loss of life or limb."

Many years later the stories of the runaway slaves intrigued Harriet Beecher Stowe. She had never visited the area, but felt that the stories about the slaves might make a powerful sequel to the novel she had written four years earlier, *Uncle Tom's Cabin*. The new book, published in 1856, was called *Dred: A Tale of the Great Dismal Swamp*. The novel sold poorly.

Even the murder of a young girl was not without precedent in the area. In April of 1898 the family of W. H. Cropsey moved to Elizabeth City. There were four daughters, one of whom, Ellie Maude, called Nellie, made an impression on a James Wilcox, who began calling on the family each Sunday. He and Nellie became close friends, Wilcox adding Tuesday and Thursday evenings to his visiting schedules. The couple also began going sailing, to the theater, and enjoying other activities together.

The girl was underage for marriage, so far as her parents were concerned, being just seventeen when the courtship began. Jim brought Nellie presents such as a gold pin with a jewel set in it, a gold ring for her birthday on July 17, and pictures of himself. She was flattered at first, but her interest proved youthful infatuation. What both Jim and Nellie thought was love gradually became, on Nellie's part, disdain.

On the night of November 20, 1901, Jim arrived at the Cropsey home as Nellie discussed her plans to visit New York. They listened to music, but the tension between them was intense. Jim decided Nellie hated him and was going to New York to meet another man. His paranoia was so intense that when she offered him a drink of water, he refused, saying that she might poison the glass.

Jim left shortly after eleven P.M., Nellie walking outside with him. She did not return to the house, nor was a search party able to find her the next day. Jim was conspicuous for not helping with the search, though he made the comment that he did not want anyone thinking he killed her.

On December 27, 1901, Mrs. Cropsey sat in an upper window and saw something floating in the Pasquotank River. Two fishermen in the river saw the same thing, went over, and found Nellie. They tied her body to a stake and brought her in to shore. She had been rendered unconscious by a blow to the head, then tossed in the water. She had not drowned, but was dead just before or just after hitting the water, no liquid having entered her lungs, as it would have if she was still breathing.

Jim was charged with murdering Nellie; his defense was that she had committed suicide. The blow to her head had undoubtedly come when she dived into the water to kill herself, his lawyer argued. The jury did not believe him, nor did the mob of men from the community who stood outside the courthouse, making disruptive noises, demanding Wilcox be punished. At 10:10 P.M. on March 22, 1902, he was sentenced to die by hanging.

Jim's lawyer gained him a new trial, the jury this time deciding that he had struck her in anger, accidentally killing her with a blackjack he was known to always carry for self-defense. The new trial resulted in his conviction for second degree murder, Jim ultimately serving seventeen years. Upon his release, he went to work maintaining the fire department engines and sometimes driving them, sleeping in the firehouse. He killed himself with a shotgun in 1933, the murder/suicide adding another tragic story for the area.

Tom Bonney was neither familiar with the bloody history of the Great Dismal Swamp Canal area, nor was he one of the people who disliked the terrain. In fact, he thought the location one of the most beautiful in the Virginia/North Carolina area, and he had loved it the moment his business partner, John McClung, first took him past the area on the way to some property the McClung family owned in North Carolina.

Tom Bonney had long tried to live in the fast lane. He had always been a hustler and a con man, using the needs of his growing family to justify the turning of a dishonest dollar when whatever "straight" job he had did not pay enough money to make ends meet.

Not that Tom couldn't work hard. He was always willing to work and to travel wherever he felt there was the most opportunity. Over the years, his family had moved throughout the South, living in Georgia, Florida, and most recently, Virginia. The land adjacent to the Great Dismal Swamp was the first he had encountered that made him want to put down roots. The pastoral setting was peaceful, quiet, a place where the pressures of daily life seemed to vanish.

There weren't enough quiet times for Tom. He was a plotter, a schemer, always looking for ways to get through life on street smarts rather than book learning.

Sometimes Tom saved his family from trouble by creating a role they could all play. For example, if he was low on money, he might glance out the window, see a nearby river, and suddenly announce a change of name. "I think I'm going to be Tom Water," he would say. "No. Waterman . . . Tom Waterman . . . Yes, I'll be Tom Waterman." Then he would call his wife and tell her the new family name, instructing her to give it to all the children. Everyone was then expected to only answer to the name Waterman, and everyone but Kathy went along with the scheme.

Not that Kathy argued against her father's name changes. She was the oldest, and had seen her father in action and understood his reasoning. He would change the family name when they were about to lose their home. Then he would rent a new place using the new identity, which had no record of bad finances. By the time this next landlord realized Tom was a fast-talking deadbeat, the Bonneys would be several months behind in their rent.

Then the process was repeated. Tom would begin looking for a new name and a new place as soon as he was hauled into court. The legal proceedings allowed at least thirty days following the formal eviction notice before they all had to move. This was plenty of time to develop his latest scam.

There were many names and numerous landlords over the years. Each time, the owner of the rental home was delighted with the pleasant family he encountered. And each time, the owner later regretted making the rental.

Tom was also a thief at times. He saved enough money to buy himself a motorcycle, then sold it at a small profit, taking the buyer's address when he made the transaction. Later that night, or perhaps in a few days, he would go to the buyer's house under cover of darkness, stealing back the motorcycle. When he was certain he was safe, he would find another buyer, repeating the scam until he felt he had taken advantage of all the potential buyers in a given area. Then he would stop, delighting in the hundreds or thousands of dollars in profit, waiting until the family moved to a different location before starting all over again.

Tom also used religion to try to get ahead. He was raised a Christian, though had come to hate God and despise Jesus, often saying that Jesus got what he deserved when he was crucified on the cross. The anger stemmed from the death of his father, a man who had abused Tom all of his life. It was only when his father was dying that he decided to reconcile himself with his son. He asked Tom, who was living out of state, to come to his bedside, and Tom raced to be near him.

Despite his best efforts, Tom arrived too late. The older man had died, a situation Tom was convinced God could have and should have prevented. Emotionally shattered by what he felt was a personal betrayal, Tom never trusted God again. The next time he was down on his luck, he tried chanting to "Omar," an entity of his own creation.

Yet Tom found that he apparently was favored neither by God nor Omar. Whatever work he was doing over the years seemed to come to an end without the prospect of further employment. He and Carol would have to gather their children and move to wherever there seemed to be the hope of a better future.

Each new move brought the anticipation that their troubles were over. Yet always, in a matter of weeks or months, the situation would be as it had been. Their income would stop. Their wanderings would be resumed. As his father always told him before he died, Tom seemed to be a loser.

Even the thirty-foot motor home he purchased came from a scam. Tom convinced the owner to give him the title so that the proper papers for sale could be prepared. He explained that transferring titles was part of his business as a salvage man, and he would be able to handle it faster and easier than the seller. Then, once the title was out of the man's hands, Tom made the transfer without paying the previous owner. There was no record that indicated any money was still owed. Tom had legal ownership and the previous owner had no recourse.

It was in the Chesapeake area that Tom finally experienced the success that had eluded him all of his life. He no longer needed the con games to stay afloat. He was able to engage in a legitimate business and still prosper.

The naval base brought a constantly changing group of young men and women, always short on money, who were looking for ways to cut their cost of living. A salvage yard proved the perfect small business in such an area, a steady stream of customers seeking still usable parts from old vehicles so they could inexpensively maintain their cars and trucks. Eventually Tom was able to expand to three locations, all of them profitable. That success seemed to make an earlier dream come true.

In the early years of Tom's marriage, back in the late 1960s, when he and Carol—a woman with only a seventh-grade education, and thus only minimal work skills—were moving from town to town, he became fascinated by the television series "The Waltons." It was a show about an extended family living in poverty in a mountain home. The parents, grandparents, and children were hardworking, devoted to one another as they struggled from day to day. John Boy Walton, like Kathy, was the oldest of the children in the television family, and planned to be a writer one day. Mary Ellen Walton was the first of the girls to be married. Everyone pursued their dreams, always devoted to one another.

Tom Bonney wanted his family to be like the Waltons, with himself as the patriarch, dispensing love and wisdom while always working hard to support Carol and their two daughters. When Kathy Bonney, his older girl, became fascinated with writing, he was thrilled. She was like John Boy, and he knew that her short stories and the mystery novels she was writing would be published one day.

Everything was planned around such a future, even the man Kathy would marry. He did not know who that would be as yet, though he had an image of the youth in his mind and would not settle for anyone less. Ultimately he and Carol would be like Grandpa and Grandma Walton, the beloved elders helping and cared for by their children and grandchildren. And always Tom Bonney would be in control, the patriarch into old age. The fact that they were finally finding financial success, that the move to Chesapeake, like the home on Walton's Mountain, would be their last, added to the image.

Death never intruded on Walton's Mountain. The children were always healthy and strong, growing into adulthood, the only danger facing the family coming from a change in the Nielsen ratings, which could result in the cancellation of the program.

Men in Chevrolet Blazers never kidnapped Mary Ellen, as such a man had apparently done with Tom's beloved daughter, Kathy. There was no rape, no torture, no untimely death by violence. The television version of the struggles of daily life always had a happy ending.

His name was "Hitman." At least that was how his friends knew him. He looked like Clint Eastwood in the Dirty Harry movies. Tall, powerful, with slightly slanted eyes as he brought his .44 Magnum revolver, "the most powerful handgun in the world," coldly to bear at his victim's head.

Not that Hitman owned a .44 Magnum. He never thought about buying such a weapon. He favored the .22-caliber revolver, a nine-shot that did not require you to reload so often.

Most people made the same mistake about handguns that Dirty Harry did. A .44 might be powerful, but the bullet will pass through anything—skin, bone, steel, concrete, even a car's engine block. Shoot a man with a .44 and the impact may knock him off his feet, but the bullet will pass through his flesh so rapidly that he may get back up and kill you before you can fire again. A .22 stays inside the body, bouncing off ribs, breaking into shrapnel that will pierce the heart, the lungs, all the vital organs. A .22 is a real killer's gun, the type favored by professionals, the type favored by Hitman.

A .22 was an easy gun to conceal. You could keep the gun under your hat if you wanted, the last place your enemies would look. Or in your car, under the seat or in the glove compartment, where it wouldn't be spotted by passing cops.

Hitman had been nervous about killing the girl. He wasn't comfortable killing women. There just was no pleasure in such an act.

In the week before he killed her, he had been troubled by what he felt he had to do. He had difficulty sleeping, unusual for him. He had taken to wandering through the house, taking the revolver from the shelf, carefully loading the bullets into the chamber, feeling the weight of the gun, spinning the cylinder, sighting with it, then unloading the weapon and placing it back on the shelf.

Kathy had seen Hitman once or twice during that period. Her awareness of him was unnerving, though she said nothing to her family, never realizing the danger. She expressed some unease to a few friends, though none of them thought she needed protection.

Normally he would have been upset to learn his victim was aware of his presence. It was unprofessional, creating an avoidable risk. Yet he had enough confidence in his own abilities that he really did not care about what Kathy had seen or who she told. He could take care of himself, handle whatever problems came along.

There had been others who knew something of his plans. The Preacher tried to talk with him, to tell him about God and man, right and wrong, all the words of the Bible that didn't mean diddly-shit. But Hitman had turned his back on the Preacher years ago. Ever since the night Tom's daddy died and Hitman watched helplessly as Tom raced to his father's hospital bedside, only to arrive too late to reconcile the harsh relationship that had existed for years between father and son.

God was a cosmic joke to Hitman. A bastard. You did what you had to do, right and wrong determined by the person who was victorious.

Hitman had been successful the day of the murder, though that, too, had not gone as planned. There were others present, witnesses who didn't have the nerve to tell what they had seen, yet who had tried to interfere.

One of them had kept him from shooting for a moment, giving Kathy a chance to grab the handgun. The trigger was pulled during the brief struggle, the noise of the explosion catching the witness by surprise. He had watched in horror as the bullet slammed into her head, sickened, in shock, letting Hitman finish what he had started.

Hitman pulled Kathy to the ground, looking at her closely. She was a pretty thing, big tits, small waist. Lots of men wanted to put it to her. And she was a willing partner for some of them. Her father thought she was perfect, but Hitman knew she could be a little slut when she wanted to be. Those Christian schools she went to didn't fool him. Wouldn't fool the cops if they ever found the body.

He stripped her of her clothes and dumped her along the canal bank. He could have arranged the body like she just had sex. Spread her legs, maybe. Some men would have raped her after death just to make it look like a sex crime. Body still warm. Like taking her in her sleep.

That kind of sex was not for him. Disgusting. Nasty. Ideas like that were for perverts, not for a professional like Hitman. Just leave her as she was, knees bent, hair in the water, clothing tossed aside. Let them figure it out.

He could hear the others who were there, watching, crying, begging him not to hurt her more. He paid no attention, though. No one laid a hand on him. No one went to help their beloved bitch. All talk. That's what they were. Witnesses to his power without the guts to ever tell the police. Let them get an eyeful of what a real man could do.

Hitman stepped back, aiming the gun, then firing. The body moved slightly as some of the rounds hit it. Not much. Not like she was trying to escape. She was dead, or so close to it that what little life might still have been in her was no more than a dying ember impossible to reignite. The movement was from the bullets' impact.

The sound was louder than he imagined it would be, though not so loud as when they had been in the car, struggling for the gun. The noise died quickly, though. The water, the grass, the trees all acted as baffles, absorbing the sound almost the instant he heard each explosion. No one outside would know what had taken place. All that would be found would be the naked corpse, riddled with bullet holes.

And that was what had happened. Tom and Carol Bonney were distraught over their missing daughter, not even knowing she was dead. The police had been around, knowing who she was, daring not express their beliefs because the Bonneys could not handle the grief if the investigators were mistaken. But no one knew what had happened. No one realized what Hitman had accomplished. And the others did not talk, could not talk. Not even the one who had accidentally caused the gun to fire the first time.

Hitman was safe. Hitman had committed the perfect murder.

CHAPTER 2

The Clues

Monday, November 23, Approximately 11 A.M.

Sleep, even when fitful, helps change a person's perspective. Tom Bonney was thinking more clearly by the time Detective Williams arrived at the A-1 Salvage Yard. The protective anger he had used to mask his fears for his daughter's safety was no longer in place. He knew she had not run off with a man for a weekend of fun and frolic. He knew that wherever she was, she was in trouble. He still could not face the possibility that she was dead. But he did know that she had to be located quickly, that any information he could provide the police and sheriff's deputies might determine whether or not he would ever see her alive again.

Tom explained to the detective that Kathy had a boyfriend, John Hoskins, who had worked for him until ten days earlier. The man had gone to work at K&T Auto on South Military Highway, though when Bonney called there earlier that morning, Hoskins had not yet reported for work.

Mention of Hoskins was obviously difficult. The man was married, the affair with Kathy an illicit one. Tom hoped there was no connection between Kathy's disappearance and John's not having shown for work, because of John's marriage. The idea of Kathy involved in an ongoing, adulterous affair was most upsetting for him.

Bonney also told Williams that he had gone into his daughter's bedroom, looking for anything that might help locate her. While there, he had come across a diary containing a letter. He expressed great shock at the contents, saying that it contained "nasty things" and four-letter words. Reluctantly, he handed the letter to the detective, embarrassed by its explicit sexual nature and the fact that Williams would know a side of Kathy that Tom had not realized existed.

The detective glanced at the first page of the letter, realized what it was, and pocketed it for possible evidence. Then he questioned Tom concerning whether or not Kathy had ever been arrested or fingerprinted. He explained that fingerprints would be of value if Kathy had been injured and was in a hospital, unconscious. Tom and Carol Bonney had already explained that her purse had been left behind, so a hospital without any other form of identification would need to rely on the fingerprinting.

It seemed to Detective Williams that Tom had not fully heard what was being said. It appeared to Williams a defense mechanism, the man not yet ready to think of his daughter in trouble. The detective knew he could not raise the issue of the corpse, at least not until the identification was more certain.

Kathy might have just run away from home, Tom suggested, though neither he nor the detective seemed to take the idea seriously. She had been thinking of leaving home in recent weeks. She had been saving her money, though it was doubtful she had enough to afford an apartment. Still, she might have gone to the Sandbridge area of Virginia Beach, where the rents were low. Maybe she was in Sandbridge. Maybe they should be knocking on the doors of the apartment. Maybe . . .

The detective listened politely. He was certain the corpse was Kathy's. There was nothing about her disappearance that indicated she might be a runaway.

Perhaps there were dental records? A photograph that showed her features better than the image on her driver's license?

But Kathy's dental records were in cities where the family had lived in years past. And the only photograph was wallet-sized and included all the children, probably giving them less information than they had with the license.

The conversation was frustrating for both men. Detective Williams could not shatter the emotions of this troubled father by telling him they needed to make a positive identification of a corpse. Tom Bonney felt he was somehow betraying the daughter he loved, the daughter he prayed would return home.

As they finished their conversation, John McClung, Bonney's partner, came by and mentioned that there had been calls on Saturday from a man who identified himself as "John." McClung said that he had not been concerned about them because he thought the calls were from John Hoskins. Now that he knew about the other John, the man with the Chevrolet Blazer who had ridden off with Kathy, he wondered if there might be some connection.

Williams asked for more details about the man with the Blazer. Tom Bonney thought for a minute, then remembered that there was a large toolbox positioned in such a way that the passenger door could not be opened. Instead, the driver had slid over to the right, letting Kathy climb onto the driver's side. Perhaps the tools would be a clue to the Blazer owner's profession.

Gently, without revealing the certainty that Kathy Bonney was dead, Detective Williams helped Tom Bonney focus his mind until he was gradually remembering more and more details. Kathy had been wearing a green sweater, Tom recalled. Green pants. And pierced earrings, the simple type with a single loop through each ear.

Tom was embarrassed when it came to talking about underclothes. But Kathy usually wore a teddy or camisole type of undergarment. Tom didn't recall the specifics from that day, though he was certain about the green sweater.

The questioning lasted no more than twenty minutes. Everyone was trying to keep busy so they would not think too much about what might be happening to Kathy. Tom was constantly being distracted by questions from his wife, Carol, or his partner, McClung. Everyone was doing what they could to avoid facing the possible horror that awaited them.

Williams left with the letter, not certain whether it would prove of value. He would have a crew dust Kathy's bedroom for fingerprints later in the day. He was hoping that they would match those of the corpse so that a positive identification could be made before notifying the family of the tragic outcome of her disappearance. Only then would they ask the Bonneys to view the body and make a formal confirmation.

Monday, November 23, Afternoon

Williams read the letter Kathy Bonney had written and left in her diary. It was apparently a rough draft which might or might not have been rewritten or sent. Whatever the case, it presented a new angle and several possible new suspects. The letter was to John Hoskins, the salvage yard's former employee and her boyfriend.

Kathy began by expressing her surprise with herself for having an affair with a married man. She told of trying to forget that fact, of putting aside thoughts of his wife and child.

The letter related her fears of men. She told of her previous boyfriend, a seemingly gentle youth with whom she had a strong relationship only he had wanted to make more intimate.

Kathy had been quite uneasy making love to him. Their sex had been voluntary, but it brought up memories of less pleasant past intimacies. She said that she thought she was going to start crying when they were finished, her mind torn between the past and the present.

The letter told how she was certain that her lover would not hurt her, yet she was confused during sex. She said that part of her enjoyed what they did very much. Part of her was thinking that he might hurt her.

Overall it was a sad, gentle, loving letter, the type that intimates might share when trying to build their relationship to a new level. Kathy was obviously emotionally committed to the man. It was equally obvious that such a letter would be very difficult for any parent to read, especially one who employed the man to whom it was going to be sent, a man who already had a wife and child.

Monday, November 23, 5:30 P.M.

Williams arrived at the Bonney residence with an agent for North Carolina's State Bureau of Investigation and a Chesapeake Police Department identification technician. They needed fingerprints from Kathy's possessions to see if they matched the corpse. In addition, they took a small mirror, a larger mirror from the dresser, a can of foot spray, some hair from her hair brushes, and a photograph of Kathy with another female approximately the same age as the victim. It was from this material that the preliminary identification would ultimately be made.

Tom Bonney stopped by the police station on Monday night, spending an hour talking with the detectives. He was sick from worry and had not slept well. His head ached. His stomach was in turmoil. The fingerprint work with the corpse had not been completed as yet, nor would it be the next day. All the detectives could do was reassure Tom that they were working on the case.

On Tuesday a photograph of the face of the corpse was shown to the Bonney family members, including Kathy's aunt, Linda Oakley, and various friends. John Hoskins had been located by then, and he, too, was shown the photograph. None of them were able to make a positive identification of Kathy. The bullet to the head and the other damage she had sustained made accurate identification impossible.

Tom and Carol Bonney kept their reactions to themselves. They were frightened, looking at the photograph, terrified they would see their daughter's face, equally frightened that they would not.

If the picture was of Kathy, then their hopes and prayers were for nothing. For Tom it would have been a repetition of his childhood nightmare where he raced to reconcile with his dying father, arriving too late. Again there was so much he wanted to say, to do. Again he would have been denied even a last few moments with the beloved child he had once thought would outlive him.

And if the picture wasn't Kathy's, then that meant the police no longer expected her to be found alive. The police were assuming that she had met with violence, perhaps torture, rape, mutilation. God knew what some sick mind might have done, might be doing, to their child. Kathy might be alive, helpless, in excruciating pain. Or she might be dead, her last hours ones of agony.

The act of bringing the photograph meant that the police were convinced there was no love tryst. Kathy had not run off with some man. Kathy was a victim, and if the picture they brought was the wrong one, the next photograph from the next corpse would be the proof they were seeking. Or the next. Or . . .

And so the Bonneys looked, terrified, saying nothing, holding in their emotions until they could be sure, waiting for a day they prayed would never come.

John Hoskins was the primary suspect. Never mind the incident with the Blazer. Unless this was a chance killing or an oddly arranged meeting with a new lover, it seemed logical that the Blazer incident had nothing to do with the missing Bonney girl. Assuming the corpse was Kathy's, and there was still no reason to think otherwise, perhaps she had had the driver of the Blazer drop her off at a prearranged meeting spot with Hoskins.

Hoskins was taken to the Chesapeake police station for several hours of questions. He was shown Kathy's writing, and he stated that he had received a similar letter from her. Obviously the note was a rough draft. He certainly denied nothing.

The police and sheriff's deputies hoped the case would resolve itself with Hoskins, but there was nothing suspicious about the way he handled himself. If anything was unusual, it was the number of men named John in Kathy's life. John was the name of her father's partner, her current lover, the man who had driven the Chevrolet Blazer. Her father knew two of them, was certain they were not the ones who had taken Kathy away. Yet the idea that she was kidnapped by the man in the Blazer was just one possibility.

The police had to examine all possibilities. The detectives considered that Kathy may have black-mailed her lover. He was married, with a child. If his wife learned of the affair, the divorce settlement could break a man who was not earning much money. They may have quarreled, Kathy making a scene. Scared, desperate to protect himself from Kathy's revealing their secret, he might have lashed out at her.

Either one of them could have had the gun, though it was more likely that the weapon was his. Perhaps the first shot was an accident, the remainder meant to cover up. Or perhaps he became enraged, out of control, firing at Kathy then firing again and again, emptying the gun, reloading, emptying, reloading, shooting until he ran out of bullets and could only click the trigger in helpless frustration.

Not that such a scenario was probable, nor did the police have a basis in fact for such supposition. It was simply their job to explore all possibilities because, in that way, they would overlook nothing and no one. At that stage in the investigation, every-thing had to be pursued.

The various investigating officers each had their suspicions, though they realized that suspicions meant little and often proved wrong. No one and nothing about the crime scene evidence could be overlooked until all facts were obtained.

There was another search of Kathy's room on Tuesday evening, this time in an effort to gain more of a sense of her life. Personal writings were tak-en, some magazines, and other items. The informa-tion would be used with the investigation, but by the time it was gathered, the technical experts had enough material to make a positive identification. The officers involved would be notified the following morning, then would have to break the news to the family.

Wednesday, November 25, 12:26 P.M.

Three men went to the Bonney home to tell the family that the corpse that had been found along the Dismal Swamp Canal was definitely that of their daughter. Detective Williams was accompanied by Special Agents Kevin McGinnis and Ken Enscoe of the North Carolina State Bureau of Investigation. They explained that there was a definite fingerprint match. There was no chance for error.

The Bonneys should have been prepared for the news. They had seen a photograph of the dead girl found along the canal. They knew that, logically, a missing daughter and an unidentified female corpse could well be connected. But humans survive on hope, and Tom and Carol Bonney were no different. They had avoided focusing on what the photograph told them was a probability. They had not let themselves think that there was no chance for their daughter's return. They either avoided thinking at all or focused solely on the actions needed to get from day to day—cooking, cleaning, working in the salvage yard, taking care of the other children.

But there was no way to avoid the news they were presented with. Both husband and wife screamed in agony on the couch on which they were sitting.

Then Tom began crying out, his words almost incoherent, his breathing abnormally rapid. He slid onto the floor, telling the detectives he thought he was going to die. Suspecting a heart attack, Detective Williams summoned a medic unit from the nearby fire station.

The paramedics found Bonney hyperventilating, not suffering from a heart attack. They had him breathe into a brown paper bag to calm him, talked with him a few minutes, then left. He remained in control as the detectives talked with him about arranging to prepare a composite drawing of the man in the Blazer. A police expert would guide him through the process in an effort to alert the public to the suspect's appearance.

News of the victim's identity was quickly conveyed to the media. Reporters from both Virginia and North Carolina radio and television stations, as well as from the newspapers, soon converged on the Bonney home. They wanted statements from the family, video coverage of the couple's grief: corpse at five, tears at eleven. How did it feel to discover that your daughter was stripped of her clothes, riddled with bullets, and dumped in the water, Mrs. Bonney? Do you want to warn other parents about this psychopathic degenerate who shoots naked girls, Mr. Bonney? I don't suppose we could go with you to the morgue to get a picture of you screaming hysterically as you look at the body, Mr. and Mrs. Bonney? After all, inquiring minds want to know.

The pressure was intense, though not because the case was a national one. The story was a big one for

Elizabeth City, but murders happened all the time in both Virginia and North Carolina. Most killings are committed by friends or family of the victim. The killers are caught quickly and, unless there is an unusual aspect to it, the story is good for the nightly news lead for no more than twenty-four to forty-eight hours. If that was the case with the Bonney death, they'd milk it for all it was worth, then get on with more important events.

There was always the chance that there was more to a murder than a violent act between former friends, though. With luck, the death would be caused by a serial killer who would strike again and again.

Serial killers, especially those who prey on attractive young women, are a reporter's delight. An assignment to the Elizabeth City area was almost as far from the big time of television and newspaper journalism as you could get. Usually the stories involved the weather's effect on the local economy, or perhaps some local official being honored by the Loyal Order Of Waterfowl Lovers Lodge #27. If Kathy's death led to a story about kinky sex, torture, bondage, and mass murder, an ambitious small-town reporter could make an instant reputation with the networks. There would be the remote with Dan Rather, Tom Brokaw, or one of the other giants of the business. There might be a sixty-second backgrounder for the "Today Show" or "Good Morning, America." And then the offers would come in—Chicago, Los Angeles, New York.

Logic and experience told the reporters that Kathy Bonney's death was not going to be part of a Hillside

Strangler or Boston Strangler type of case. But hope springs eternal in the hearts of the desperate, and there is nothing so desperate as a young journalist covering a backwater beat. The Bonneys were intensely pressured to make their grief as public as possible, a situation that added to the nightmare they were experiencing.

The news reports were avidly watched by a number of clergymen throughout the Chesapeake, Norfolk, Elizabeth City, and surrounding areas. This was the type of event on which they thrived, on which they built their Sunday sermons. And those sermons were as varied as the members of the diverse religious community.

Many churches added the Bonney family to their prayer list. They prayed for Kathy's soul, for the parents to know the peace of the Lord, for the change of heart of the unknown killer.

Some preachers were not so accepting of life. Among the sermons preached following the news were ones that stressed that men and women die as they lived. Kathy Bonney was found naked and alone, a death that awaits any woman who is disobedient, who wears sinful clothing and mocks the ways of the Lord. Bible passages concerning the fate of harlots, the devious ways of Satan, and the ultimate retribution of Jesus, sent chills down the spines of the upright, uptight members of such congregations.

Among the more extremist church groups, there were parishioners who told of becoming suspicious of outsiders. Some found themselves videotaping every newscast that appeared on television in order to have a complete picture of what was taking place. "I don't know why I did it. The Spirit led me to the VCR and told me to put in the tape," said one woman who lived near the Bonney family. "I made a scrapbook of clippings from the newspaper. I kept everything I could find, trusting in the Lord to show me what the purpose was. My husband thought I was crazy, but he's new to the Lord and not so strong as I am. I just knew that I was being led, and someday I'll know the reason. Someday I'll need all that."

The woman's home was filled with books, many of them unread, relating to the speaking in tongues, the end of the world, and the ways the Lord will bring people to Heaven. There were pictures of Jesus, a well-worn Bible on a stand near a rocking chair, needlepointed sayings from the Bible, and a cross on the wall. The television in one corner was large, a shelf filed with videotapes marked according to the different television evangelical programs that had been recorded, apparently, since the VCR was first purchased. She smiled as she talked, comfortable in the belief that she was safe from Satan, though understanding the risks everyone else—those "of the world"—were facing.

To some of the police officers, the "nuts had come out of the woodwork." They talked of people coming to them with the names of the murderer, names that came to them in visions, dreams, or through the direct speaking of the Holy Spirit.

Other officers seemed to be more resigned. They had seen it all at other times, usually involving violent, temporarily unsolved crimes. One explained that he felt it was the way the people gained a sense of control over the chance happenings of life:

> Blame the victim and you can be safe. If you think that someone is running loose, choosing his victims at random, then anyone might be killed. That's too scary for these people. They make the Devil real. They make killers conform to rules of their creation. They bless themselves and spend a little more time in church. And if all their "magic" fails, they feel that they won't suffer what others have suffered because they will be taken immediately to Heaven.
>
> I don't find it any crazier than anything else we do to try and make us feel in control. I'm no braver than the next guy. Most of my work is pretty routine. I've drawn my revolver a few times, but that was for show. I never really expected to use it. Yet the only reason I feel safe going into situations no one in their right mind would normally go into is because I've got my gun and my nightstick. They're my talismans. They make me special. It's bullshit and I might not come home some night. But I feel better. I feel more in control.
>
> If some of these people want to use their belief in Satan the same way, I won't argue with them. They've got their way to cope, I've got mine. We're all just trying to stay alive and enjoy old age. We're all just trying to make some sense of the unexplainable.

And constantly the media reminded the public that a teenage girl had died, her killer at large. They reported the news with an intensity that fanned the flames of fear, intolerance, and superstition, while frightening the viewers and readers with their constant reminder of human mortality.

There had been a time when Tom Bonney would have loved the media's attention. It would have made him feel important, like John Walton, Sr. He would have delighted in getting videotaped copies of the broadcasts, playing them and replaying them for Carol, Kathy, and the other children.

Tragedy had a way of turning the fantasy world of television into a sick reality. Tom's favorite television shows would have had a happy ending to the crisis. The corpse would be that of some other girl. His daughter would be lying in a hospital bed somewhere, the victim of traumatic amnesia, from which she would miraculously recover the moment she saw her mother and father. And it would all take place—the crisis, the anguish, and the joyous reunion—in no more than two hours, including commercials and preview of next week's attractions.

Kathy's death was that aspect of real life no parent ever wants to face. Parents envision themselves growing old, then dying peacefully in the loving care of their adult offspring.

Kathy Bonney's death was particularly painful for her father because Tom felt himself responsible. He was the one who had made arrangements for John to let Kathy examine and test drive the Chevrolet Blazer. He was the one who had driven Kathy to the convenience store where she climbed into the vehicle to see how it handled. He was the one who had stayed behind, not even checking the Blazer's license number, waiting in the family car while his precious daughter was alone with a stranger.

Yet Tom had been through similar circumstances hundreds of times before. Nobody wants to cheat the salvage man. The customer wants money. The salvage man has the cash to pay for the car. The vehicle is examined, test driven, then an offer is made.

But murdering Kathy? It made no sense. The man must have been a psychopath overcome with violent lust, driven to a frenzy in a way that could not have been anticipated.

Yet he should have been suspicious, Tom told himself. He should have protected his daughter. He should have . . .

Linda Oakley, Kathy's aunt, had gone through some of Kathy's papers just before the family learned of the girl's death. Among them was a letter Kathy had written to the editor of the Virginia *Star-Pilot*. The letter, which expressed outrage over the leniency given to a murderer, was waiting to be mailed when Kathy was killed.

Kathy's rage had come after she learned that a man who admitted to killing his daughter, a two-month-old infant, was sentenced to just six months in jail. She was irate that so short a sentence could be imposed for so violent a crime. The letter made those who saw it wonder if perhaps she had been the victim of a killer who had also been shown too great a leniency in the past, a man or woman who had been released from jail only to kill again.

Kathy's unpublished letter addressed the feelings of the child who had been murdered, a child who might have begged her father to spare her life. She complained that children have no rights, and because they have no rights, some are no longer alive.

The letter continued, berating the defense lawyer who asked the judge not to give the father any jail time so that his career with the U.S. Navy would not be interrupted. And she expressed her anger with the judge for only giving the father the six-month sentence.

She went on to ridicule the fact that the father expressed regret for what he had done. She related regret to what someone might feel when you accidentally bump someone else in public and say "I'm sorry." She felt that regret in the case of a man who killed his daughter should not be a factor in sentencing which, Kathy believed, should have been far harsher.

Kathy's family also wondered if her killer had also been someone who had been given a second chance by some judge; if he, too, had said he was "sorry."

There had been a time when Tom Bonney felt at home in Chesapeake. Five times in six years the Bonneys had been uprooted, moving to a new location in search of more work and a better life. It was only when they reached Chesapeake, when the salvage business began making high profits, when they could finally afford a nice home, that they thought their frustratingly nomadic existence was at an end.

Tom and his partner, John McClung, had become financially successful with their ownership of several salvage yards. Tom had been living in a shack when he met John, his family seldom having adequate food to eat. But John had the business sense that Tom lacked, and Tom had the street wisdom that John needed. Together they had made money, their business bringing Tom a standard of living better than any he had known since he finished his military service twenty years earlier.

Kathy's death soured the previously sweet success. He did not know why Kathy had been murdered. He did not know if the death was somehow personal or just a random act of violence such as had never been experienced by himself or his family. Either way, he felt that staying where they were meant exposing his wife and surviving children to potential danger. Moving would be difficult, but it was better than having some other family member hurt or killed.

Tom needed money to move, though. The family had acted in the same manner as young couples experiencing their first well-paying jobs. They bought whatever they needed, then whatever they wanted, too delighted to finally have money coming in to ever think about saving. The Bonneys were past the limits of safe debt, and in financial straits that might force them into bankruptcy.

The salvage business was seasonal as well, not a comforting thought when creditors were hounding you. Tom and his partner were experiencing the period when costs were fixed while income was down. There were a lot of pressures on him, pressures that were making him extremely agitated. He frequently complained of headaches, and his stomach was in turmoil no matter what he ate. He would survive because he always survived. However, there were no savings to be used to move the family to another area where they could start fresh, safe from the horror of the violence they had just endured.

The media were sympathetic to the Bonney family. The couple seemed to represent an earthy version of the American dream. They lacked the education to ever go from poverty to great wealth. But they had established a comfortable middle-class existence against all odds.

Tom Bonney's struggles and concerns were more than matched by those of his wife. Carol had known rough times from the time she was a toddler. When she was two years old and playing in her home in the small community of Summerville, Georgia, her mother was cutting a relative's hair. Backing up to look at the hair, her mother's housecoat came too close to a heater. The material burst into flames and Carol watched in horror as her mother went running from the house, screaming, too out of control to think about putting out the fire. By the time help arrived, her mother was too badly burned to survive.

Carol never knew her father, though she was aware that she had numerous half brothers and half sisters. The children were divided among the relatives, Carol moving in with her aunt and uncle, Willie and Lee Brown. Apparently there was a problem with the Lees having custody; Carol was moved to a foster home for a while after the community's Social Services agency stepped into the case. However,

Carol felt the only love and parenting she had ever known came from the Browns, ultimately returning to them.

Carol was twelve when she had the next serious trauma in her life. Her aunt Willie asked her to go to a small store and buy a few items she needed. Along the way a boy Carol knew pulled alongside the road in a vanlike vehicle. It was filled with adolescent males out for a good time at any expense. When Carol got into the truck, they drove her to the woods, tore off her clothing, and took turns raping her. Only the last one, a boy she did not know, refused to get involved. He showed her a path through the woods that would lead her back to the road on which she had been walking. He had her put on her clothing and flee.

The aftermath of the gang rape was predictable for a small town. The sheriff came and took the report, then Carol went into the bathroom and washed herself in a tub filled with hot water. She cleansed her body again and again, trying to erase the physical memory of the event. Then she went to bed, experiencing such depression that she did not leave the room for three weeks other than to go to the bathroom.

There was never any prosecution, though Carol knew one of her attackers by name. She lived in the type of small town where scandals are best not mentioned, especially when the victims are "only" female and "no long-term harm" is done. Even her aunt and uncle shared such sentiments, clamping down on her as though she had been the aggressor, not the victim. Carol was placed under a strict curfew, not allowed to go out at night. Eventually she was able to obtain a job, though her future was severely limited by the repressive nature of the aunt and uncle who raised her.

Carol had been taught that success came through others. A woman could never be independent. Her role was to get a job only until she could get married. Then she became her husband's responsibility, her future being endless days of raising babies and shopping for whatever the family could afford. The more possessions she acquired, the greater her status in the community. And the more people would forget that she was involved with the rape.

Carol Bonney could barely read or write. She had never obtained a Social Security number and did not have a driver's license. Kathy was her link with the world at large. Kathy was chauffeur and confidante. Kathy may have worked for Tom Bonney, a man who tried to dominate his daughter's life, but she earned three hundred dollars a week, enough money to give her real independence. She also had the zest for life and the desire to experience the world at large that Carol had known until the adolescent rape experience and its aftermath. Kathy's death meant more to her mother than the loss of a daughter. It meant the end to her awareness of an existence outside of home and immediate family.

Carol was not the only person who relied upon Kathy. The teenager was known to have encouraged troubled friends to stay in school. She had developed a strong social conscience the last year of her life, making plans to give her outgrown clothing to the needy. She had even convinced her family to let her fix a simple Christmas meal rather than the elaborate feast they had planned to celebrate their growing prosperity. The food they otherwise would have consumed was to be donated to one of the shelters.

The pain of such a loss was so great that Carol told reporters, "I want him caught. If police can't do it, I will figure out a way to do it myself. I will not let a murderer walk around free. It ain't right."

The newspapers and television crews were becoming emotionally involved with the story. What had once seemed like a ticket to network success was increasingly a human story. The more the reporters interacted with the family, the more they were moved by the tragedy they were witnessing. When Tom Bonney explained his desire to leave the area in order to protect his family, the television crews gave him airtime to ask the public for money. He had already borrowed his limit to pay the unexpected funeral bills. The additional money would help the family get away, to start over somewhere else.

And the public responded. No one is certain how much money came in, but John McClung reported that the family began receiving five dollars from one person, ten dollars from another. The amounts were usually small, though they represented all the public had to give. It was an incident that touched the hearts of many, who wanted to help in any way their circumstances allowed.

KATHY C. BONNEY

CHESAPEAKE—Kathy Carol Bonney, 19, of the 400 block of Briarfield Drive, a secretary, died Nov. 22, 1987, in Camden County, N.C.

Miss Bonney, a native of Norfolk, attended Bethel Baptist Church. She was employed with A-1 Auto Parts Inc., in Virginia Beach.

Survivors include her parents, Dorothy Carol and Thomas E. Bonney of Chesapeake; two sisters, Susan C. Bonney and Jennifer A. Bonney, both of Chesapeake; three brothers, Richard Bonney of Norfolk, Tom Bonney Jr., and John Bonney, both of Chesapeake; and maternal grandmother, Mary Louise Bonney of Norfolk.

The funeral will be conducted at 2 P.M. Sunday in Hollomon-Brown & Snellings Funeral Home, Great Bridge Chapel. Burial will be in Forest Lawn Cemetery in Norfolk.

The family will be at the funeral home from 7 to 9 P.M. Saturday.

Virginia Pilot
November 27, 1987

Friday, November 27, Approximately 6 P.M.

Tom Bonney arrived at the Chesapeake Police Department's Detective Headquarters in Great Bridge to meet with Robert Castelow. Bonney was the only witness to his daughter's apparent kidnapper, and he agreed to do whatever was necessary to locate the man known only as John.

Bonney appeared to be in a stupor when he arrived. It was as though the emotional turmoil of the past few days had drained him of all feelings. He had a bad headache and was bothered by stomach problems. "He asked me if I had ever felt like that, and at the time, I replied I had," Castelow, the police artist, said later. "It was usually the morning after I had had too many drinks the night before."

But Bonney was not hung over. He had not been drinking. He was deeply hurting, though the more he talked about his troubles, the more his voice developed a whining tone to it. Even the most compassionate officers found that the sound of his voice was grating, and they wished he would help complete the sketch as quickly as possible and get out of there.

Detective Castelow ignored the voice and went to work. "In doing composites, we get a general description of the person that we're doing a composite of, and we have a standard set of questions we ask, such as sex, male. He stated he was a Caucasian male of medium height, medium build, young age—he stated in his earlier twenties—with brown hair that was cut not short but not long. A small amount of straight brown hair. Stated he was wearing a hat and had a mustache."

The composite begins in a general manner, utilizing the height, weight, and build. A standard face with standard features is completed, then the person is asked what is wrong with the drawing. The shape of the face is corrected if necessary, then the size of the nose, the mouth, the eyes, the amount of hair. One feature at a time becomes the focus, allowing the witness to remember each detail.

The work is handled using an Identi-Kit made by

Smith & Wesson. The kit contains a series of over-lay films for each feature, each film coded. When the work is completed, it can either be duplicated with a copier or the codes can be used by another technician utilizing the same kit to produce an identical match.

Detective Castelow was encouraged by the composite because the face looked familiar. However, when Bonney left the station, one of the other officers glanced at the Identi-Kit image, then informed the detective that he had drawn a self-portrait. As occasionally happened when working with overwrought victims, Bonney had described the officer handling the identification instead of the suspect. Such a situation was frustrating for everyone, though there was nothing more to be done about it.

Tom Bonney returned to the police station around five o'clock that evening in order to talk with Detective Williams. He was asked to go over what happened again, Williams knowing that each time a witness is asked to repeat what was seen, the memory becomes clearer. Minor details, overlooked during the first few tellings, are recalled. Sometimes such details add very little. At other times, the details provide the answers that lead to an arrest.

Williams later stated: "He said that John had called the house around dinnertime on the previous Saturday, that being the twenty-first. He said that Kathy, Dorothy, and Susan were at the store at the time of the call. Tom had told John that his wife would be back in a short while. He said they got back in about twenty-five minutes after the conversation. Mr. Bonney told Kathy about the call and the Blazer, and then he and Kathy got into the car, went to the 7-Eleven, Battlefield Boulevard and Old Drive." He and Kathy took the Chevrolet Impala that was used as a family car.

"He said that while at the 7-Eleven he pulled his car up beside the Dumpster, which is on the side of the lot, and waited until John arrived. That took about twenty minutes. He said the Blazer pulled up right beside his car, the Chevrolet. John got out of the car, walked over to Tom and Kathy. They got out of their car and Kathy said, 'Hello, John.' He responded, 'Hello, Kathy.'

"Kathy got behind the wheel. John got in. Mr. Bonney said he was going to go along [ride in the cab of the truck with the other two during the test drive] but because the toolbox was in the way, he couldn't get in. Kathy said she'd be right back, in approximately ten minutes or a few minutes, and [the car] headed north on Battlefield Boulevard.

"Mr. Bonney said he waited at the 7-Eleven for Kathy Bonney to return for between thirty and thirty-five minutes. He then went home to see if possibly she had gone there to show the Blazer to her mother. She was not at home. He said he stayed home the entire night waiting for Kathy to come home.

"He told us that Kathy had once stayed out all night, but that was when they had lived in Virginia Beach on Bow Creek Boulevard. Since she had moved to Chesapeake, Kathy didn't have any friends, and neither he nor his wife knew how to contact her or even how to try to contact any of her friends.

"Mr. Bonney said he didn't talk to anyone that evening. But he couldn't remember what time he had gone to bed. He did say that he had locked all the doors and the windows so that he could tell if Kathy was trying to get in or trying to come home. She—according to him—she did not have a key to the house.

"[Bonney] said, Sunday morning, the twenty-second, he had got up approximately seven o'clock. Kathy still wasn't home. He checked the bedroom. He said about a half hour later he went to our police headquarters. His wife, Dorothy [Carol], was home cooking breakfast. He said there he saw Officer Hardison. He was told to wait twenty-four hours before making a report, and she had only been gone about ten hours."

The rest of the statement was familiar. Tom Bonney again described the clothing his daughter was wearing, and the fact that she had left her purse on the seat of the Impala. He mentioned that she had a favorite ring made from silver, with a turquoise stone, but said that she had not been wearing it. The detectives had already found that ring during the search of the bedroom.

Bonney said that when he checked his daughter's room, Kathy's diary was missing. He did not know if that had any significance. She was extremely private about the book, writing everything that happened to her on the pages. Only once did she voluntarily offer to let someone read from it, and that offer had been made to John McClung, who refused. Tom admitted that he had tried to sneak a peak at it when the family lived in Virginia Beach, but Kathy caught him, took it, and left the house, staying out all night. She wanted to worry him, as punishment for invading her privacy, and it had worked. He had not tried to look at it again.

"He was asked whether or not he had had any firearms," Williams continued. "He said he had a .22 sawed-off rifle that had been stolen from his wrecker earlier. Said the rifle had a scope on it, but he couldn't tell us the brand, serial number, or anything that would identify the rifle. Also, there was some ammunition taken during the theft. He was not certain about how long the rifle had been missing, but he believed it was just before John Hoskins was fired from the business."

Bonney remembered one other detail, though it was not very helpful. The Blazer owner had gotten out of the vehicle for a moment. That was the reason Tom had been able to estimate his height. Yet he could recall no other details, no special distinguishing marks that would help them locate the suspect.

John McClung loved Kathy, being treated as part adopted brother, part uncle. He wanted to do anything he could to help, so he, Tom, and some of the police detectives got into Tom's Chevrolet Impala and drove around the area, looking for the Blazer. Then, a day or two later, Tom sold the Impala to a black man over at Ingram's junkyard on Indian River in Norfolk. The price was five hundred dollars, a fair one for the car. The sale was not unusual, Tom frequently selling the family car whenever he could make a profit, then get a different one for them to use. However, both McClung and the police wondered if the vehicle wasn't too filled with unpleasant memories.

The detectives felt that they should keep tabs on the vehicle, never knowing what might provide important information. They talked with Tom the Monday after the funeral, learning that he had not paid much attention to the name of the buyer. It was Herrington or something similar, and the man had promised to bring the tags back to Bonney's home. The man said he would call as soon as the tags arrived, to set an appointment to come over, but as the days passed, the buyer never telephoned.

John McClung was less able to continue business as usual than Tom. He was thirty-two years old, single, and though a partner in the salvage yard, he was using the money he earned to go to school to learn video production, journalism, and related fields. The salvage yard was Tom's life, and he was able to busy himself with the routine. John McClung was more creative, less dedicated to the physical labor at the yard, even though he had worked with Tom Bonney for several years, knew the family, and had helped them go from abject poverty to a comfortable way of life.

Officially the two men were partners, though Tom was enough of a con man so that it was he who handled the money, frequently seeing to it that John was shortchanged. Still, McClung did well, averaging around $30,000 in a good year. Since the business was growing and John cared about Tom's family, he was not overly concerned about being cheated. He had more than enough for his needs.

The one area of dissension between Tom and John McClung came when the younger man became actively involved with a church. Bonney hated Christianity, mocking Jesus, cursing God. He had been the victim of an abusive father, a man who had been a game warden for part of his career, who loved to hunt and ridiculed Tom for the boy's refusal to kill any living creature. There had been emotional and physical batterings over the years, and then Tom was unable to get home in time to reconcile with his dying father, which had left him bitter toward God. If there was any love to be had from Jesus, he felt that he had not seen it. Still, he liked to read the Bible enough to paraphrase stories and throw out quotes, implying to those who never read it that he was a religious man. He often carried a Bible with him, yet those close to him saw such actions as another con, something that would generate trust among the deeply religious people in the area where he lived and worked. All Tom was certain about was that God did not love him.

By contrast, John McClung's Christian faith was what kept him partners with Bonney. John was concerned about the welfare of Carol Bonney and the children. He had known them when they were so poor that even meeting necessities was difficult. Even now that they were successful, he frequently bought the Bonneys food or clothing whenever John felt that Tom was squandering money on unnecessary personal purchases. It was John who thought that Kathy might benefit from parochial school, and John who had paid the tuition.

Kathy saw John, a youth fourteen years her senior, as someone in whom she could confide. He was close enough in age that he was not a father figure. Yet he had the wisdom and life experiences of an adult. He was also totally accepting of her, never judging her, even when she confessed to having been intimate with one or another of her boyfriends over the years. He did not approve of such actions, but he also did not condemn her, as her father would have done.

Kathy also became interested in religion, and was pleased when John paid her tuition for a Baptist parochial school. Some of the teachings were a little extreme for both Kathy's and John's beliefs, but she ignored those aspects with which she disagreed and delighted in the quality of education in the basics, especially English and writing classes.

Kathy was writing all the time. She wrote stories, especially mysteries, and kept a personal diary. She felt an intense privacy toward the diary, a need for secrecy as intense as only a CIA agent, or a teenager in the throes of adolescence, can experience. That was why McClung was deeply touched when she once offered to show him some of her entries. He refused, though, explaining that anything she wanted to share, she should share verbally. He did not feel comfortable invading her privacy.

It was to John McClung that Kathy first confided her desire to move away from home. She was better-educated than her family, more intelligent as well. Home life seemed stifling to her, and she wanted her own apartment. She knew her father would not approve, even if she took a place near to the family home and continued working in his salvage yard. That was why she was saving her money to find a place, intending to move out without warning. Her father would be hurt, but when he saw that nothing had changed except where she ate and slept each night, she was certain he would forgive what he would see was the abruptness of her actions.

Kathy's sudden death overwhelmed John McClung. He could not relate to so vibrant and beautiful a young woman suddenly ceasing to exist. He was angry with anyone who had ever hurt Kathy or caused her any unpleasantness. In his mind, they were all suspects in her murder, even her father.

The police were also beginning to wonder about Tom Bonney. There was no evidence linking him with the murder, no reason to suspect that he had killed his daughter. Yet there was something wrong with the things he was saying, the way he was acting.

The crime scene evidence indicated that either the murder was committed in great anger or it was an accident and the crime scene manipulated to seem like something worse than it was. The bullets had been fired by a revolver, .22-caliber handguns usually holding five, six, or nine bullets, depending upon the manufacturer and model. At the very least, the killer had to shoot until the gun was empty, reload, shoot some more, reload, and fire the remaining rounds of ammunition. A total of twenty-seven bullets had pierced her body, the type of violence most often associated with lunatics and jealous lovers.

Could Tom Bonney have been having an incestuous relationship with his daughter? Could he have discovered that she knew the Blazer owner, that she was having an affair with him? Or was it some other man? Was it caused by the letter she had written to John Hoskins? Or some other letter, as yet unfound, addressed to yet another lover?

Or were there other possibilities? The corpse seemed to have been positioned in a manner to suggest a sex crime. The clothing had been removed, yet there was no evidence of intercourse. Perhaps the shooting had been an accident, the killer panicking, removing Kathy's clothing, then shooting her again and again until there were no bullets left. If Tom Bonney was involved in such a crime, he may have waved the gun at his daughter to scare her, his finger pulling the trigger when he did not mean to do so.

Yet the detectives had to admit that Tom Bonney really did not fit either image of a killer. His voice had a self-pitying whine to it. His body posture, his attitude toward others, all gave the indication of a man without violence. Neither his wife nor his business partner had given the police any indication that he was capable of such extreme action. And Bonney had the relaxed manner of an innocent man, a grieving father trying to cooperate with law enforcement in order to catch his daughter's killer.

The detectives had many years of experience among them. They knew when someone was lying; they could tell a phony, a person whose emotions were barely in control. Tom Bonney had to be placed on the list of suspects because the last person known to be with a murder victim always was placed in such a category. But the detectives were also certain that whoever had murdered Kathy Bonney was not a relative.

The problem was, there were no strong leads other than the owner of the Chevrolet Blazer. Kathy's boyfriend did not appear to be a suspect. John McClung was not connected with the death. There was simply no evidence connecting anyone with the murder.

Tom and Carol Bonney returned to the police station to look at a series of photographs of possible suspects developed from the composite he had made. The detectives hoped that if they pulled a series of photographs of criminals with facial features similar to the police artist, they might get lucky. For the sake of accuracy, they included a photograph of Detective Castelow as well. Tom instantly recognized the Castelow picture, saying that, of course, he was not the man. Unfortunately, his memory was no better than when he had made the mistake with the composite, a not unusual situation with witnesses, but always a frustrating one.

Again the detectives talked with Tom, having him relive the night of the murder one more time. His memory was better, his emotions more in control. He remembered distinctly that the Blazer had come to the 7-Eleven store between eight and eight-thirty, an hour later than his earlier estimate. He also told the detectives that he and Kathy had definitely been using the Chevrolet Impala. Earlier he was confused, saying it might have been the Chevrolet they had driven and it might have been the salvage yard's wrecker.

He told the detectives that he had not noticed what Kathy did with her purse when she left the Impala. He was not thinking about whether she had it with her, because legally she would need the driver's license she kept in it when operating the Blazer. His interest had been on the vehicle he was thinking about buying, and it was only the next morning that he found Kathy's purse on the seat of the car and realized she must have left it when she got out.

Tom remembered more of the conversation with the mysterious John as well. He said that John claimed to be new to the area, though whether he meant new to Great Bridge or Chesapeake, Tom was uncertain. However, the man did know Route 168 and was familiar with the location of the 7-Eleven store where they met.

Hitman was wondering why he had let the others come along when he killed Kathy. Ego, probably. Committing the perfect murder is like shooting a hole-in-one on the golf course. It's not half the fun if there's no one along to see you do it.

Besides, Hitman knew they were weak, knew they wouldn't go to the cops even if they thought he might try to hurt them later. What he hadn't expected was the pestering, especially from Mammy. The old lady wanted Hitman to take them all out to the grave to get Kathy, bring her inside where it was warm and safe. The cold ground was no place for the child to be spending her days and nights. Not when there were loved ones available to take care of her.

Loved ones. Hitman hated the bitch. That was why he had killed her. And the others, the wimps, had let it happen.

The old lady was making Kathy some sort of saint

now that she was dead. If the hag loved the bitch so much, why hadn't she kept Kathy out of his way?

In the end, he went along with them, though. It was a copout, he knew, but it was worth shutting them up. Only Viking had gone along with Hitman, wanting to leave her where she was, though no one much cared what Viking said.

It was easy getting Kathy. No one wandering the cemetery noticed anything special about the odd little group when they went to Kathy's grave site. No one saw the special way they took her, the way they made certain that, when they left, everything looked undisturbed. Even a careful check would show that the dirt was tamped down just as it had been following the interment.

Even Hitman was proud of the way they took her, the stealing of Kathy from the grave as perfect a crime as her murder. It was a nuisance, but the idea of Tom going out to visit a buried, empty coffin delighted him. And if the others stopped nagging him now that he had helped, so much the better.

Friday, December 4

The detectives decided to look more closely at John Hoskins. Their search of Kathy's room had revealed more rough copies of her letters. One of them, a deeply emotional one that would later become a part of the murder trial, showed the depths of her feelings as she explored her growing sexual desires.

The letter, addressed to a man named "John," was apparently in response to something the couple had discussed. She described it as "kinky," but the images she created were quite normal.

Kathy talked about being with John in an intimate setting, a fire in a fireplace, champagne available for sipping. The couple would kiss passionately, then slowly undress one another. Eventually they would stimulate one another until they felt compelled to have intercourse, Kathy's orgasm being extremely intense. And then, sated and happy, they would fall asleep in each other's arms.

The letter was one no different than the type of thing any lover might write to someone else. However, it was just explicit enough that it would be upsetting for any parent to discover. Not only was it obvious that Kathy was no longer a little girl, it also was clear that she had been intimate with John at least once and possibly more times. And while there was nothing unusual about such experiences for lovers everywhere, parent/child relationships are always such that children have difficulty picturing their parents as sexual beings, and parents have trouble with the idea that their children have reached a level of physical and emotional maturity where sex is a part of an ongoing relationship. It was also a letter that undoubtedly would cause some embarrassment for Hoskins if anyone else witnessed Kathy's words.

Hoskins admitted to receiving the letter from Kathy when the detectives showed it to him. He was quite open about the affair. He gave every indication that his marriage was over and divorce so imminent that he was not worried about what his wife would think, or he was foolishly confident that he would be able to extricate himself from the compromising situation because Kathy was dead. Either way, the detectives felt that Hoskins had neither anger toward the victim, nor was he a blackmail victim who had turned on the person who threatened him.

But if not Tom Bonney, if not John Hoskins, then who might the murderer be? The man with the Chevrolet Blazer had not been spotted by any law enforcement officers and was presumed to have left the area. Yet even if they found him, the detectives sifting through the list of suspects were uncomfortable with this other "John" being the murderer.

The detectives reasoned that the Blazer owner would have wanted to protect himself from discovery. He would have asked Kathy where she lived, a logical question considering the business deal they were arranging. Then he could have gone by the house, watched to see where she went, how she lived. He would come for her when she was alone, taking her off when there were no witnesses. Certainly he might be a psychopath, but the detectives had encountered psychopaths before. Always they used some judgment. Meeting a girl's father, a man who might have taken down the license number of the Blazer, and then driving off to murder Kathy, made no sense.

John McClung was obviously shattered by Kathy's loss. Of that the detectives were certain. He also had an alibi for the time she was missing.

The detectives returned to basic textbook evaluation of the crime. Who had the motive, the means, and the opportunity to commit the murder?

Tom Bonney had the most obvious motive. He was angered and embarrassed by Kathy's affair with a married man. He knew she had been sexually active, had known about at least some of the writing she had done to John Hoskins. And Kathy was planning to leave home, a reality with which her father seemed to have had difficulty coping.

What kind of father was Tom Bonney? He seemed to be strict with his family. He carried the Bible around with him, quoting it a lot. The detectives wondered if he was the type of man who took too literally the idea that if you spare the rod, you spoil the child. Did Tom beat the children, perhaps thinking that it was for "their own good"? Had Tom beaten Kathy in the past, perhaps a little too often, a little too hard? She had dropped out of school. She was planning to leave home. Those could be signs of an abuse victim trying to flee her abuser without alerting friends or teachers that she was having trouble with her father.

Maybe Tom and Kathy got into a fight after the test drive in the Blazer. Maybe Tom thought Kathy had been flirting with the owner. Maybe Tom drove her over the border so they could talk.

The detectives could imagine a scenario where Kathy became angry with the way she was treated, picking up the gun Tom often carried with him. Maybe she pointed it at him, screaming, almost out of control. Tom would have struggled with her, tried to get her to put down the gun before it accidentally fired.

The detectives had seen people panic when they accidentally shot a friend or loved one. Tom might have thought that no one would believe the truth. He might have decided to create the impression that a murder had taken place. He could have taken her clothes, dumped her body, and shot her repeatedly.

Tom would have grieved just as intensely, the detectives reasoned. Tom would have gone into shock seeing the photographs, perhaps mentally reliving the event that shattered so many lives. A father accidentally killing his daughter would fit the motive. Tom's being alone with Kathy when they went to see the Blazer provided the means and opportunity.

That would mean that Tom's whining, his headaches, his upset stomach were all reactions to his nervousness. Instead of being furtive, avoiding the detectives as others in such a situation had done to them, perhaps Tom was revealing his guilt in ways where the officers had failed to spot the signals.

Tom was brought to the police lieutenant's office, where several officers were present to question him. He was not under arrest. He did not have to consider having an attorney present. They just wanted to talk with him, to make it clear that they did not believe him, that they thought he might somehow be responsible for his daughter's death.

The interview lasted between two and three hours. Six investigators from police and sheriff's departments in North Carolina and Virginia were present, everyone crammed into the small office.

The police told Tom that the murder weapon was a nine-shot, .22-caliber revolver, a gun identical to the one Tom had owned. What happened to your gun, Tom? What did you do with it?

Tom said that he had sold his revolver to a black male in Virginia Beach. He was vague about the description, but he was vague about the appearance of most of his salvage business customers. And that was how he looked at the transaction. Everything in Tom's life had a price. Everything he purchased was to be cherished only until someone came along and offered enough money more than you paid so that the profit was too hard to resist.

Was Kathy someone with a price, Tom? Had he reached a point where she, like the items he took in for salvage, was ready to be dumped?

The detectives showed Tom photographs of his daughter at the crime scene. The images were vivid ones, the bullet holes readily visible, the skin distorted by the blood pooling. They were the type of pictures the police normally avoided showing to a victim's family because there was no way to harden oneself to their impact. All the pain, suffering, and fear that the victim must have suffered in her last moments were vividly evident.

But Tom did not react the way they had hoped. There was no emotional breakdown, no sudden confession.

Tom focused on the distortions caused by the battering that occurred when the bullets slammed into his daughter's flesh. The girl in the photographs was dead. He agreed with that. But the pictures were not of Kathy. Kathy's skin was not bloated when he last saw her. Kathy did not have bullet holes in her body when he let her out of the Impala at the 7-Eleven. Kathy was whole, happy, vibrant, filled with life. The police had some horrible pictures, but they were of some other girl, some other father's daughter.

The denial of what he was seeing, the stoicism in the midst of the endless questions, all caused the detectives to realize that, whatever the truth, there was going to be no dramatic confession. Tom had not become angry or defiant. It seemed he understood the reasons they were trying to get a confession from him and could only shake his head in amazement.

When Tom left the station, it was almost as though he had compassion for his interrogators. They had not wanted to hurt him any more than he wished to be hurt. They had put him under such pressure because it was necessary in order to assure that the investigation moved forward. Now they would be able to look elsewhere, to find the real killer. As some of the officers watched Tom walk the approximately four blocks to his home, the body language they witnessed seemed to reflect Tom's sadness that such an ordeal had been necessary.

Thursday, December 10, 12:15 P.M.

Detective Williams received a telephone call from an excited Tom Bonney. His voice had a sound of happiness the investigator had never heard before. Tom had found the Chevrolet Impala in which he and Kathy had driven to the 7-Eleven. He had been looking for the car for days, realizing too late that he should not have treated it as part of his business, selling it so quickly after the murder. He felt that it was his job to locate the car, especially if it might help the detectives resolve their problems. And now he had found it! He was going to get the keys and drive it to the station.

The detective was concerned about Tom's attitude. Yes, it might be a help to have the car they were seeking. But there were other concerns. There could be trace evidence Tom would not know about, could not avoid obliterating. It was important for technical experts to be sent before Tom touched anything more than he might already have.

Tom would not listen. Apparently he remained upset by the way he had been treated during Friday's interrogation. He understood why he would be a primary suspect. He understood why the police would put him under so much pressure. Yet now he had succeeded where they had so far failed. Bringing the car to them would be his way of tweaking their noses for their foolishness.

Detective Williams ordered a check for Tom Bonney's whereabouts as soon as Bonney hung up the telephone. An officer quickly drove to A-1 Salvage, though Tom was not there. Other officers were alerted to look for him as they went about their routine patrols.

Tom again called the detective approximately forty minutes after his first call. He said that he was in Virginia Beach, using a telephone in the office of London Bridge Motors, located on Virginia Beach Boulevard. In response to the detective's request, an employee of the company took the receiver and confirmed both the location and the presence of Tom Bonney. Then Tom got back on the line, complaining that, although he had found the car, the employees of the company would not let him take it from the lot.

The detective was relieved to hear of Tom's problems. He ordered Bonney not to touch the car. He then arranged to go to the company to retrieve both Tom and the vehicle. However, although Tom agreed to the plan, by the time Williams arrived, Tom was gone.

Tom Bonney felt confused, uncertain what to do next. He had had his moment of triumph, his vindication when he found the Impala. But he had no reason to wait for Williams. The detective would do whatever detectives did with cars like the Impala. Tom could be of no further service, and he had done enough gloating over the telephone to satisfy his desire to get back at the police for the way he was treated.

Now there was nothing more to be done. He knew he should stay at home, care for his wife, his children. But they had enough food and money to get by for a few days without him. He needed a chance to think, to clear his head. He owned an old motor home, which, like the other vehicles in his life, was battered yet serviceable. He thought he'd take it and drive, perhaps to Florida where the family once lived, perhaps somewhere else. He could eat and sleep in the motor home. He could think. He could have some peace while the police located his daughter's killer.

Tom Bonney did not realize that law enforcement officers were anxious to question him again, now that the Impala had been located. While he quietly drove downtown to a gas station where he filled the motor home's tank with fuel, police and sheriff's deputies were searching for his truck. They did not realize that he was fleeing the area in a big, clumsy, slow-moving, high-profile vehicle. If Tom Bonney was guilty of murder, if his leaving Chesapeake was a means of fleeing law enforcement, then he was making the perfect getaway. Tom Bonney was hiding in plain sight.

The police were unaware of Tom Bonney's actions, but Hitman knew. The bastard! Leaving town would change everything. The cops would think Tom was guilty.

The police would dig deeper, look more closely at the evidence in their possession. Hitman's success depended upon the cops broadening their investigation, not narrowing its focus. All Tom had to do was stay home with his wife and kids, work his job, and be available for what was becoming an endless series of interrogations, and Hitman was home free.

Hitman had planned so carefully. Not for the witnesses, of course. Not for the way the initial shooting had happened by accident. But the fact that the witnesses would not, could not, come forward: that, and the way he had handled the body after the first round was fired, showed his brilliance.

The one thing he hadn't counted upon was Tom's not withdrawing. The wimp should have fallen apart, staying at home with his wife or sitting around the junkyard with that asshole, McClung. That's what Hitman had come to expect from Tom.

That's what he had expected when the police investigation began.

But driving to Florida? It wasn't fair. It wasn't right. It wasn't the way Hitman had so carefully planned.

CHAPTER 3

The Arrest

No one knows for certain exactly what happened during the next few days and weeks. From comments Tom made to the various psychologists, psychiatrists, the police, and others, the following re-creation is believed to be as accurate as can be known.

Kathy Bonney first spoke to her father as he was driving toward Maryland. He supposed he had expected it. That was why he didn't lose control of the motor home the first time he heard her voice speaking softly just behind him.

Tom had known the photograph the police showed him was wrong. It looked a little like Kathy, sure. So did the girl they buried. That's why he had been so upset, everybody thinking it was her. Tom knew it wasn't the same girl, yet that poor victim was so much like his daughter, he was overwhelmed with grief just from the possibility that Kathy had died. And now, here she was, inside the motor home, talking to him, all embarrassed by what she had put him through, yet happy they were together.

Tom smiled as he listened to her mirthful voice. He didn't turn around, didn't glance in the mirror. It was enough to let her gently lilting words envelop his mind, his heart, his body.

She was repentant about what had happened, about the things she had done with John Hoskins, about the nasty things she had written. She didn't like having hurt her daddy. What she liked was pleasing him. They were so close, Kathy and Tom. Friends, really, more than father and daughter. That's why she was so pleased that at last they were alone together.

What a daughter he had! Scaring him the way she did with what had obviously started out to be a practical joke. She must have really felt awful when she heard about that other girl dead along the canal bank, heard how she was mistaken for Kathy, heard about her daddy being a suspect in the killing. That's why she didn't come forward until now.

She was only nineteen, Kathy was. Still a kid in some ways. No wonder she waited. It was just a good thing he decided to take the motor home. She probably had been hiding there for days, scared, wanting to make things right, yet frightened to show herself to the police.

The motor home had beds, a place to wash, to make food. The whole family had lived in dwellings that weren't as nice. It was the perfect place for Kathy to have concealed herself. Tom was just sorry he hadn't looked there before. It would have saved him a lot of grief.

He should have had more faith in Jesus' hand in all this, of course. Tom realized that as he let the sound of Kathy's voice recede in his mind.

He should have known that no matter what fool stunt Kathy pulled, Jesus wouldn't let her die. Jesus loved her, loved him, wouldn't want either of them to suffer too much pain. That's what the Bible said, and he read the Bible all the time. Talked about it too.

Driving on down the highway, Tom wondered if maybe all the hell he had experienced the last few days wasn't just Jesus' way of telling him it was time for a change in his life. He had thought about that possibility from time to time in recent months. He had thought about a new line of work, then let himself get so busy that he never did anything about the idea.

Now he and Carol and the kids had been through so much, the scare about Kathy, being chased by the police . . . Maybe this was Jesus' way of forcing him to make a decision. Maybe, when everything was straightened out, he should give up his business and become a preacher full time.

He'd like that, being a preacher. Going around and telling stories from the Bible. It was a nice way to make a living.

The smile faded from his face just like the voice of his daughter had faded from his ears. Jesus loved him, he thought. Jesus loved his daddy too. That's what everyone said. That's why Jesus took his daddy to Heaven before he could get to the hospital to see him all those years ago.

There was a sound in the motor home, a sound like somebody sobbing. He had heard that plaintive cry before, heard it in the hospital when he learned his daddy had died before they could talk just one last time.

Jesus had done that to him then. Jesus had prevented him from confronting his father at last.

All the way driving to the hospital, Tom knew what he was going to do, knew what he was going to say. He planned to tell his father that he was a man, not a wimp. Tom deserved his daddy's respect. Daddy couldn't call him a wimp no more. Daddy couldn't call him a bastard! That's what he was going to say, and the old man was going to listen to him just once before he died.

But Jesus interfered. Jesus took his daddy before he could say the words, end the hurt, free himself from the years of pain.

Jesus was the wimp, Tom thought, his hands gripping the steering wheel more tightly. He was glad Jesus had died on the cross. Jesus could take his daddy like that but couldn't save Himself when they hammered in the nails.

It was right to crucify the bastard. Jesus had let his father die too soon. And now Tom hated him, hated Jesus, hated his father, hated the B word. Bastard! Bastard! Bastard . . .

Tom was startled to feel the mucus running down his nose, onto his lips, to feel the tears stinging the corners of his eyes. He realized the sobbing he had heard was coming from his own throat, realized he was bawling like a wimp.

Had to get control of himself, had to be a man for Kathy's sake.

It would all work out. He'd get away for a few days, talk with Kathy, read the Bible, get things sorted in his mind.

When he got back, he'd see about being a preacher. He could sell the salvage business to his partner. Talk with people about the Bible, about Jesus, about . . .

Carol Bonney's heart and mind were so racked with pain that she could feel everything and nothing. The loss of her daughter, the disappearance of her husband, the chance that Tom had killed Kathy . . . Too many things were happening. Life was at once overwhelming and incomprehensible.

An outsider might have said that she should have seen this coming, seen the violence of the man, taken the children and left him. But Carol Bonney had no life outside of Tom. She had little education, little work experience. She could cook, though never to Tom's satisfaction. He hated what she made, used to complain all the time. Every once in a while it seemed like too much trouble to fix the family meals, causing him to buy hot dogs and complain all the more.

Still, being put down by a man was nothing new for her. She seemed to have been put down and used all of her life. Tom made demands on her. The kids made demands on her. And they were all constantly moving, chasing some dream of Tom's that made sense for a while, gave her and the kids hope for a better tomorrow; and then the dreams seemed to fall apart somehow in ways neither she nor Tom could fully comprehend.

Hope had become a fragile thing for Carol Bonney, too easily shattered for her to risk cherishing it anymore. She had accepted living in the present, knowing that tomorrow would mean more of Tom's erratic behavior, more threats, demands, more complaints about the pains in his head, in his stomach, the quality of the food.

For Carol, abuse by Tom was familiar, predictable. She learned to go from day to day, gaining whatever pleasure she could, enduring the pain, desensitizing herself to the idea that life could hold something more for her than the here and now.

Carol Bonney didn't know what to think when Kathy disappeared. She and her daughter had been close. Kathy would tell her things, especially about boys, that she would never tell her father.

Like the time Kathy thought she was pregnant, bought a pregnancy test, found that it was negative. She couldn't tell her father, but she could confide in her mother. Her father would have become enraged. Her mother just accepted the fact, like she accepted everything in life that most people feared. The bad was so familiar that the emotional impact was dulled for her.

Of course, Tom had found out about the pregnancy scare, like he found out everything. He never asked about the boy, never wanted to know who did it. Kathy tearfully spoke of a rape, but he could not comprehend the idea of his daughter being violated against her will. He decided that Kathy had failed him.

Though the test results showed that Kathy wasn't pregnant, Tom would not let that fact interfere with his preconceived ideas. She was carrying another man's child and that could not be tolerated.

Tom had balled his fist and punched Kathy in the stomach. Kathy. His favorite child. Just punched her as hard as he could where the baby grew, Carol remembered, then pushed the girl down some steps. Tom never believed in doctors, wouldn't have let her go for an abortion if the test had been positive. Handled it his own way. Kill the baby and teach Kathy a lesson about obedience, all with one punch. That was Tom's way when he went a little crazy. That was the Tom she had endured over the years.

Then Tom found those handcuffs, left in a car someone sold to the salvage yard. Handcuffs and a key.

Carol didn't know why the previous owner had them. Tom probably didn't know either. Maybe the car belonged to a police officer or a security guard. Probably the man thought he had left the cuffs in his locker or in a drawer at home. Maybe he didn't even know they were missing.

There were other possibilities, of course. The owner could have been involved with sadomasochistic sex or some other kinky activity. But such ideas would not have crossed Carol Bonney's mind when Tom brought them home. She was not the type to read about such things, to fantasize about sex.

Tom had been violent with her before he found the handcuffs. Social workers had documented a history of family violence over the years. Carol had once gone to a battered woman's shelter. Yet always she returned, always they had tried to work things through because Tom, no matter how he might act, was still familiar. He was the only type of man she had ever really known, perhaps the only type she thought she deserved. Yet nothing in the past had prepared her for the circumstances she was facing.

Grief-stricken over the death of their daughter, Carol Bonney had wanted to lean on her husband, to use his strength, his wisdom, to help her through the crisis of losing a child. Instead he had acted strangely, sometimes withdrawn, sometimes so violently angry that she thought he might lash out at her. And in between the mood swings, he complained about his head, his stomach, about an endless list of trivial annoyances he made sound like the most important things in his life. Yet never could she talk with him about her sadness, about how they would get along without Kathy, about any danger to their other children.

And then he had brought out those handcuffs. It didn't make sense. Kathy was dead and buried, and he was acting in ways she didn't understand.

Tom had taken her into the bedroom, she admitted to the reporters after he took the motor home and left Chesapeake. He handcuffed her to the bed, violently raping her. There had been no reason for it, nothing in their past together that would indicate he was capable of such craziness.

Carol Bonney made it clear that Tom's actions were not some sort of kinky sex. Couples in grief often use sex as a way of avoiding, at least for an hour or so, the horrors they have been experiencing. Sometimes the lovemaking is quiet. Sometimes it is kinky. But Carol was adamant that what happened was neither an act of tenderness nor the result of intense lust fueled by the need to escape the horror they had so recently shared. It was as though he hated her. Or perhaps he was punishing her for bringing Kathy into the world, creating a daughter who could get herself into circumstances where she could be killed by a stranger.

Tom's sudden disappearance left her even more alone, confused, in pain. She began to think of herself as Tom Bonney's second victim, to suspect that he might actually have had something to do with Kathy's death.

The newspaper reporters were cautious in discussing Tom Bonney's disappearance, seemingly not wanting to prejudice any police case that might evolve. But the articles they wrote gave the distinct impression that something was seriously wrong, that perhaps Tom Bonney was more involved with Kathy's death than anyone had suspected. For the first time the possibility was raised that Tom Bonney might be the murderer.

Mary Louise Bonney, Kathy's grandmother, thought differently of Tom. "I don't believe any of what I read in the papers," she said of reports hinting possible involvement. "I think he's just gone off to think things over for a while, and I think he'll come back. I just have that belief. It's the only thing I have to hang on to."

Tom would have liked to have heard his mother's statement as he drove, to have known that he had her support. In the past he always believed that his brother was the one she loved, and he had spent years spending money on the older woman in order to impress her. Tom took on her bills when his father died. He helped pay her living expenses. Yet she never seemed grateful, never was impressed with the fact that, no matter how hard he was struggling to support his own family, he still was able to help her.

The seeming estrangement from his mother was one of Tom's great sorrows, a personal anguish he shared with his friends. He never knew how to please her, never knew how to gain her respect. And now, the one time she publicly stood up for him, he was hundreds of miles away, unaware of what she had done for him. Such ironies seemed to form the story of his life.

Hitman stared out the window of the motor home as it slowly made its way to Maryland. Kathy and Tom were prattling on, oblivious to his presence. He just wished he could block out the sound of their voices as well. Kathy was apologizing for the trouble she had caused, and Tom was alternately acting like the father on the Waltons or whining about his stomach and headaches so Kathy would speak soothingly to him.

Another problem was that Tom was thinking too much for himself. Tom could have kept the

Chevrolet Impala awhile longer. Sure, eventually the cops would get wise, find the bloodstains and the evidence that a bullet had been fired within. But not at first. Letting the police know where it was located so soon after the funeral was dangerous. Didn't Tom know there was a death penalty in North Carolina? The wimp could die if they ever caught him.

And the escape . . . The logical thing would have been to take the wrecker. It was in good shape, with a powerful engine. It was meant to haul cars, the engine being one that could make the truck move out on the highway when nothing was attached. He couldn't outrun a cop car, but he could move quickly enough for a decent getaway.

Nobody made their escape in a thirty-foot motor home. Sometimes it seemed that you couldn't outrun a bicycle in it unless you were driving downhill with a good gust of wind giving you an extra push. Yet it was so ridiculous that Hitman realized no one would look for Tom or the others inside such a vehicle. Tom may have made another of his stupid-ass blunders, but this time luck was with them. Hiding in plain sight was the perfect way to go. If Tom and Kathy would just shut up for a while, Hitman might actually begin to enjoy the trip.

On Friday, December 11, Carol Bonney filed a Missing Persons report concerning her husband, saying that she had not heard from him since he telephoned her at four-thirty on Thursday afternoon. It was the same Thursday that the police had discovered bloodstains in the Chevrolet Impala Tom Bonney had been driving the night his daughter was murdered.

Four days later, on Tuesday, December 15, 1987, a first-degree-murder warrant was issued for the arrest of Thomas L. Bonney. It had been three weeks since his daughter's bullet-riddled body had been found along the banks of the Dismal Swamp Canal. During that time the police had searched for the mysterious "John" who owned the Chevrolet Blazer Tom Bonney claimed he and Kathy were thinking of buying. The investigators had intensely questioned John Hoskins, the man to whom Kathy had written at least two love letters, and they had interviewed Tom's partner, John McClung. As Special Agent Kevin McGinnis of the North Carolina State Bureau of Investigation explained to reporters, "We traced down a lot of people, a lot of people named John, but Bonney became a suspect late last week."

The police would not discuss Tom Bonney's motive, but McGinnis's comments about the forensic evidence indicated the way law enforcement was thinking. Hair, blood, fiber, and carpet samples were taken from the car. In addition, the laboratory was checking to see if Kathy had been raped. It was speculated that Tom Bonney was a jealous lover, enraged over his daughter's affair with Hoskins, driven to rape after discovering the letter she had written. It was a sick, perverted relationship that was suspected, incest and murder in what was previously believed to have been a loving family. But no evidence to support such speculation ever emerged. The truth would ultimately prove far more shocking than any of the original suspicions.

* * *

The newspaper reporters began seeking everyone who had known Kathy Bonney or her family. They began uncovering a very different image of Tom Bonney than the one they had drawn when interviewing him after his daughter's death.

An affidavit filed as justification for one of the search warrants disclosed previously hidden information concerning the family's involvement with Social Service agencies shortly after Kathy's murder. One of the other children spoke to both a social worker and a detective, telling them that she was physically afraid of her father. The daughter said that her father had threatened her mother with a gun.

Neighbors discussed the fact that they had thought Tom Bonney was overly protective. One boy who had dated Kathy mentioned that neither he nor any of her dates were allowed in the family home. He said that Kathy frequently fought with her father for being so restrictive. He insisted that she accompany him on her errands so that she would always be within sight.

Kathy had attended the Open Door Christian School in Virginia, where most of the girls saw her as quiet and somewhat of a loner. Few of them ever got close to her. She was different from them, not particularly communicative in class, and never participated in the athletic activities that formed the bulk of the students' social lives. She also did not participate in what they called their "proms." The school did not believe in dancing; the prom was actually a formal party for the students that included a dinner and an inspirational speaker. It was the high point of the year for those attending classes there.

The few friends that Kathy did make were usually the rebels. Jill Kelly, who rebelled at the strictness of the school and later moved out of state, described herself and Kathy as desperate for help and attention, turning to acts that they hoped might achieve such an end. They threw a brick through the school window, for example, but Kathy was never caught. Even if she had been, help probably would not have been provided. The school was better equipped to expel the troublemakers than to counsel them. Although a number of the students had been placed in the school by their parents in order to correct what were perceived as discipline problems, the girls were more likely to be sent back to public schools if they upset the others. The staff and the majority of the parents wanted their children to have a solid Christian education in the form in which they believed, not to have the school serve to reform delinquent behavior.

Public school was not an option for Kathy because Tom Bonney was afraid that she would meet the wrong man there, Jill Kelly related in interviews with reporters. She said that Kathy frequently confided her father's wild mood swings.

There were others who mentioned the results of Tom Bonney's actions, though they never directly witnessed the violence. For example, some told of Tom discovering that Kathy thought she might be pregnant when she was seventeen. They related the incident that had troubled Carol, when Kathy was punched and thrown down the stairs. They had seen their friend badly bruised, her normally well manicured fingernails broken and bloody, and they believed her story of what had happened.

A neighbor told of Kathy and her mother fleeing the house, then going to the police station to take a warrant against Tom. She also said that the family reconciled and went back together.

Those who knew Tom Bonney also talked of his mood swings, of his being like two different people. John McClung told of Tom being gentle, helpful, a skilled salesman in his salvage yard, talking a customer into making a four- or five-hundred-dollar purchase, most of which would be profit. Then, when the transaction was almost completed, the money about to change hands, Tom's eyes occasionally seemed to glaze over. He would pause for a moment, no longer focusing on anything, then suddenly explode. He would curse the customer, using extremely foul language, sending the person fleeing from the yard without completing the purchase. It was an action that made no sense, though it happened infrequently enough that it had not caused a serious rift in the relationship between the two partners. It was simply an unpleasant reality that McClung questioned but could do nothing about.

A former boyfriend told reporters of an experience when Kathy had sneaked out of the house to go on a date with him. She was eighteen and they met in a shopping mall where Tom discovered them together. He started calling his daughter a "tramp," slapping her hard across the face. Then he turned toward the youth, his face enraged, but the boy ran off. Bonney chased him for a while but never caught him.

Jill Kelly said that even she, a girl, was not allowed to call Kathy at home. Kathy was terrified of how her father might react if she did. Kathy also told her that her father had warned aloud that he might kill the family, then explained that he had sold a gun so he would not use it. However, John McClung mentioned that Bonney was always buying and selling weapons, seldom without at least one in his possession. The idea that he would sell a gun so as not to kill seemed out of character. Tom would not have thought that way. He also did not stop the buying of guns, so if he believed there was a risk he would harm his family, apparently he was comfortable taking it.

There would be more such information coming out, most of it as friends and acquaintances compared notes at the trial. But the little the press was uncovering seemed to greatly change the public's perception of what had occurred.

Tom Bonney would have been upset to read the newspaper accounts of his personal life. He was convinced that, under the best of circumstances, few people ever spoke the truth about him. He felt they tended to lie about him, to say he did things that he not only could not remember, but that he also would not do. The idea that strangers were interviewing his family, his friends, and anyone else who knew him, would have enraged him.

Now, Tom's aimless wanderings took him far from home, into areas where no one had heard of his daughter's murder. He traveled through Maryland, then on to Dover, New Jersey, where he sold the motor home to a dealer at AMA Cars, Incorporated. The deal was a good one. He received a 1978 or 1979 gold, two-door Chevrolet Nova he could use for transportation, and five thousand dollars in cash he could use to live on.

The car was in good condition, two new tires on the front, two all-weather tires with plenty of tread remaining on the rear. The engine ran well and got good mileage. He was proud of the deal, even though he had no intention of keeping the vehicle. He used it only to drive as far as Cleveland, Ohio, pulling into the parking lot at Hopkins International Airport, where he removed the license plates before abandoning the vehicle.

Tom obtained an airline ticket for Daytona Beach, Florida, where he thought he could have some peace and quiet. He needed to think, to decide what to do next, and Florida was a state with which he was familiar, a place where he could lose himself for a while.

Daytona Beach, like much of Florida, was a city where transients came for the season. Strangers were commonplace and rents were as likely to be paid by the week in Daytona Beach as they were by the year in other parts of the country. Thus no one was suspicious when Tom arrived, obtained a Florida driver's license, and used some of his cash to rent apartment 101 in a complex at 421 Atlantic Avenue.

Although he was trying to avoid any encounters with law enforcement, he instinctively followed old patterns. There came a point when he decided to stop paying rent, though he still had much of his money and was working spot labor jobs for from twenty-five to twenty-eight dollars per day. He bought a four-door, 1976 Plymouth Valiant for just under five hundred dollars from Don's Used Cars in Daytona Beach. Then he moved all his possessions into his car so that if the landlord changed the locks or tried to hold his goods until the rent was paid, there would be a way for him to escape with everything he owned.

Most of the time, Tom worked or thought or watched television. There were times, though, when his mind returned to his family, to Carol and the children, all of whom he missed. He seemed to envision the family waiting patiently for his return, concerned for him yet respecting his need to escape. It was like "The Homecoming," the Christmas special that introduced the Waltons to television. John Walton, Sr., working in the harsh weather, trying to earn money for simple gifts for his family, who only wanted him to return safe and healthy. Tom "Walton" Bonney seemed to sense that his family was like that, everyone looking to his return.

While Tom Bonney had visions of a family looking hopefully toward his return, the reality was quite the opposite. Tom thought of the Waltons. Carol Bonney thought of one of the popular slasher movies where a psychopathic killer keeps reappearing when and where you least expect him. Terrified that Tom would return and hurt one of the other children, she let one of the Social Service agencies place all the kids in foster care with the understanding that they would be returned after Tom was in jail.

At first Carol talked freely with reporters, saying that she was having frequent nightmares of Tom chasing her through the house, beating her. She said that when she didn't have nightmares, she would have visions of Kathy. "She tells me not to worry, that everything will work out fine," Carol related.

Carol also said that she was convinced her husband had murdered Kathy. "He hit her, or she hit him, and all hell broke loose. I think he just flipped out," she said, stressing that she was convinced the murder was accidental. She felt that everything that followed, the stripping of the body, shooting Kathy repeatedly, the dumping of the corpse, all of that had been done to make it look like someone else had been there. Despite what he did to her, Carol was convinced that Tom never raped their daughter, never considered assaulting her.

Carol gave the reporters more details about the violence she experienced after Kathy's death. She discussed the incident with the handcuffs, then mentioned a second time that he came at her while the children were outside playing. Tom had been hiding in a closet, waiting to catch her alone. Then he leaped out and grabbed her, and she fought with him, moving through the rooms until she was able to grab a kitchen knife. She slashed at him, lightly cutting one of his arms, convincing him to leave her alone. "You're crazy," she recalled his saying to her.

"And I said, 'You're the one who's crazy. You started the whole mess.' He said, 'You're my wife and I got a right.'"

Carol told reporter James Pate of the Virginia *Pilot* that Tom had called her; it was several days after Tom began his roundabout trip to Florida. "He told me he loved me and said he'd be home in seven and a half hours." He claimed that he had been hit by a car and was injured, but he would be coming home soon. "I think he's cracked all the way up. He sounded different—like he wasn't aware of what was going on. I said, 'Tom, they think you did it.' And he said, 'I figured that.' He claimed he never done it."

Tom did not return, nor did he say from where he was calling. It did not matter. By then Carol Bonney thought he was guilty. She said that after Kathy's disappearance, even before she knew her daughter had been murdered, "Tom turned mean as a damned rattlesnake."

The more she talked, the more frightened she became. Finally Carol went into hiding, refusing to reveal where she was staying until her husband was caught.

On January 15, Tom Bonney, frustrated by his inability to locate his wife by telephone, called his former business partner, John McClung, Jr. He was not at home, his father said when he took the call.

For the next half hour John McClung, Sr., listened to Tom talk about trying to find Carol and his children. The elder McClung did not know where they had gone or how to reach them; but Tom, who sounded dazed, needed to talk.

Tom claimed to not remember why he had left Virginia or why the family had split up. He still loved Carol and wanted to see her, to talk with her. There was no sense of his understanding the magnitude of his actions or the results.

Tom Bonney was too restless to stay only in Florida. He drove to Georgia once, then drove to Indianapolis at the end of January. That city was unfamiliar to him. He knew that Interstate 40 would take him south to areas from which he could find his way, but he did not know how to get there. Finally, the gas low, frustrated and lost, he pulled into a parking lot, turned off his engine, and left on his parking lights.

An Indianapolis police officer was walking her beat when she spotted Bonney sitting in the car. The area was predominantly black, and a single white male, sitting alone in a vehicle with out-of-state plates, looked suspicious to her. She radioed the license number to headquarters about the same time that Bonney saw her and waved her over, asking for directions to the Interstate.

The computer check indicated that the car was registered to Tom Bonney at his address in Daytona Beach, Florida. But the National Crime Information Center, through which the check was made, also indicated that Bonney was wanted on a North Carolina murder charge. The officer drew her gun, had Bonney get out of the car, and made the arrest. He offered no resistance.

At eight-thirty on Monday morning Bonney told Indianapolis detective Gerald Cole that the charges were wrong, and he refused to allow himself to be extradited to North Carolina. He was angry and hurt by the matter, yet less than two hours later, when Cole returned to see Bonney, Tom was suddenly cooperative. He apologized for not having signed the waiver earlier. He said he wanted to go to North Carolina to clear up the charges pending against him.

Chesapeake, Virginia, Detective Williams and North Carolina SBI Agent Kevin McGinnis flew to Indianapolis to question Tom, then return him for trial. There was no resistance, no problems with the extradition. In fact, Tom became comfortable enough to engage in conversation with them, something that was anticipated. A tape recorder had been carried by the officers so that anything said could be accurately retained.

Special Agent McGinnis began talking with Bonney in the car as they drove to the Indianapolis airport and again when they were in the Airport Security Office, waiting to board the plane that would fly them back to the Norfolk airport. Bonney began talking more freely than he had in weeks, as the conversation was being tape-recorded by Agent McGinnis and Detective Williams. They began by mentioning the draft of the sexually explicit love letter that Tom had found in Kathy's possessions, a letter he had shown her in the car.

MCGINNIS: You showed her the letter and, uh, what happened then?
BONNEY: Well, the gun was on the front seat of my coat.
MCGINNIS: Was that your nine-shot .22 pistol?

BONNEY: Yeah.

MCGINNIS: It's a nine-shot .22 pistol. Where is that pistol now, Tom?

BONNEY: I just throwed it away in the river somewhere.

MCGINNIS: You just throwed it away right there?

BONNEY: No.

MCGINNIS: No? What river did you throw it away in; do you remember?

BONNEY: Up by the bridge.

MCGINNIS: What bridge was that?

BONNEY: It crosses Battlefield.

The tape continued:

MCGINNIS: So you shot her right there. Tom, do you remember reloading the gun to shoot her again?

BONNEY: Well, some of it, strange as it may seem, I can't think of it. I can't remember.

MCGINNIS: I understand that.

BONNEY: Some of it I can and some of it I can't.

MCGINNIS: Do you remember how—

BONNEY: I have no idea why.

Bonney was asked if he remembered how many times he shot or if he reloaded the gun. "I guess I did," he replied. "I don't know. I probably did." He then said that after shooting her, he "just went crazy. That's all there is to it. There's nothing to explain."

The interview continued, Tom saying that he drove straight home afterward. Then McGinnis asked Tom when he put Kathy in the trunk of the Impala.

"She never was in the trunk," Bonney replied.

MCGINNIS: How did the blood get in the trunk, Tom?
BONNEY: I have no idea.

McGinnis explained that some blood was found in the trunk, to which Tom replied, "It never was opened. It never was opened. The trunk never was opened."

MCGINNIS: Okay. Did you throw her shoes and pants and everything in the canal right there?
BONNEY: Yeah.
MCGINNIS: You did? Everything was right there. Okay.
BONNEY: That's impossible for blood to be in the trunk.

McGinnis asked about a hole in the roof of the car. The police assumed that Tom may have made it when trying to dig out one of the bullets, but Bonney explained that the hole had always been there.

The interview continued, Tom saying that he had been gone with Kathy less than ninety minutes. He was surprised that McGinnis had guessed that Kathy had lunged for the pistol as they argued over the letters. However, he repeatedly said that he could not remember moving Kathy, getting out of the car. He remembered the gun going off and he remembered driving straight home. Everything else was rather vague in his mind.

McGinnis changed the subject, returning to the gun. Tom said that it had been found in one of the junk cars, that it was old, rusty, but it still worked. He explained that on the night of the murder, he had it under his coat on the front seat. Then he talked about the drive to the area where she was found, an important consideration for determining jurisdiction in the murder since the body was found not far over the North Carolina line.

MCGINNIS: Okay. So it ended up, you know, that Kathy lunged at the gun and the gun went off, and you ended up shooting her some more times. Is that correct? Is that what happened?
BONNEY: Whatever you tell me. I don't know. Whatever the papers say. Whatever you say.
MCGINNIS: Well, the papers don't know anything, Tom. What I'm saying is, tell me what happened after the first shot. What happened?
BONNEY: I just went crazy, I guess. I have no idea. I couldn't stop. I know that.
MCGINNIS: You just kept shooting?
BONNEY: Probably.
MCGINNIS: Well, you never reloaded?
BONNEY: No. Gosh, no!
MCGINNIS: When did you stop shooting?
BONNEY: I mean, I guess I did, though.

MCGINNIS: Yeah. When did you stop shooting and take her clothes off?
BONNEY: I don't know that either. I was gone less than a hour, though. That's all I know. Now, does that help you when I say I was gone less than a hour?
MCGINNIS: Uh-huh. Okay. You don't remember taking her clothes off or anything?
BONNEY: No. Good gosh, no! That's for sure.

Bonney said that he didn't remember what he did with the clothing but it should be where the body was found. He also said that he didn't cut off any of the clothing.

MCGINNIS: Did you have to cut her underwear off, her underwear off and all, or her pants or anything?
BONNEY: I don't know if they'd be hard to get off or not.

The tape was turned over, some of the questions being lost in the process. McGinnis stressed that Tom shouldn't lie or say "what's best to say." He said that he needed to know what actually happened. But Tom could not remember how Kathy got out of the car after he fired the first shot. "Maybe she got out, took a walk or something. I don't know. I don't know. All I know is she should have been left there right where she was and—"

MCGINNIS: You don't remember picking her up and putting her down the . . . down the bank?

BONNEY: Good gosh, no!
MCGINNIS: You don't remember taking her clothes off?
BONNEY: I hurt so bad, even I can't pick up much of anything at all.
MCGINNIS: Do you remember taking her clothes off of her?
BONNEY: Probably.

But Bonney was being vague again. He said that he probably took off Kathy's clothing on the ground. Then he said that he "just throwed 'em here and there. Just here and there. No special place."

McGinnis explained that some of the clothing had been found, but not all of it. The shoes were still missing, and any jewelry, though Tom said that she had not been wearing any.

Tom continued to describe the way he drove returning home, then how he made the Missing Persons report. He tried to remember what he and Kathy had said to each other, but he had difficulty with that as well. He also said that the memory of how the gun came to be used was vague, uncertain in his mind.

"It's strange how some things come to mind and some things just don't. I don't know if it's because this is the period of time that is trying or if it's just confusing. I get confused an awful lot anyway. But I'm gonna be honest with you. I'd be going hungry. I can't think which way to turn. Golly day."

Tom remembered that he was in the car when Kathy lunged for the gun. "I can't remember no more. I just . . . it's a bad feeling. It's a feeling I don't know how to get straight. When you go over the end, the edge or something, you just . . . it's like you're on remote control. It don't stop. It's just like you don't get control. It don't . . . it don't stop. It's just . . . it's just like it's programmed and then you just go out and that's it,'cause you just . . . you just crack. That's all. I believe that. I actually believe I cracked. I really do. I . . . I know. I know I did."

Tom was then asked about some of the items taken from Kathy's room. There were two men's magazines, a *Playboy* and a *Hustler*. There was also a pair of handcuffs that lacked a key. Tom did not know about the magazines, but the handcuffs had been found in the shop. The kids often went looking through the salvaged material to see what interested them.

The conversation returned to the gun and the fact that Tom had deliberately taken it with him when he and Kathy went to go look at the Blazer. He was certain that she knew it was on the seat, underneath the coat. He also said that he took it because it was getting dark and he had no idea where they might drive for their talk. "I just made a left there and a right there, a left here, a right there. And wherever I wound up at."

Then he added, "All I know is I just been under a big strain, and I've been under a big, gigantic stress and I had no idea where I was gonna go and what I was gonna do when I got there. I do not know. I have no idea. That's the truth. . . ."

A second tape was made as the discussion continued. They talked about the wrecker and the fact that the shell casings had been found in its gas tank following its repossession by the authorities searching for evidence related to the murder. Tom said that he probably transported the shells in his pocket, though he didn't remember for certain. He just knew that he always carried extra bullets with him, usually on the dashboard of the wrecker.

Once again the questioning returned to the murder itself, this time with Detective Williams asking the questions. He said, "From the time when Kathy lunged, lunged at the gun and the gun went off, what did she say?"

Tom responded, "What did she say? I don't know what she said. Probably just hollered and screaming or something, I imagine. What did . . . I don't know. I have no idea what she said."

WILLIAMS: Was there anything said by her?
BONNEY: That's when all the excitement went on then. I don't know. It's just . . . I don't remember. I don't know. That's history.
WILLIAMS: Do you know if she screamed?
BONNEY: I would think so. Somebody got shot. It just scared me half to death. I turned white as a ghost. I remember that. And from then on I don't know what happened. And I would pass that on a lie detector test too,'cause I have no idea. Not at all. Like I said, guy, I hope you never have to face it. See, I have nothing to hide right now. It's all out in the open. I'm trying to help you guys. How's it gonna help me if I tell a story? How's it gonna hurt me if I tell a story?

The taping ended. The men boarded the airplane for the flight home. It had all been without incident except for Tom's rather vague, somewhat disjointed admission that he had killed his daughter. The detectives knew they had the right man. What they still did not have were both the details and the reasons for the murder.

At 1:58 A.M. on Wednesday, as Tom Bonney was being driven by the Camden County Sheriff's office, he insisted upon talking with reporters. The action came as a surprise to everyone, including the sheriff, who at first allowed the action. Bonney had been keeping his jacket over his head so he could not be readily seen and photographed. The sudden switch to open confessor had not been anticipated.

Bonney told the reporters that he and Kathy had argued about her lover, during which time he was holding a gun that went off. "Jealousy had nothing to do with it," Tom Bonney said. "We just had a disagreement. The gun just went off."

One reporter asked, "Why was your daughter shot twenty-seven times?"

"I just cracked," Bonney replied. "I just cracked."

The sheriff, Bobby Berry of Camden County, stopped the interview, but not until a tired Tom Bonney said, "It was temporary insanity. It's like somebody going over the edge . . . when you go over the edge and crack up, you aren't responsible. You just aren't responsible.

Bonney also explained that the love affair had caused heartbreak in the family. "My daughter was seeing a married man who had a baby . . . I wasn't jealous, but it just wasn't right.

"My wife and I found a letter in her bedroom," he said, explaining that after he confronted her with proof of the romance, "she went to hootin' and hollerin'."

Bonney also managed to explain that he owned a salvage business and had to carry a lot of money. That was why guns were kept around in the office as well as under the seat of the truck. What he did not explain was why there was a gun in the Impala, though he originally said that he and Kathy had been traveling in the wrecker. He said of the murder weapon, "It was throwed in the canal."

Shortly after Bonney's statement, the press learned that the shell casings from the murder were found in the bottom of the gas tank of the wrecker he had used in the salvage yard. The wrecker had developed engine trouble, and a mechanic had drained the fuel tank to check the lines. The sound of rattling metal was heard when the gasoline was removed, and a check revealed the cartridges. Only the revolver remained unlocated, and there were doubts that it would ever be found.

Carol Bonney was one of the first people to learn of her husband's statement. As was normal with reporters, they went to get her reaction before writing their articles.

They hoped for a dramatic response that would add to the media impact, and they were not disappointed.

"How could you be insane and kill somebody like that?" she said. "He probably did it because one minute he would be himself and then the next he would flip and not even remember it.

"If he did something like that, then they need to fry him—pull the switch so he won't do nothing like that to nobody else."

The story should have ended there, a simple tragedy that would lead to an uncomplicated trial and conviction. The police had the father in custody. He had told reporters that he'd killed, and while there might have been some problems resulting from that statement, the worst would have been a change of venue for the trial. That would have meant hearing the case in a different county, an area where there had been little or no publicity about the Bonney murder and his statements to the press.

Bonney admitted to having no money, and his family was unable to be of any help. His children remained in the care of the Social Service agency. His wife was forced to live with friends. People in the community read of the fate of the Bonneys with sadness or momentary anger, then turned the page of their daily newspaper, knowing that it would be a matter of time before Tom Bonney was sent to death row.

John Halstead, a well-known criminal defense attorney, was assigned the Bonney defense as a court-appointed lawyer. Halstead is a complex man, tall, caring, a hard worker who jokes about receiving the cases that no one else wants. He has frequently defended the unloved and unwanted, ranging from alleged child molesters to murderers. Many of his clients are guilty, the only issue being the degree of that guilt and how well the prosecution has prepared its cases against them. Others are perceived as being guilty, the crimes of which they are accused so unpleasant that other lawyers are not anxious to have their reputations connected with such individuals, even if they ultimately triumph.

Halstead's reputation is that of a man who is caring about his clients and about the law. Some of the town's attorneys and media representatives find him an excellent defense counsel. Others rate him as only average. Yet all say that he truly is concerned with the legal system and the rights of the defendants. He takes matters to heart, recognizing that for clients like Bonney, he literally has someone's life in his hands when he walks into the courtroom.

Many defense attorneys are arrogant, overly self-confident in order to live with the fact that their skill may be all that determines whether or not an accused criminal may live or die. They are like surgeons and others in high-risk professions where lives are totally entrusted to their care. They talk of "cases," not people. They see the courtroom as an arena for gladiatorial confrontation. They are more concerned with beating the prosecutor than they are with the ultimate future of the man or woman whom they are defending.

John Halstead is not arrogant. Intense, hardworking, perpetually tired, he takes the results of his cases personally, working longer hours than he should, his escapes from the office being all too brief in the eyes of his staff. He is a good man in the roughest venue in which a lawyer can function.

The facts facing John Halstead were not pleasant ones for a defense counsel. Tom Bonney was present at his daughter's murder. Tom Bonney made statements indicating that he killed his daughter by accident. But Kathy Bonney had been shot twenty-seven times. A nine-shot handgun had been emptied into the young woman, reloaded, emptied, reloaded, and fired again. At some point the body had been stripped naked. At some point the clothing had been tossed away. Had a stranger committed such violence, it would have been heinous. The idea that a father might do it was chilling to Halstead, who knew it would be at least as horrifying to the jury that would decide Tom's fate.

Yet when John Halstead first met Tom Bonney, Bonney gave no indication of being a cold-blooded, out-of-control killer. Tom was a weak, whiny man complaining of headaches, stomachaches, and the poor quality of the food he was being given in jail. He seemed alternately self-centered and worried about his family. He did not seem like a man who was capable of shooting his daughter twenty-seven times, yet there was no way of knowing for certain. Every experienced criminal defense attorney has learned that there are few limits, good or bad, concerning the potential for violence of the average person.

Information concerning the Bonney family was being uncovered by both law enforcement officers and the press. There had been enough abuse within the family that, when they lived in Norfolk, Social Services had taken the children for a prolonged period following the accusation that their parents had neglected them. Another child, eleven years old at the time Tom was arrested, had a different last name and had been living with a different family for several years. That child had been removed when he was eight months old, returned briefly to the family when he was four, then taken away again.

Carol Bonney had given up her children when Tom fled, but Social Services was working to prevent their being returned even though Tom was in jail. The agency's concern was heightened when Carol showed up with a black eye.

Yet all of this information did not seem to show a family history of the type of violence that could lead to murder. Something was not quite right, yet none of the available facts seemed to indicate the full story of what had taken place. All John Halstead knew for certain was that the case was going to be a difficult one. The death penalty was certainly going to be requested by the prosecutor, a penalty with which the jury was likely to be comfortable if they found Tom guilty.

John Halstead did not believe in sentencing someone to die, no matter what their crime, though he could live with the law if the person was truly guilty. He also knew that if an innocent person received such a sentence, it would be as much the result of a defense attorney's failure to adequately defend his client as it would be the skill of the prosecutor. The difficult part was the client who fell somewhere in between, such as a man who was both guilty and insane.

Tom Bonney did not yet fit comfortably into any category. Something was completely out of kilter, and Halstead had no idea exactly what it was or what to do about it. Fortunately, there was time to learn more: yet one fear Halstead had was that even with time, the facts might never be fully understood.

H. P. Williams, the prosecutor in the Bonney case, had none of the concerns that were troubling the defense counsel. He was a career district attorney, a young man with a dedication to the law. "My client is the Constitution of the United States," he says proudly. And he speaks with greater pleasure about a time when he obtained the freedom of a man he had previously convicted of a crime, a man he later learned was innocent, than of his high conviction rate. He is quick to point out that the man he had freed was a career criminal guilty of enough other crimes that everyone genuinely thought he was guilty. It was a case where all the known evidence worked against the man he prosecuted, only later information revealing the truth. Yet he was willing to return to court, embarrassing himself in the eyes of some of his colleagues, rather than let the man stay in jail for a crime of which he was innocent.

Williams admits that the man he had freed went on to commit other crimes in a different state, yet he feels no responsibility for that. The man deserved jail time only for those crimes he committed, not because he was a bad person. Being freed from a sentence he did not deserve could have proven an inspiration to change the man's ways. No one could predict that the man would not use such an opportunity. What mattered to Williams was that the man's rights were protected and society benefited in the long run, regardless of what happened before or after. The Constitution had been upheld and society was better for that fact.

Williams did not see the Bonney case as one of much importance other than on a personal level, since H. P.'s father was coming to see his son in action for the first time. The murder seemed clear-cut, simple to try. He saw no reason to bother preparing for it until the last minute, only making a serious effort a week before he had to go into court. They had the man. They had ample evidence. They had an apparent confession. Everything pointed to Bonney's guilt. Williams would present the facts and let the jury decide.

The news media delighted in the way the Bonney case was progressing. The reporters had to admit that it was coming down to a seemingly simple example of domestic violence. But the way it had unfolded, the missing girl, the unidentified, naked corpse, the distraught parents, then the unexpected flight of the father, all had managed to keep it continuously in the newspapers and in the television news. Many reporters felt that it was one of the biggest stories to take place in North Carolina and Virginia in all of 1987.

Now the case seemed to be rapidly heading to a close. The reporters decided that the father was guilty, their only question being why he had done it. Still, they kept talking with anyone involved who would grant them interviews, follow-up items appearing every few days on the inside pages of the papers.

The public was still curious for details, including one man whose interest would dramatically alter the tone of the trial. That man was Paul Dell, Ph.D., and when he came forward, the seemingly simple case would change in radically unexpected ways. Although he did not realize it at the time, Dell would ultimately reveal a conspiracy to kill Kathy that involved more than a half-dozen individuals who thought they had committed the perfect murder.

CHAPTER 4

The Sins of the Fathers

THE father wasn't a tall man, but he was lean, muscular, powerful. He worked as a game warden and a fireman, jobs involving extensive physical activity. He liked duck hunting and fishing, enjoying the challenge of the kill as much as the fresh game with which he fed the family.

To the son, the father was a giant with a booming voice and a fearsome presence. No matter what the son did, his actions always seemed wrong to the father. His mother might disagree with her husband's harshness toward the son, but she would not interfere.

The son had been given the job of cutting the grass, something he had been doing quite responsibly until, in the middle of the job, the lawn mower broke. The son was scared, though he had done nothing wrong. The lawn mower was an inexpensive one, not well-maintained. The rough ground was covered with sticks, pebbles, and other debris that was forever getting caught in the rotating blades. Sometimes it just flew out, often striking the person pushing the mower. Other times it would shatter in the blades, chipping away at the cutting edge, making it less efficient.

The lawn mower had broken in the same manner when the father used it, but this day the father refused to remember that fact. This day he was in one of his moods, looking for any opportunity to vent his anger, no matter how unjustified.

"Bastard! Little bastard!" the father roared, his booming voice echoing through the house, reverberating from the walls like a slap across the face. "You broke the mower, you little bastard!"

The boy cringed with each word. His stomach hurt and he thought he might vomit. He had to control himself, though. His father would only yell at him if he was sick. His father didn't understand. His father . . .

"Bastard! I told you to cut the grass. I told you it was going to be done today."

"But the lawn mower broke. I didn't mean to do it. I was just trying to—"

His mother started to intervene, to explain that he couldn't be held responsible for the old mower no longer working. They would simply have to let it go, get the mower fixed, cut the grass another day.

"The little bastard won't get out of it that easy. If he can't use the mower, he can use a pair of scissors."

His mother looked at her husband in surprise. Surely he didn't mean it. Surely . . .

But the boy knew and started to cry. He hated himself for that, hated the tears and the snot dripping from his nose, hated how his face was reddening and how he couldn't even get a tissue to clean himself. Salt from the tears mingled with mucus and dripped down his chin.

"Wimp!" said the man, looking at the pathetic figure of his son. The boy wouldn't go hunting with him, wouldn't even try to kill a duck. He couldn't sit still in the boat for fishing, then cried when told he had to clean the catch. And now this. Snot dripping all over him. He looked disgusting. A wimp. A bastard.

"Here's the scissors and a flashlight, you wimp bastard!" the man said to his son. "You go out there and cut the grass until it's done. I don't care if it takes you all night."

"But Daddy, I've got homework to do. I've got school."

"The boy needs to get his sleep," added his mother, hopeful that this time there might be a change, a difference.

"Wimp bastard has to learn to be responsible. He'll cut the grass until it's done. That'll teach him."

There was no arguing. He took the scissors and the flashlight and started outside. As he left, his mother whispered, "Don't worry. When it gets dark and he goes to sleep, I'll come out and let you inside."

And that was it. He had to get on his hands and knees and start cutting the grass. The air got cool after sunset, too cool for the clothing he had been wearing in the heat of the day. He began to shiver, but he dared not go inside for a jacket, and no one in the family came out to comfort him.

With the darkness came the shadows, the unfamiliar sounds and smells of night. He was terrified to look up toward the house, terrified to stop in case his father should be watching, should come outside and yell at him again. All he could do was cut a small patch, then inch his way forward and cut some more. The tears kept coming, the anger, though he suppressed that. If he ever let the rage escape, ever fought back, he was certain his father would kill him. He was so big. So big. And calling him that . . . that name. Bastard . . . He hated the man. Wanted to kill him.

Bastard. A nasty name. Nasty. He hated him for it. Hated . . .

He shivered and kept cutting, overwhelmed by fear, by rage, by sadness. Too much . . . Too much . . . He'd kill him one day. He'd kill him.

His mother came outside, warm, comforting. His father was asleep. It was okay to come inside. She would awaken her son before dawn, before his father arose for a new day. The boy would have to go outside again, take the scissors, cut more of the grass. His father would have to think he worked through the night, without sleep, coming in only in time to go to school. That was the punishment that had been ordained. That was the punishment he would have to think was carried out. But at least Tom could have a few hours of warmth and rest. They were all his mother could give him, but she felt better about herself. She did not have to face the fact that by not standing up to her husband she was, in her own way, just as abusive to their son. Yet the boy never thought of killing his mother. Only his father. Only the man who called him bastard!

Words, not bullets, represent the deadliest force one person can use against another. Words can generate feelings of love and affection. Words can bring peace to a troubled heart. Yet words can also shatter self-esteem or force someone into a corner from which he or she feels the need to fight to the death. Words can generate rage so intense that, if only for an instant, no act one human being can do to another seems unspeakable. And because they leave no obvious marks, words are the ultimate act of aggression and human torture.

Inflict physical pain, and the sufferer will either heal or quickly die. Inflict emotional pain, and you may sentence your victim to a lifetime of nightmares from which there is no escape.

Police officers patrolling the streets of any city understand the threat of physical violence. They carry nightsticks and handguns, wear bullet-proof vests, and drive cars equipped with shotguns and two-way radios so that they can instantly summon an even greater armed response.

Dangers to the body can be anticipated. A furtive movement in the shadows of an alley. The sound of footsteps on an overhead roof. A group of sullen, angry men who suddenly divide, positioning themselves like a box to entrap anyone foolish enough to try to walk through the opening they have created. The click of a bullet being placed in the chamber of a rifle. A scream, cut off as abruptly as it began. Instant silence in an area where, just a moment before, the sounds were intense. So many warnings. So many chances to protect the body.

We often talk about the streets as a jungle. Some sections of a community form a peaceful oasis where, like an African watering hole, anyone may gather, day or night, without cause for alarm. Other sections seem to have predators lurking everywhere, waiting to pounce upon the unwary and the foolish.

But there is a second jungle, far more dangerous than the first because the menace it contains is less obvious. This is the jungle of the mind, the last frontier, the hiding place for villains more evil than all the fantasy creatures of comic books, television, film, and literature.

The problem with the jungle of the mind is the fact that there is no physical protection from the dangers it contains. The detectives who must investigate its deadly twists and turns enter alone, armed only with words, never knowing when those words might backfire, creating an explosion that shatters all in its wake.

Paul Dell, Ph.D., was a detective of the mind. He had chosen to daily walk those streets where the menace is invisible, yet ever present. He traveled alone, armed only with words—a video camera and tape recorder his only backup. When he succeeded, the jungle changed, the predators vanished, the peace of the watering hole expanded to the outer reaches of the mind. When he failed, he could condemn a person to a continuing internal hell, unseen on the outside, yet like a time bomb waiting to destroy either the individual in which it was contained or those who had the misfortune to cross the person's path.

Like all good detectives, Paul Dell was curious about people. He was drawn to the extraordinary, the different. He wanted to know why people were the way they were, not just observe their actions or restrain them from further harm. Fear was overridden by his constant quest for knowledge. And like all detectives driven by more than an animal need to avenge those who had been made to suffer, he could be so blinded by his quest that his actions could occasionally be viewed as folly.

A police detective is constantly studying the streets, evaluating what is taking place, looking for hidden meanings. Is the man standing in the darkened doorway, watching the street, a mugger waiting for his victim? The lookout for a group of criminals in the process of committing a burglary, a robbery, or perhaps a drug deal? Or just an honest citizen waiting for a friend to pick him up, standing in the doorway both to escape the wind and to be out of the path of pedestrians hurrying to and from home, jobs, and places of entertainment?

Are tensions rising because of recent confrontations between police and private citizens? Because of unusual storm fronts that have left the city hot, muggy, and the average person unable to sleep well, and thus tense, tired?

The detective watches the flow of car traffic, the movements of prostitutes, how business people travel to their places of employment, how they handle their banking. The detective studies the eyes of possible junkies, the movement of the person who may be so borderline drunk that, though he seems in control, he has had one too many to be on the highway.

The detective of the mind has other concerns. Sometimes this is the immediate, the person who hears voices, who hallucinates images, who becomes violent for reasons that make no sense to the average individual. At other times this concern is for the past, for events long forgotten by the conscious mind yet which can mold and twist and change a person in ways that ultimately create an individual who may one day explode in an orgy of destruction too horrible to want to anticipate.

Paul Dell's detective work of the mind had long ago taught him that the child is father to the man. The ideals of youth, the fantasies, the joys, the verbal and emotional violence we sustain, all of these form the subconscious mind and affect the way we first see life as adults. Sometimes these are nurturing experiences, leading a child to become a caring, sharing, giving individual regardless of what profession he or she enters. Sometimes these are destructive, creating a negative self-image that can lead to shyness, withdrawal, insecurity, the inability to try to reach one's potential for fear that others will discover the "hidden truth" that is often quite the opposite of the person's reality. And sometimes the abuse leads to a rage so intense that violence is the only answer. Internalized, the rage leads to depression and thoughts of suicide. Externalized, the angry child within the adult can trigger great violence and even murder.

The Bible speaks of the sins of the fathers. Psychologists use terms like child abuse, trauma, and post-traumatic stress, among others.

Yet good or bad, we all have choices in life. We all have the opportunity as adults to put our lives in new perspective, to come to terms with ourselves, our pasts, and our present. We can choose to stop the abuse by not passing it on to the next generation. We can take a stand, saying, "I won't do to others what was done to me."

Or we can become angry, withdrawn, deciding that the world is no good, that only the strong survive. We can choose to perpetuate what happened, this time becoming the aggressor, this time taking the power position for ourselves. It is not a mature reaction. It is not emotionally healthy. But it is a choice.

Or, in a few cases, we can act out all the roles. The abused child becomes so overwhelmed by the trauma being endured that feelings become isolated, compartmentalized, rigid. The personality fragments so that, instead of being capable of a full range of emotions, the individual develops multiple personalities. When there is reason for anger, the personality meant to handle violence will dominate. During intimate moments, someone else will handle sex. There will be someone to endure pain, and perhaps someone else whose job it is to work, to provide income to support body and soul. Sometimes each personality thinks that he or she is the only personality, acting out accordingly, then constantly being troubled by "lost time," periods of minutes, hours, days, weeks, or longer when the body functions but there is no awareness.

At best, the person passes through life viewed as normal. He or she successfully hides the inner turmoil. At worst, the inappropriate personality takes control and creates a nightmare. The angry personality appears during sex, and gentle lovemaking suddenly becomes violent rape. An innocent, child-like personality gets behind the wheel of a car that a different personality learned to drive, awkwardly manages to get it moving, then finds himself going too fast in the wrong direction on the freeway.

However the adult behaves, the seeds are planted and nurtured in the child. The parent only decides whether the soil will be made from venom or from love, whether childhood will father a healthy, happy adult or a monster.

The truths of child rearing have always been the same. The Bible is filled with stories of incest, abuse, rage, and goodness. Ancient literature and drama told tales that read much like a modern psychologist's casebook. Yet the discussions of such abuse and their impact on the mind are modern phenomena.

Child abuse was rampant in the United States at the turn of the century. Overcrowded tenements led to physical violence and incest, and the lack of child labor laws turned children into chattel, tiny money machines whose life spans were often cut short because of the demands placed upon them.

It has only been since World War II that the issue of child abuse and the study of its effects has been of serious importance to therapists. It is only within the last thirty years that efforts have been made by schools and religious organizations to try and spot a child coming from a troubled home so that a trained counselor might intervene.

And it is only within the last ten years that extreme disorders of the mind such as the concept of multiple personality have been taken seriously. *The Three Faces of Eve* made headlines in the 1950s, but most therapists thought that it was a unique phenomenon. Then came *Sybil; The Five of Me; I'm Eve; Tell Me Who I Am Before I Die; The Final Face of Eve; The Minds of Billy Milligan; Nightmare*; and numerous other books. Both the American Psychiatric Association and the American Psychological Association began having meetings and conferences concerning issues such as multiple personality and adult victims of child abuse. The issues became of great importance, though still facing much skepticism in the profession.

By the time of Kathy Bonney's murder, some therapists routinely looked for multiple personality and similar problems in people whose actions were extreme. Severe mood shifts, unexpected and unexplainable quirks of behavior, acts of violence so unusual as to not be logical, and other occurrences, were all studied. Sometimes this was in clinical settings with patients who had come to see the doctor. And sometimes, as in the case of Dr. Paul Dell, this was taken more broadly in society. Yet always they were acting as the detective, reading the "streets" of the mind, trying to both understand and anticipate.

Dr. Paul Dell was an academic, a man accustomed to seeking knowledge through the writings, not just the actions of others. He was a clinician as well, spending an average of thirty hours a week with his patients. But it was the academic side that often dominated his life. He frequently used newspapers as tools, using the documenting of the follies, glories, passions, and actions of humanity provided by the press as a way of constantly trying to understand the often hidden aspects of life.

"It's funny what you can find in the paper if you pay attention," Dr. Dell commented in an interview after the Kathy Bonney case was resolved. "I mean, to give you an example, I was reading the sports page one day, and there was a news story about some local high school pitcher who was something of a phenomenon because he pitched both left-handed and right-handed. Now I have heard of switch hitters, but being able to pitch left-handed and right-handed is a phenomenal degree of ambidexterity, and I said to myself, 'That's the kind of thing a multiple could do.'

"I wondered and I read the story closely, and sure enough, there, in the story, is a report of abusive behavior on the part of the father . . . The boy had showed left-handed behavior in early childhood. The father, who wanted to train the boy to be an athlete, had decided that left-handedness was a disadvantage. He didn't want the boy to be left-handed, and he tied the boy's left arm behind his back . . . so he couldn't use it.

"There were accounts in the story of major behavior problems early in high school, psychiatric treatment, and episodes where the boy would go out of control, tear up a room, then shift mood and say, 'Gee, I'm really sorry.' These are the kinds of things you can find in the paper if you look."

There were other stories, all of which were clipped for file and for occasional use in teaching. However, the psychologist never followed up on them because he did not feel it appropriate for him to try to force himself into someone else's life.

There was something a little different about the Bonney case, about the fact that Kathy had been shot twenty-seven times with small-caliber bullets. "And I said to myself, when I read it, this is an incredibly intense level of violence. This is the kind of violence you get either with somebody who is intensely psychotic or dissociative.

"One of the things that goes on with dissociation is you are able to get this incredible purity of behavior and effect, and when I get that kind of—twenty seven shots, I mean it was clear that he had to reload the gun. And I thought, 'I wonder if she was shot by a dissociative killer?' Nothing more than that.

"It was the extreme of the violence. So then some period of time went by—I don't know how long it was—and the man was arrested out of Indianapolis. Got picked up out there. And I said, this is the guy that shot his daughter twenty-seven times. I wonder if he is dissociative. That's what went through my head."

Dr. Dell began watching the news concerning Bonney. He noticed that when Bonney came in from the airport, and when he went to be arraigned, he covered his head so he wouldn't be seen. He obviously wanted to avoid any contact with the press, as well as avoiding having his picture taken. Yet when the sheriff was taking him to jail, he insisted upon the car being stopped so he could talk with the press.

"So they stopped the car. He talks to the reporters who were there and confessed to the killing. And again the thought went through my head, 'I wonder if this guy is a multiple, because that sounds like a switch.'

"I mean, these are the thoughts going through my head as these different events were rolling by with Tom Bonney. Then I read the newspaper the following morning and that's what really took me. I think there were a couple of newspaper reports. I got one in particular, the Virginia *Pilot*, February fourth, 1988, front-page story: Bonney caught officers by surprise when he demanded to make a statement to reporters just before he was driven to the Albemarle District Jail in Elizabeth City, North Carolina. And he says this stuff about being depressed, and he got into an argument and says some stuff about cracking up. There was temporary insanity, went over the edge."

Dr. Dell then quoted the statement: " 'When informed of her husband's statement that he had shot the daughter, Dorothy Bonney, his wife, says, "How could you be insane and kill like that?" ' He probably did it because one minute he would be himself and the next he would flip and not even remember."

There were other aspects of the case about which he was reading that helped Dr. Dell form his opinion. He mentioned that when Bonney was asked what happened to the gun, he was quoted as saying, "It was throwed in the canal."

To many people, a quote such as "It was throwed in the canal" would imply that the speaker was uneducated. But Dr. Dell became convinced there might be a deeper meaning. "This is dissociative language. What a person would say who is not dissociative is, 'I threw it in the canal.' 'It was throwed in the canal' is the statement of one alter (personality) or a dissociated person describing something that they know or saw themselves do that they did not experience as their own behavior." So convinced was Dr. Dell that the language quoted in the article was significant as a clue to Bonney's motivation that he called John Halstead, the defense attorney, whom he had casually known in the past.

"I said, 'John, I think I know what is going on with this guy.' I said, 'I'm not positive, but I have an idea I know what is going on with him, and I would be interested in taking a look at him if you want.'

"John talked with me for maybe three or four more minutes and hung up. Then I didn't hear anything more about it until approximately three-and-a-half months later. John called back and said he had been evaluated down there by the State Forensic Institute and Dorothea Dix Hospital and did I want to evaluate him for the defense?

"I said, 'Okay.' So that's how I got in on it."

Paul Dell may have been a detective of the mind like most psychologists and psychiatrists, but he never wanted to be involved in murder. He was essentially a family therapist working at the Eastern Virginia Medical School in Norfolk. He had trained at the University of Texas in Austin, studying to be a clinical psychologist. Then, after graduating in 1973, he did a two-year clinical internship and obtained his fellowship in family therapy. Finally he went to the medical school to become director of the Family Therapy Institute within the Department of Psychiatry.

Dr. Dell's work had been relatively routine for several years. He saw cases of spouse abuse, of couples with sexual problems, couples unable to communicate, and all the myriad difficulties that are encountered when two people attempt to interact over a long period of time.

Dr. Dell's world changed dramatically after a couple, Judy and Pete Tyson (a pseudonym), had been receiving counseling from him for a year. The approach he was using had worked many times before, yet something was different this time. The wife was becoming increasingly depressed, so much so that Dr. Dell felt that he should see her individually, not just with her husband.

One day the woman was depressed to a level where Dr. Dell thought she was likely to commit suicide. He was certain that if he let her leave the office, she would take her life at the first opportunity, leaping from a window, dashing in front of traffic, or some other self-destructive act. As they talked, she moved from a chair to the floor, slowly curling into a fetal position, as though desperate to return to the safety of her mother's womb.

The doctor had never seen anyone in such a state before and knew that the problem required drastic measures. He was calling the hospital to see if there was a bed available on the adult unit for Judy when she spoke up, her voice extremely weak, and said, "Judy isn't here. Judy is not here . . ."

Judy was placed on the psychiatric ward, where she was diagnosed as a multiple personality, a field about which Dr. Dell knew very little. His awareness of such problems primarily stemmed from the popular culture. He had heard about the book *The Three Faces of Eve*, the pioneering study in the 1950s that led to an Academy Award–winning performance by Joanne Woodward in the movie by the same name. She had played the roles of Eve White, Eve Black, and Jane, three radically different types of women all "sharing" the same body.

Dell had also read the book *Sybil*, then seen the television adaptation starring actress Sally Field. But again, these were written for the popular market. Detailed information about the causes of such a phenomenon, as well as information concerning how to help the patient heal, were not included in any of the work.

"I didn't know how to treat her," said Dell, who later learned that the personality who had spoken to him from the floor of his office was a highly abused personality who was hoping that the doctor would reject her. "I hadn't the foggiest idea. Nobody I could find in the Department of Psychiatry had anything they could tell me, and I did the only thing I could do. I started reading. I'm an academic, and so I read and I read, and I dug up literature and I read and read and remembered."

Judy had revealed herself just after Dr. Dell had learned of the First International Meeting for Multiple Personality and Dissociative States. He did the therapy the best he could for the next several months, attending the Second International Meeting in order to gain more practical experience.

Over time, Dr. Dell became extremely knowledgeable about what is known as dissociative phenomena. According to Dr. Dell, this relates to the way the mind can block different aspects of human experience in order to insulate the body from stress. This ability differs with the individual and the experience.

The concept of hysteric dissociation or multiple personality always starts with a trauma, according to Dr. Dell. "The source of the trauma can be physical. It can be a result of being terribly beaten or tortured. It can also be psychological. It overwhelms your ability to cope.

"You or I might be able to cope with somebody tromping on our toe very hard, or perhaps being scared by a loud noise, but if the trauma goes beyond that, say, to the point of being mugged, you may be able to cope with it or you may not. The person who is not able to cope with the mugging will find some way automatically to block out part of the intensity of the assault, and it's when you begin to get this automatic partial shutting down of the body's defense systems."

Dr. Dell explained that the crucial aspect of trauma is that "it's overwhelming. And what may be overwhelming for one person may not be for another. There are, indeed, differences from one persona to another person."

Multiple personality, which is triggered by trauma, "means that an individual has more than one separate personality. More than one, where you have at least two personalities which recur over and over across time, over and over, taking control of the body so that you've got two internal centers or more that are capable of taking control over the body."

Dell continued: "Dissociation involves a splitting apart of some kind of the functioning of the individual. It's hard to think of human beings as having separate parts, and dissociation has to do exactly with that. It has to do with part of our functioning separating off from the rest of us.

"Dissociation is a major defense mechanism of the human mind. What I mean by that is that there are a variety of automatic bodily physiologic defense mechanisms that everybody is familiar with. For example, when you run a temperature, when you have a fever, that, in fact, is the physiological defense mechanism going into action trying to throw off a bug or a germ, or whatever it is that you've gotten. Similarly, if you get a blister, that cushion of fluid under the skin where you've been burned or where you've rubbed yourself too much is the body again trying to insulate itself from the burn to protect itself. It's a defense mechanism that occurs automatically.

"Similarly, when you cut yourself and your blood starts clotting, that's an automatic physiology defense mechanism of the body to protect you from bleeding to death. The blood clots and the bleeding stops.

"In the case of trauma, one of the things that the human body appears to be wired up to do is . . . dissociate to protect itself in the face of overwhelming stimuli.

"What's overwhelming? A large number of things. Anything from a child being physically abused, a child being sexually abused, a woman who is raped, soldiers in combat, even an automobile accident or severe accidents of various sorts can be overwhelming, so that dissociation can automatically click into gear for us in exactly the same sense that blood clotting automatically clicks into gear, or running a fever automatically clicks into gear to protect us."

Dr. Dell gave some specific examples of dissociation. "You may have heard that some dentists use hypnosis for pain relief. I mean, not all dentists just routinely use novocaine or whatever it is. Some dentists use hypnosis. They'll hypnotize the person and they will, in essence, turn off the pain.

"Another way of saying it is that when you have that kind of hypnotic pain control, the pain is dissociated. It is split off and you don't feel it. I mean, the dentist is still drilling holes in your teeth and the injuries to you are still very real, but you don't feel it. And hypnosis in that sense is something of a dissociative mechanism intentionally used by the dentist for pain relief.

"There are many women today who do Lamaze technique when it comes to childbirth. The Lamaze procedure works well to help many women go down into trance, and it helps dissociate a lot of the pain, so that is a quasihypnotic procedure. There is a splitting off of the pain.

"Now some psychiatric patients will spontaneously develop dissociation where they can't feel something. They may have a whole arm go numb and they literally can't feel. You can come up and stick a pin in it and they won't feel it. It's a psychiatric symptom that just occurs spontaneously."

Dr. Dell explained that some people create a trancelike state by just staring at a fixed object. This is especially obvious with children who stare at a television set, so riveted by what they are watching that they stop being aware of what is taking place all around them.

"There are a couple of psychiatric symptoms of dissociation. One is called 'derealization'; another one is called 'depersonalization.'

"Derealization is when you become disconnected from your sense of things around you being real. It's a fairly common experience. It's a brief period; you know you're doing things, but you feel a little bit alienated and disconnected from everything, and it's not real.

"The other term is 'depersonalization,' and, if anything, depersonalization is even a more common phenomenon than derealization. It's the kind of thing where you feel a little bit disconnected from yourself. You are busy doing whatever, and you just really feel separate from yourself. Not a great deal separate, but you look at your hand and you know it's your hand, yet it doesn't have the same feeling of 'youness' as it usually does. It's a very common experience."

Dr. Dell explained that one common dissociative occurrence is known as sleep paralysis, and usually lasts no more than a minute. It occurs when you first awaken, know you are awake, yet for a few seconds cannot move your body. Such an experience is considered dissociation since, for a moment, your mind cannot control your body.

"Another example that many people would consider to be a dissociative phenomenon is the occurrence of speaking in tongues. When speaking in tongues occurs, the individual does not experience themselves as saying what comes out of their mouth. They feel it is disconnected from them. It's like they are speaking without trying to. And they may also have certain emotional experiences while speaking in tongues, and it doesn't feel like their own emotions. It's like these emotions just come through them or that they are just there. They happened to them. And this is a dissociative phenomenon. Disconnected. Split off."

The doctor explained that another dissociative disorder is the "fugue state." He related the fugue state to amnesia. In amnesia, you have full awareness of what you are doing except for a blank of a few minutes, a few hours or whatever, during which you cannot remember. Everything before and after that time is clear, though. Only one section is forgotten.

With a fugue state, there is not only amnesia, but "something happens and you take on another identity." He explained, "You take on another identity and you spend some period of time in this other identity until you come back to yourself. And then suddenly you find yourself someplace else. You don't know how you got there. You have no memory for what has occurred in between, and everything's a mystery to you. And if you find people who interacted with you during that period that you can't remember, they will describe to you what you did, what you said, and they will usually tell you that you claimed to be somebody other than who you are." It is a very rare experience, but it is something that occurs routinely within the disorder known as multiple personality.

Other researchers in the field of multiple personality stress that it is a coping mechanism of a young child overwhelmed by trauma, often sexual in nature, from which he or she cannot escape. Usually all of this takes place before the person is seven years old, and it never starts any later than preadolescence, according to researchers.

The trauma is frequently abnormal child abuse. Something that the child does that results in great love from the parent one day may result in a beating the next. If one parent is abusive, usually the other parent is either absent from the home or is known as the passive abuser, aware of what is taking place yet not intervening to stop it. There is also one overwhelming trauma from which the child feels unable to flee physically, and so the child flees mentally.

For example, Christina Peters documented such a childhood in her autobiography *Tell Me Who I Am Before I Die*. The final trauma was a rape by her father when she was five years old. Unable to mentally handle what was happening, her mind created a personality that was all rage and violence to try and fight her father. But the rage of a five-year-old is no match for a violently mentally ill adult man, and she was almost instantly overwhelmed. Then she created a personality whose job it was to endure the pain she was experiencing, both then and throughout her life. And when it was over, she created a personality to get her through each day because she no longer could cope as she had before.

The personalities become like real people, though always limited in what they can do. Henry Hawksworth, whose multiple personality case was documented in *The Five Of Me*, had Peter, the playful child who thought he was Peter Pan stuck in the wrong body. He had the violent Johnny whose hobby was going into bars frequented by Marines, then beating up all opposition. And he had Dana, the brilliant, high-paid insurance executive. Yet any of the personalities might take over at any time. As a result, Dana sometimes found himself sitting in the water near a beach, a crudely made sand castle by his side, while he was dressed in an expensive suit and should have been meeting with a client. Or Johnny would come out in the office and attempt to sexually assault an attractive secretary, then Dana would be dumbfounded when she quit.

"Many children who are severely abused in childhood, physically abused, or an adult who was physically abused in childhood, will tell you that often they got to a point where they didn't feel pain: 'I knew he was hitting me. I could see the marks. I was even bleeding. But, no, I didn't feel the pain.' So there is a dissociation of the sensation.

"Same thing happens in combat. A lot of soldiers will go through a firefight, and only after the battle is over do they realize that they are severely wounded and bleeding, and in bad need of medical attention. It was a spontaneous dissociation of sensation. It's an emergency response of the body."

Dr. Dell also explained what are known as out-of-body experiences. "The one I run into most often is when I'll talk with a woman about her childhood sexual abuse experience, and what she may tell me is, 'Daddy was doing this, but it was like I was floating in the corner of the room over there. And I was watching him do it to that little girl in the bed. I know it was me, but it wasn't me. I was up there watching it happen.' That's an out-of-body experience that is not an uncommon one at all in times of severe trauma. I hear that frequently in child sexual abuse."

Rape victims sometimes experience the same situation. They describe the rape from above, looking down on their attacker and being able to describe him from the back. However, though the experience seems real to the person involved, it is definitely a way for the mind to cope instead of being an actual experience of leaving the body. Detectives and police psychologists say that while the victim remembers seeing the back of the rapist and may mention scars or other marks seen only when floating above the body, when they catch the man, those marks are not there. Only what the victim saw under normal circumstances is accurate. Everything else was created by the mind during the illusion of being out-of-body as a way of protecting the mental state of the victim. As Dr. Dell explained, such victims dissociate both the physical sensation of the rape and "they will also dissociate the emotion by getting themselves out of the body. It's a good, protective mechanism."

Multiple personality can involve dissociation of emotions, memory, physical sensation—all facets of the experience. The person may act radically different, then not remember any of the experience until therapy.

This is not to say that the multiple personality individual is permanently dissociated. When the therapist helps the patient uncover the trauma that caused the split, to remember and deal with it, the person can go on to function like anyone else. They are not "insane." They utilized the coping mechanism of a healthy child's mind in crisis. And as an adult, with help, they can return to acting like everyone else. Yet while the person is multiple, he or she may commit acts of great heroism, selflessness, or violence. Some multiple personalities have been both dedicated church leaders as well as prostitutes, the prostitute shocked to discover religious materials among her papers, and the church leader horrified to discover extremely revealing clothing in her closet. Neither personality remembers acquiring what has been found. Neither remembers anyone leaving it there. Yet it cannot be denied, and is for them an extremely troubling fact. It is such unusual behavior that often sends the person to a therapist in the first place, and it is this unusual behavior that may help the therapist diagnose multiple personality.

Dr. Dell had been working with multiple personality patients for four years when he read the newspaper reports of Tom Bonney's arrest. He had a handful of such troubled individuals in his practice.

He also worked as a consultant to other professionals working in the field, in addition to his teaching. He was respected, though occasionally at odds with other therapists who were unfamiliar with dissociative behavior.

"I knew about the powerful link between trauma and dissociation, and when a violent crime was reported in the newspaper, I would often read the account closely, wondering if any dissociative stuff should happen to pop up in the newspaper again."

John Halstead was desperate. Paul Dell was curious. There seemed little question that a jury would be convinced that Tom Bonney had pulled the trigger of the gun that killed his daughter Kathy. The psychiatric evaluation of Bonney at the state hospital had brought about mixed results. There seemed no question that Bonney was dissociating, yet exactly what that meant was uncertain. Even worse, North Carolina followed the M'Naghten Rule for insanity. This meant that if someone committed a crime while understanding the difference between right and wrong, they were sane and could be sentenced to death.

On the surface the M'Naghten Rule seemed fair. The problem was, an extremely disturbed individual could know the difference between right and wrong, yet still be mentally ill to an objective observer. For example, there was a case in Ohio where a man killed strangers. He killed once, went about his daily life, then killed again without knowing the person, seemingly without motive. The murderer was eventually caught and readily confessed.

God told him to kill, the man explained. God had come to him and asked him to kill. For weeks the man had argued with God, explaining that he had read the Bible and knew that God had made killing a taboo. He quoted the Ten Commandments to God, giving special emphasis to the words "Thou Shalt Not Kill."

But over time, God asked the man to study the Bible. God told him to look at the number of times God took lives, such as when the Egyptians pursued Moses and his people as they fled bondage on their way to the Promised Land.

"That's all right, God," the man reportedly explained. "You can do anything you want. You're God. But I'm just a mortal, and Your book tells me not to kill."

Neither the prosecutor nor the defense questioned that such a dialogue raged within the mind of the man sitting in the courtroom. Ultimately God convinced the man that he was God's chosen avenger. It was his job to kill for God. The Lord explained that He could use any means desired, and He chose the man who was now charged with murder.

The man knew that what he was doing was wrong. Yet he was doing it for God, and that meant he was obeying a higher authority, an authority who could not be disobeyed. The jury was convinced that the man was seriously mentally ill and truly believed that he was acting on behalf of God. They also found him guilty of first degree murder as charged, because, under M'Naghten, so long as someone knew the difference between right and wrong, they were legally responsible for their actions.

Tom Bonney knew the difference between right and wrong. Sometimes Tom Bonney talked as though he had murdered his daughter. Sometimes he talked as though someone else must have done it. And sometimes he decided that she was still alive, a belief he held strongly in the Albemarle District Jail, where he was being held pending his trial.

Dr. Dell's curiosity and background left him unprepared for what he was about to do. Tom Bonney was being charged with murder, the ultimate taboo in American society. It is the irreversible crime, the one act for which an individual can never say "I'm sorry." As Kathy Bonney had stated in the letter to the local newspaper written just before she was killed, "I'm sorry" is something you say when you bump into someone else in public, not when you have killed.

There are seemingly far more heinous crimes than murder. The rape of a child, for example, is so despicable that when a man is convicted of such a crime, even hardened criminals are likely to harass him, torture him, even castrate him in his cell—if they let him live. Yet a child who has been raped and brutalized can eventually lead a normal life, given intense therapy for many years following the horror he or she has to endure. There are crisis centers established to help adults who have been battered and assaulted. Most people believe that though a violent trauma may cause psychological and, perhaps, physical scars for many years, it is possible to help such individuals return to normal existence.

There is no second chance with murder. A corpse cannot be given counseling. A corpse cannot be healed and rehabilitated. Death is forever. As a result, a prosecutor involved with a murder case will feel it is his or her duty to shatter any defense arguments easing the impact of such a crime. If this means discrediting a weak witness for the defense, so be it. And Paul Dell had set himself up to be a weak witness.

"Gung-ho" curiosity is fine in a clinical setting where the ultimate goal is to heal the person in pain. Had Tom Bonney come to Dr. Dell as a patient, the psychologist's attitude and actions would have been commendable, lauded by his colleagues. Dr. Dell was anxious to learn the truth behind the man as quickly and as effectively as possible. He wanted to satisfy himself intellectually. He wanted to ease the pain and suffering of a disturbed mind if, indeed, Tom Bonney was dissociative. He understood that, if his beliefs were correct, Tom had endured a nightmare of a childhood, something that had haunted him all of his adult life.

Good intentions have no place in a criminal trial. The moment Paul Dell called John Halstead, he established himself as biased. H. P. Williams or any other competent prosecutor would justifiably be able to say that the psychologist entered the case with a preconceived notion, then made an effort to find answers that only matched what he believed. The tragedy of the Bonney case is that what Dell found was both so accurate and so shocking that it would be a relief for a jury to not believe the story. By volunteering his services, he may have unknowingly created a situation where Tom Bonney was destined to be sentenced to death.

Dr. Dell traveled to the Albemarle District Jail in Elizabeth City in order to visit Tom Bonney. His first impression was not a good one, though there was no sense that Bonney was a physical threat. He found Tom to be "talkative, bubbly, whiny, friendly. He would just rattle on about insignificant stuff, complaining about the way the jailers would treat him, the food, and this and that and everything else. When I would ask him questions, he didn't know the answer to almost anything.

"I would ask him, 'How old are you?'

"He would make a long pause, then say, 'I don't know. I guess I'm about forty-four or forty-five.'

"And I'd ask him how tall he was, and he'd fumble and mumble and then he would say, 'It's been a long time since I was told how tall I am. It's probably the same as it's always been.'

" 'Well, how tall are you?"

" 'I don't know. Maybe . . . I guess about five-ten or whatever it is."

"And almost any questions I asked him, I would get this stuff. I'd ask him how old his children were, and he didn't know. He didn't remember. He didn't remember much of anything.

"He sounded pretty dumb. They had diagnosed him over at the state mental hospital as pseudo-dementia, a psychiatric version of dementia that's not real. There's no organic deterioration of the brain that would produce all this forgetting. And

I mean he had driven them nuts when they tried to evaluate him at Dorothea Dix.

"What I wrote here in my notes is, 'Slow, dull, gives the picture of a nice, simple, dull, country, retarded bumpkin.' That was my impression of him. Whining, childlike, depressed, slow."

The memory was a constant problem. "I would ask him a question, and either he wouldn't answer it or he wouldn't know the answer. Or I would get this vague answer or he'd stop for a second and he wouldn't say anything, and then he would just start talking about his meal last night or whatever it was . . . I would go down there and I would see him at, say, one o'clock or one-thirty in the afternoon and interview him, and he wouldn't know what he had for lunch. He wouldn't know what he had had for breakfast. And these are some of the basic orienting questions you ask, and he didn't know. He didn't know from nothing."

Dr. Dell was trying to be careful not to make observations that would only support his preconceived ideas about Tom Bonney. He had reviewed as much of the family history and police records as were available, in addition to making note of what he knew from the newspaper. He prepared a list for himself prior to going to see Bonney in jail so that he would know where there was any personal bias.

Because he was working for the defense counsel, Dr. Dell was able to review all reports, including confidential background information available concerning Tom Bonney. These ranged from statements made by family members, to medical reports and internal information prepared by the Social Service agencies involved with the Bonneys. They were critical for his use because they were considered a more objective overview of Tom's recent past life and behavior than anything Tom might say. As a result, there were some surprises that reinforced Dr. Dell's suspicions that Tom was a multiple personality.

For example, many months before Kathy's murder, Tom was working on a station wagon he had purchased for the salvage yard. The vehicle was on a jack, Tom was underneath the car, and there were several witnesses present.

Tom had used the jack improperly, and the slight movement caused by Tom's preparations to strip the undercarriage resulted in the station wagon slipping off its holder and smashing down on Tom. The car did not drop far, but its weight was so intense that Tom instantly went into shock with internal damage, a broken shoulder, broken collarbone, and broken ribs. Had he been alone, he might have died before anyone found him. Fortunately, John McClung was able to raise the car, freeing Bonney just before the paramedics arrived.

The paramedics did what they could, bandaging the damaged areas so Tom would not cause himself further harm through unnecessary movement. Then they prepared to transport him to the hospital, where, based on similar accidents, they expected him to have to spend up to several weeks recovering. To their amazement, Tom refused to go with them.

The paramedics tried to explain that he was in shock, not thinking clearly and still in great danger. They had handled the preliminary treatment of the most obvious injuries. However, damage such as he had sustained could easily be far more severe than was obvious. People had died as a result of internal damage after similar accidents.

Tom still refused. To everyone's amazement, he climbed into his wrecker, which still had a car attached, drove himself home, went inside and went to bed, where he rested for weeks. The pain had to be intense, yet Tom took no medication, nor did he try to ease the pain through nonprescription drugs or alcohol. And when he felt strong enough following the prolonged bed rest, he returned to work, where his still amazed friends and coworkers nicknamed him "Bones."

Dr. Dell knew that the shock following trauma can prevent a person from feeling pain for a short period of time. It is one of the body's defense mechanisms to try and keep itself alive until the injured person can get help. Yet in his experience, and in his reading about the mind, he had not encountered someone who could experience such intense injuries and then block the pain for the entire recovery period, unless they were able to dissociate. And that dissociation was the normal way for a multiple personality to survive.

Having gathered all this background, Dr. Dell prepared the following list prior to meeting Tom. He also placed in parentheses the sources for the information so he would better understand the family dynamics after questioning Tom.

I. What I knew from the newspapers & media:

1) Bizarre extreme murder—27 shots. Had to reload gun to do it.
2) Refused to admit or talk to reporters, & then underwent a sudden change & asked police to stop car so he could talk to reporters. Confessed.
3) Wife—"One minute he would be himself & then the next he would flip and not even remember it."
4) Dissociative language—"It was throwed in the canal."

II. What I knew before interviewing Tom Bonney:

Broad Screen
1) One parent cold & critical & rejecting (sister)
2) Abusive relationship in adulthood (wife)
3) Guilt (ISB) & low self-worth
4) Can block pain (DES)
5) Flashbacks (attorney interview)
6) Split personality (wife, Jill Kelly, John Hoskins, Bruce Hansberry)
7) History of sleep problems
8) Hears voices—DES
9) Family history of dissociation—Kathy
Fine Screen: Harder core items
1) Amnesias—wife, DES
2) Discovery of items among his possessions that he cannot account for—DES

3) Does not recall a large chunk of childhood—sister
4) Voices commenting on his actions—DES
5) Moody (sudden mood swings)—media reports, sister, wife
6) Little forgettings—DES
7) Peculiar forgettings—wife (newspaper), DES
8) Spontaneous trance states—DES
9) Dissociative experiences—DES
10) Visual hallucinations—attorney interview
11) Marked differences in manner, voice, etc.—wife, jail captain

(After the first interview with Tom and the review of a psychiatric report, Dr. Dell added the following to his earlier list.)

III. Additional data gained in interview and Dr. Lynn's report before hypnotizing Tom Bonney:

1) History of depression—Dr. Lynn, Tom
2) Childhood history of abuse—Tom
3) Shifting symptom picture—Dr. Lynn
4) Reports of psychic abilities—Tom
5) Sexual difficulties—Tom
6) Long history of being blamed for things he did not do—Tom
7) Thought withdrawal—observed in interview
8) Made feelings
9) Influences playing on the body
10) Headaches—Tom & Dr. Lynn's report

In addition, Dr. Dell used several tests devised by therapists throughout the country that were meant to determine patterns that indicated possible multiple personality. These were conducted with Tom before he was placed under hypnosis.

The moment Dr. Dell decided to use hypnosis to interview Tom Bonney, his decision would have far greater impact than just determining the issue of Bonney's possible multiple personality. The use of hypnosis has long been controversial. The nature of hypnosis is well understood. It is related to the fight/flight syndrome that all humans experience under stress.

In ancient times human safety required us to either flee or destroy that which attacked us. If an animal wanted to have us for dinner, we instinctively knew to either grab the nearest large rock and smash it on the head or to run away, climb a tree, or take some other physical action in order to get away.

In more sophisticated times we talk about the adrenaline rush that comes when confronted by a mugger, or when called upon to instantly maneuver the car we are driving because another vehicle is approaching head on in the wrong lane, or some other experience. We also know the overwhelming sensation of not being able to react as we wish, such as when we are being yelled at by a superior on the job. The natural reaction of a man in a three-piece suit faced with a verbal assault by the president of his company is no different from that of Og the caveman confronted by a sabertooth tiger. However, taking a rock and smashing the head of the president will result in a jail term for murder. And fleeing from the office will get you fired.

Hypnosis, like the fight/flight syndrome, is a mechanism of the mind that is actually positive. Through a number of means, either under your own power (self-hypnosis) or guided by someone else, you escape from the "fight" desire into the hypnotic state. The body and brain feel safe within their environment and you become highly suggestive. The normal defense against suggestion is eliminated and there is a condition of deep relaxation.

Hypnosis, as Dr. Dell intended, can eliminate defenses in the subject. It is possible, in a hypnotic state, to recall past events, including those that have been deliberately forgotten. This is what makes it popular as a police tool.

For example, Dr. Martin Reiser, director of the Behavioral Sciences Services of the Los Angeles Police Department, is a pioneer in the use of hypnosis as a tool for law enforcement. He has routinely used hypnosis as a memory aid for many years, proving its worth in criminal cases.

In one instance, a police officer was shot in the abdomen when responding to a burglary call. His gun was stolen and the suspect got away. Both the wounded officer and his partner tried to help a police artist prepare a composite drawing of the burglar, but the results were quite different. Finally it was decided to place the wounded officer under hypnosis to see what he remembered, since he had seen the man more clearly than his partner, even though it was only for the few moments of the shoot-out.

The wounded police officer was guided into a deep hypnotic state, during which times he helped the artist revise the original drawing of the burglar. When he came out of hypnosis and looked at what was done, he stated that there was no question that the drawing was accurate. Several months later a man was caught. His appearance was identical to the drawing and he was found to still have the police officer's revolver in his possession.

Similar cases have been made with rape victims and others who have either experienced or witnessed crimes. Frequently an intense trauma, such as a gang rape, is completely forgotten. The victim cannot handle the overwhelming physical and emotional pain that comes from such a memory. The mind deliberately creates amnesia concerning the incident and no conscious effort works.

Courts have long accepted the value of hypnosis as a memory aid if the person uses it to focus his/her attention on the past in order to remember an event more clearly. It is the suggestibility under hypnosis, when the protective barriers are down and the person remembers, that can become a problem.

Suggestibility can be positive. For example, a rape victim might be hypnotized, then told, "As you describe what happened, you will become more relaxed. You will feel better about yourself, safe from harm. All the tension you have been feeling will drain away and you will lose the fear that has been keeping you from sleeping." The conscious mind created a barrier to the memory because of the terror that had been experienced. The hypnotist, having broken through the barriers erected by the conscious mind, uses suggestion to prevent the hysteria that might otherwise accompany the subject's reliving the horror she previously endured.

However, unlike the fantasies of movies where the therapist completely controls the subject, the hypnotist is rarely able to force someone to do what they would not otherwise do. There have been instances where hypnosis was a factor in a crime, according to research done by Dr. Reiser and others, but these are rare. More common is the implanting of an idea that causes the hypnotized subject to accept it as his own. And it was with this type of suggestibility that Dr. Dell would find himself in trouble.

Paul Dell was pressured as he sat with Tom Bonney in the Albemarle District Jail. He had entered the case in part because of his curiosity, and in part because of humanitarian concerns. If Tom Bonney was a multiple personality, he was the victim of child abuse and was daily suffering his own internal horrors. The fact that he may have killed his daughter was horrible, but it was the action of an intensely troubled mind. The man needed psychological help, not the death penalty.

Time was short. Dr. Dell was used to family practice consultation where therapy could extend for weeks, months, or years. Everyone was reasonably cooperative. Everyone was committed to the change needed in order for the family to again know happiness. Yet now there was a deadline. The trial of Tom Bonney would be starting soon and he would have to serve as the key witness. What he did, what he found, would in part determine whether Tom Bonney was allowed to live or die. He had never encountered such personal pressure before. He was out of his element, nervous, yet driven by the detective's desire to know the truth.

If Paul Dell had been a detective of the streets, he might have resorted to other forms of interrogation for a witness denying his obvious involvement in the murder of his daughter. He might have taken the man into a soundproofed interrogation room, utilizing his fists, a blackjack, or some other device to literally beat Tom Bonney into confessing. He might have tried to cause Tom enough pain so that telling the truth and facing the consequences of that action were preferable to experiencing the violence he was being forced to endure.

Not that violence would have jogged Tom Bonney's memory. Beatings could not penetrate the barriers the mind erects when it has been overwhelmed by trauma. But with time limited and knowledge the only hope to save a man's life, any effort would have been used by a street detective.

For Dr. Dell, hypnosis seemed the only answer. It would have been preferable to talk with Tom Bonney without the suggestive state. It would have been best to have the luxury of hour after hour of conversation, working with Tom to get him to relive the events of the day his daughter was shot. There would be no chance of tainting the evidence presented in the court, no chance of making a mistake that was irreversible. But trial would be starting in a matter of weeks. The first interview was held July 16, 1988, and time was limited.

Dr. Dell's initial interview lasted approximately three hours and did not include hypnosis. He observed that Tom occasionally seemed to go into a trancelike state, and he knew that such a condition had apparently happened before when Tom was being evaluated at Dorothea Dix. However, he also realized that "psychiatrists know a hell of a lot more about neurological stuff than they do about dissociation. So if somebody trances noticeably, they are going to think petit mal seizure before they are going to think dissociation."

Toward the end of that first interview, Dr. Dell began asking Tom about his daughter. He said, "Tom, who shot Kathy?"

The doctor also asked him how many times Kathy was shot. And Tom did everything possible to avoid answering the question.

"I just kept harassing him about it," Dr. Dell recalled. "I said, 'Tom, who shot Kathy?' And finally, squirming and with great distress, he said, 'I don't think she was shot at all.'"

Tom Bonney had good reason to believe his daughter was not dead. She had been shot twenty-seven times. The photographs of her shattered body had been repeatedly shown to him. He had been present at her funeral. Yet despite all that, Kathy Bonney had returned. While Tom was in his jail cell, his daughter reached out to him. She could not get into his cell, but her voice had come through loud and clear to him. More important, it wasn't a hallucination. Had Dr. Dell, the police, or any other inmate stood in Tom's cell, they would have heard Kathy Bonney speak to her father. At least it was such an identity that the very real voice claimed to have.

Emily Weston, a young woman, was in the Albermarle District Jail at the same time as Tom. Her father, emotionally disturbed, was repeatedly jailed, until the day when he became so despondent in his cell that he hanged himself. Ironically, not only was Tom Bonney kept in the same cell that Emily's father had been in the day her father killed himself, it was connected by a vent to the cell in which she was being held.

Tom Bonney had no sense of the idiosyncrasies of jail construction and the ingeniousness of inmates who like to establish their own communication system. No matter how well-built a jail might be, there is almost always some way for inmates to establish a prison "telephone" system. Many old jails have the plumbing for the toilets connected in such a manner that you can empty the water from the bowl, then shout through the pipes to cells on other floors. In other jails, such as the one in which Tom and Emily were incarcerated, the ventilation system serves as an intercom. Yet because it was necessary to speak in a louder than normal voice in order to be heard through the vents, Tom had not realized that it was possible to hear a voice from another cell.

"Daddy," Emily called out one night, speaking directly into the vent, hoping to have a little fun with Tom Bonney. "Daddy, why did you do me like that? Why did you shoot me all them times, Daddy? I didn't do anything. . . ."

"I mean, I changed my voice and everything," Emily later said. "I was friggin' out."

Tom, hearing the voice, thought it was an invisible but very much alive Kathy returning to talk with him. He became intensely serious as he spoke to Emily, and his response was unsettling.

" 'Because you're pregnant,' he says," Emily recalled. " 'You're pregnant too.'

"I was scared then," said Emily, the practical joke no longer funny. "That son of a bitch was right in the same jail with me, right in the same cell my daddy had hung himself in.

"How do you think I felt? Shit, I got down from there. It was like I was talkin' to my daddy, like trying to bring him back. Freaked me motherfuckin' out!"

The conversation had been brief, yet what Emily did not realize was that her voice was further proof to Tom Bonney that his daughter was still alive. The belief was reinforced as other female inmates, learning what Emily had done, tried it themselves whenever they were in a cell where the vent could pass the sound.

Neither the prosecution, the defense, nor Dr. Dell knew about Emily when Tom first learned that his daughter was definitely "alive." Dr. Dell just knew that Tom suddenly was not acting as he reportedly had in the past. "He denied that he had told the police or reporters that he shot Kathy. So I came out of the interview and wrote in my notes, 'Very dissociated. Much characterological avoidance, suppressions, distractions, and histrionics.'

"I kept bugging him and bugging him about Kathy, and then, all of a sudden, after denying that he and Kathy had a fight, and denying that they had been in a car on this road, etcetera, suddenly he said that

Kathy had pointed a gun at him and that she was really mad, and he was reading this letter to her from John Hoskins. But he didn't remember what had happened after that.

"He was very difficult to interview. His memory was all over the place. He didn't remember all kinds of things. He denied having done things that I knew he had done. And I suspected that he was probably multiple, and I didn't think I was going to get much further with him without resorting to hypnosis."

The psychologist paused, then said, "Now, I think today, knowing what I know now, I probably wouldn't have done it. I probably wouldn't have used hypnosis for a couple of reasons.

"One is that I was convinced—naive person that I am about the courts—that I could get what I needed to get across in the courtroom, that based on the information that I had at hand, there was good cause for me to use hypnosis and to begin to ask some very blunt, pointed questions with him." Dr. Dell was concerned only with learning the truth, but his methods would later cause the prosecutor to have ammunition to use against the psychologist.

Dr. Dell also said that he was later convinced by forensic experts that an interview not under hypnosis is the best way to handle a person who appears to be a multiple personality. Such an interview might last eight or ten hours without a break. The person is emotionally battered through constant prodding, constant questioning. In theory someone who is a multiple personality will not be able to handle such stress and will be forced to "switch," to let another personality take over. Such action, videotaped as Dr.

Dell did with all his sessions, could not have been discredited. There would have been no questions. But such knowledge came after the fact.

In the movies and fiction, hypnosis is often an extremely dramatic experience. Sometimes the hypnotist stares deeply into the subject's eyes, seemingly taking control of the person's mind. At other times he has the subject focus on a crystal or gently swaying watch. Then, when the subject enters a trance, there is a dramatic change in personality. A quiet, demure woman may be transformed into a wildly sensual vamp. Or a boisterous, aggressive, physically powerful man may suddenly be hiding behind a chair, sucking his thumb and quaking in terror like a four-year-old who is home alone and terrified of a thunderstorm.

Real life is quite different. The second time that Paul Dell met with Tom Bonney, Bonney agreed to be hypnotized, then did everything he could to avoid what that experience might mean. "He'd whine and say, 'I don't want to talk about that. Besides, do you know the jail captain? Can you talk to him?'" And then Tom would talk about the problems with the food in the jail or some other trivial detail.

"I would say, 'Tom, I need to talk to you about Kathy.'

"'Oh, Kathy, I just love Kathy so much. Do you know that she used to come and see me every day at work, at lunch, and we would go and we would have the nicest time. Do you know . . .' This is what he would do. So any time I would try to get him in [a hypnotic state], he's gone.

"He was an uncooperative subject. He was anxious about going into hypnosis. I had to really exert a fair amount of persuasion to get him to do that, and then he fought it the whole way."

Dr. Dell preferred to have his subject's eyes closed for the induction, but Bonney refused. Finally he agreed to focus on a spot, yet he began "squirming around the chair, with large body movements, and saying, 'Oh, this chair is terrible.' And he starts rocking the chair. 'They have such terrible furniture here, Dr. Dell . . . ' I'm trying to hypnotize this guy who is doing this stuff."

When Dr. Dell finally was able to hypnotize Bonney, he used a technique for communication that involved finger signals instead of voice response. Dr. Dell touched one of Bonney's fingers and told Bonney that he should raise that finger each time he wanted to answer "yes" to a question. Then the psychologist touched a different finger and told Bonney to raise that one when he wanted to respond with a "no."

Although it seems odd to the casual observer, hypnosis experts have found that the use of the finger response is often easier for the subject than speaking. Yet no matter how the subject responds, the idea that someone under hypnosis has no control over what they say is a myth. The subject is highly susceptible to suggestion, but he or she is not psychologically compelled to tell the truth. The person may readily choose to lie.

"I began by asking to talk to a part of Tom's unconscious mind. That was my phrasing, 'a part of Tom's unconscious mind.' I asked if the part knew things that Tom's conscious mind didn't know.

"I wasn't getting any response. The hand was just dead, like a dead fish. I said there must be parts that know things that Tom doesn't remember.

"I kept pushing, trying to get responses on the fingers. Nothing was happening.

"Then I began really pushing, saying, 'I know you're there whether you speak or you don't. I know you're there.' I said [to the "part"] that Tom's memory comes and goes, and I told [the "part"] that I assumed that was, that the voices he was hearing were the other parts of his mind talking to him. I told the parts that they could talk if they chose, but it was up to them. I told them they were up against the wall because the police had all the evidence they needed to convict them. They had a confession. They had, you know, all those reporters that witnessed the confession. They had all this material evidence. . . .

"I told them my job was to help Mr. Halstead prepare for an adequate defense, and I said that meant that I needed to know exactly what happened. And Tom couldn't tell me that because Tom was 'out to lunch.' I told them that 'I know you guys are there.' And I said, 'It's not really a secret.' I told them that the wife knew that they were there. I told them I knew. I told them that I told Mr. Halstead that they were there and I wasn't getting anywhere with them.

"I kept talking. I finally began to get the fingers to respond. I asked if it was a surprise that somebody finally really realized they were there, and I think they said yes. I tried to get a part [Note: Dr. Dell is using the term "part" the way other therapists use "personality"] to agree to come out, and that was when Tom woke up and wanted water."

While Dr. Dell's explanation seems rather involved, his actions were both simple and potentially prejudicial against the case he was trying to build for the defense. Paul Dell believed that Tom Bonney was a multiple personality. If his diagnosis was true, each personality was, in effect, a part of the mind of Tom Bonney. While a normal person goes through life experiencing and remembering everything they do, the mind of a multiple personality is like a storage closet filled with many sealed boxes. In one box is the memory of every time a parent beat him. Sealed in another box is the memory of every act of loving kindness by that same parent. Another box may hold the memory of all love affairs and sexual encounters. While a fourth box holds the memories of every act of violence the person ever committed. It is only by opening all of those boxes and combining all the memories they hold that the multiple personality is able to heal and remember like everyone else.

Dr. Dell's request to talk with one or another "part" was his way of trying to look inside one or more of the sealed boxes stored in the closet of Tom Bonney's mind. All the boxes could be opened and their contents merged together only after therapy. But by requesting a "part," Dr. Dell hoped to open the box that held the mental "file" of the murder.

Tom's thirst had caused him to go out of the trance. After he had his water, he was again placed under hypnosis, the psychologist continuing with the finger response instead of letting Tom speak. "Why didn't I want him speaking? Because I didn't know who I'd have, and Tom had been driving me crazy. I was trying to get rid of him." The finger method required Tom to only answer questions with "yes" or "no."

Through questioning, Dr. Dell became convinced that there were at least six personalities inside. He began pushing to have them each reveal itself so that he could obtain another piece of Tom's memory that he had forced from his conscious awareness.

The pressure of the questioning would ultimately leave Dr. Dell vulnerable to the charge that his well-intentioned actions may have created a multiple personality where none really existed. As Dr. Dell admitted, the concept was proposed by himself, not Tom.

"Tom Bonney never claimed to be multiple. Tom Bonney never tried to use being multiple to get off. I made the diagnosis. I picked up the signs of dissociation, and I followed the trail of bread crumbs through the forest."

Critics of the idea of multiple personality being mentioned in a criminal case say that the mention of the psychological disorder is a way for a criminal to try to avoid taking responsibility for his or her actions. Many people, including psychologists, look upon multiple personality as an attempt to create an insanity defense. Their hostility becomes greatest in a crime as horrible as the one of which Tom was accused, the brutal murder of his own daughter.

Dr. Dell's belief, based both on his personal experience and the available published research of others, is that the true multiple personality goes to great lengths to deny the possibility. She or he does not use the condition to avoid responsibility. Instead, they often fight the very idea that it might exist.

Yet questioned further, Dr. Dell explained that there have been multiples who are guilty of a crime but will have an innocent personality come out to deny any responsibility. Since that personality was not involved, the MPD (Multiple Personality Disorder) patient may be able to pass a polygraph test or other examination meant to determine the truth of what is being said. And this fact was a potential problem with the Bonney case. Would a man who might be provably guilty of murdering his daughter have a personality appear before the police and the court "honestly" denying guilt for something another personality did? Even worse, could Dr. Dell's suggestion that Bonney was multiple, a suggestion made when Tom was hypnotized and highly sensitive to such suggestions, create a condition that did not exist?

Dr. Dell did not anticipate that he might be accused of inducing MPD in the mind of a man who was simply a reprehensible killer. However, he was comfortable with the fact that, assuming Tom truly was a multiple, he would not use the disorder as a defense. "The overwhelming majority of multiples are guilt-stricken and they are horrendously upset by what they do, and they hold themselves guilty for things they shouldn't hold themselves guilty for. Like the abuse that was done to them.

"So the important bottom line to this, because multiples avoid admitting they are multiple, because they avoid dealing with their multiplicity, is it's often the case that a therapist will begin to strongly suspect the presence of MPD and not be able to get anywhere with the case for a long time because all of the alters are hiding out. The host personality doesn't know they are there, doesn't want to know they are there, and it takes a long time to kind of coax them out in the open."

And so Paul Dell continued his walk along the streets of the mind, searching for what he hoped would be the truth about Tom Bonney.

"I got all kinds of inconsistent answers that were not helpful. I kept trying to get them to come out and talk to me. I finally got around to asking if one or more of them shot Kathy. They said 'No,' and I said, 'Well, I think one of you did shoot Kathy.'

"They said no. I asked if they knew who did it. 'Yes.' So then I began running down the names of all the people that were involved with Tom Bonney. Went down a long list and finally got down to John McClung, who Tom calls 'John the Jew.' I don't know why, but that's what he calls him. Anyway, I got down to that and I said, 'How about John the Jew?' And the finger said 'Yes.'

"I said that doesn't make sense. John McClung? They said 'Yes.'

"I said, 'You guys telling me the truth?'

" 'Yes.'

"I said, 'Were you there when it happened?'

"They said 'No.'

"I said, 'Did you see him do it?'

" 'No.'

" 'Well, how do you know he did it?' Of course there is no answer to that." No evidence ever indicated any chance that McClung would have been involved.

Dell kept discussing the case with Tom, increasingly frustrated by the responses. He began to repeatedly warn the personalities that Tom was going to be convicted if they didn't cooperate, that he could die. Throughout both the second session and, periodically, in other sessions, he would remind Tom, under hypnosis, that to not cooperate could result in the death penalty.

"I would periodically say, as I was trying to get these guys to deal with me, I said, 'Look, you guys got three options and only three.' I said, 'Either you go to court and you get convicted, then you get sentenced to prison for a long time. Or you can go to court and you get convicted and you get sentenced to death.' I said, 'Or the third alternative is you go to court and they decide that the place you belong is in a hospital.' I said, 'Those are the only three alternatives here. So you guys going to talk to me?' "

For approximately eleven hours the work continued. All the work was directed toward getting the identities of the personalities, to learning about their early years, and to understanding what happened the night Kathy was killed. The questions could only be answered by yes or no. The work was seemingly endless, tedious, frustrating. And then there was a stirring of the body, the mouth opened, and Viking, another of the personalities, came out, sobbing, his voice high-pitched, scared, pleading. No longer were finger signals being used. No longer was Dell dealing with the whining Tom Bonney.

"No. No. Don't . . ." He was sobbing. Inside that storage closet of the mind, Tom Bonney had opened the sealed box where some of the memories of the night Kathy was killed were stored. The personality named Viking was reliving the murder. "He's going to shoot her. No. Don't. No. No. I've got to protect her. I've got to protect her. Don't shoot. Don't shoot her. Don't shoot her." His body was twisting and turning. The movements were not dramatic, yet it was obvious that he was in great emotional agony, uncomfortable with what he was seeing. "I've got to protect her. Don't shoot her. I'm going to protect her. I love her. Don't shoot. He's going to shoot her. Don't. Don't. Don't."

The voice sounded panic-stricken. Within the mind of Tom Bonney, the present had become the future, and he, along with the other personalities, began reliving the events leading up to the murder. Kathy was still alive, still in the house prior to going to look at the Blazer. And Viking was trying to convince her to not go along with her father. "Tell him no," he said. "Gotta tell him no. Don't go. You don't know. Tell him no.

"You gotta know what he is going to do, Kathy. Kathy.

"Listen to me. Listen to me. You gotta listen to me. No. I'm protecting you."

But the living memory of Kathy was not responding, perhaps had not heard Viking. He began begging her, trying to convince her to avoid the fate he knew awaited her. "Don't go with him in the car. I'm telling you, don't get in the car. Tell your mama. Don't let you get in the car. He won't listen.

"Kathy, come here. Don't get in the car. . . .

"Kathy, I'm trying to help you. You can't hear me. I've been trying to help you all these years. Don't get in the car. He's going to kill you.

"Get out and run. He's going to shoot you. Run as fast as you can. He's going to shoot her. Please don't shoot her."

Mental time raced ahead, events compressed, the memory advancing across the motion picture screen of the mind like a videocassette recorder operating at triple normal speed. His voice varied from anguished pleading with Kathy to a desperate effort to stop the murderer from killing her.

"Kathy. Kathy, listen to me, Kathy, listen to me please. I have helped you all these years since you have been born. Don't get in the car with him. I have watched him all these years. I was at the hospital when he was born. I was there. You didn't even know I was there.

"I have been watching you all these years and trying to protect you. Your daddy loves you so much. Don't get in the car. He's got a gun. He's got a gun."

Then, confronting the murderer: "Don't you shoot her! I said no!"

But the pleading seems to be to no avail. His voice breaking, he says, "Oh, no, leave her alone. Don't you shoot her.

"Daddy loves her so much. All these years . . . Don't shoot her."

Stronger. "Run! Run, Kathy! He's going to shoot you. He's gonna fill you full of bullets. He's sick.

"There he goes. . . ." The voice trails off to wailing and sobbing, then the body seems to slump. After a few minutes Dell is able to coax Viking back out, to relive what was happening that night. This time Viking is remembering Kathy's life and the times when he supposedly protected her. He starts by talking about when she was a baby and had a mouth full of rat poison. "I made it come out so you wouldn't die."

Then, speaking to what proved to be another personality, he said: "Satan, why did you have to do that? I have been looking over that kid all these years and don't you remember the night in the car? You were trying to get her. I tried to protect her. Now you have killed her. You have killed Tommy's first baby."

Apparently turning back to Kathy, "When boys wanted to take you, I stopped them to protect you. Now you are lying on the ground and he keeps on shooting you. I told him to stop and he keeps on shooting. All the years protecting, and now look at what you did. I loved her. Her daddy loved her so much.

"You keep shooting her. Stop shooting her. Shoot me! Don't shoot her no more.

"I'll get you for this. I'm going to get you one of these days. I'm going to get you. You just wait."

Shortly after this, Dr. Dell asked Satan, "Is what Viking has been reliving here true? Is it the truth?"

And Satan said, "Yes."

CHAPTER 5

The Growing Cast of Characters

The discovery of Tom Bonney's other personalities was made in pieces. It was like watching the reruns of a long established soap opera with every segment shown out of order. All the information was there. All the characters had their moments upon the stage. But unless careful notes were taken, names and events charted, it was difficult to tell who had done what to whom, and why.

Fortunately we now have the advantage of hindsight. It is possible to put together the cast of players in original order, something that will help make sense of the unfolding drama.

Tom

It might be said that there are two "people" named Tom. Tom Bonney is the name of the healthy child whose mind functioned like anyone else's. It was Tom Bonney who experienced the physical and emotional trauma that led to the coping mechanism of forming multiple personalities.

"Tom," an alter personality, answered to the name "Tom Bonney," but was different. He was formed after the mental "split." His job was to run the body most of the time. But because he was formed as a child, he remained childlike, dependent, loving, friendly, seemingly simpleminded, and somewhat of a hypochondriac. He is much like a whiny pre-teenager who has learned to feign illness in order to avoid going to school. You could picture him in bed just long enough to miss the start of classes, then going off to play with his dog, read comic books, or otherwise pass the time in what, for him, were pleasurable pursuits.

Tom's memory is highly selective. Because he did not shoot his daughter, he genuinely has amnesia about the event. He cannot tell the difference between people who are real and people who were created in his mind. That is why Tom can convince himself that Kathy is alive, since he "sees" and hears her inside his head. The Kathy personality the "original" Tom Bonney created after her death has an active life that, while invented by the mind, cannot be distinguished by Tom from the flesh and blood offspring of the same name.

Tom is a prudish man. He reads the Bible daily, loves his family, writes constantly of his adoration of Jesus, and has difficulty discussing sex, which he calls "nasty stuff."

Because Tom cannot distinguish fantasy from reality, he does not realize that the personalities that are a part of his existence are fabrications of his mind. He is also constantly surprised that he is being forced to confront the often harsh consequences of his own actions, especially since he suppresses the memories of what took place. A common statement by Tom is: "I don't understand why I'm in trouble all the time, but everybody says I'm in trouble."

Satan

Satan was a strong protector, not the personification of the Devil, as his name might imply. He apparently was created somewhere around ten years of age when Mammy, Tom's beloved grandmother, died. Tom, overwhelmed by the loss, ran crying into the woods, staying there until it was so dark he was terrified to come home. Satan was formed to take care of the body, eventually becoming so strong that he could also endure seemingly unbearable physical pain.

It was Satan who emerged when the car on which Tom was working crashed onto his chest. It was Satan who refused medical attention, preferring to take the "body" home to bed.

Satan became convinced that he was invulnerable, needing neither doctors nor emotional attachments with others to not only survive, but to triumph in the world. Dr. Dell found that Satan insisted that he "knows everything," "can do anything," controls everything, and has extrasensory perception.

Although Satan did not consider himself to be the Devil, he hated Tom's talk about what he called the "Jesus stuff." He had no use for God because God let good people, like Mammy, die. He claimed to dominate everyone, including Tom, "the wimp."

But the truth was that Demian was stronger, able to control Satan any time he desired.

Mammy

Mammy was the second personality to split off from Tom. She is literally Tom's grandmother, his mind so overwhelmed by her death that the only way he could cope was to re-create her in the rooming house of his disturbed brain. Mammy is limited in her knowledge of the other personalities, especially Satan and Demian, but she tries to watch over the family that Tom created, and serves as the caretaker.

Mammy was "born" at the funeral. Tom, overwhelmed by grief, took a flower from the grave as a way of holding her near to him. He came to believe that she was alive in the coffin, just waiting for that action so she could rise from the grave, pass through the flower and into Tom's mind, where she has lived comfortably ever since.

Demian

Dr. Dell estimated that Demian was the third alter created, splitting off no later than Tom's thirteenth birthday. He is angry and violent, hating most people, and especially Tom's father.

Demian probably was created when Tom's father was being physically and emotionally abusive to his son. He hated the fact that his son refused to hunt ducks, and frequently called him both a "bastard" and a "wimp."

In order to protect the body from Tom's father, Demian took on many of the older man's characteristics. He is the one who would make unrealistic demands on the family. He was the one who had explosive rage, beating both Kathy and her mother. Demian was probably the one who handcuffed Dorothy Bonney and raped her before Tom fled the city. It is also quite likely that Demian molested Kathy Bonney, his power to isolate himself from the others preventing any of them from "seeing" or knowing about the incest.

Demian likes to use Satan as his front man, controlling the latter's actions without his awareness. It was probably Demian who was involved with the violence against Kathy, though his actions were undoubtedly indirect, not letting the others know he was in charge.

Viking, Tommy, Hitman, and Preacher

Tom was thirteen, still in the early throes of adolescence, when he could no longer handle the abuse of his father. The older man apparently overwhelmed what few emotional defenses remained. As he was being violently kicked by his father, Tom formed Viking, Tommy, Hitman, and Preacher.

Viking and Tommy are quite similar, helpful, friendly, and kind, as though by being good, the violence would stop. Preacher is the man of intellectual reason. Preacher's job was to use religion to convince the father to stop using violence and foul language.

There was confusion about Hitman. Dr. Dell felt that Hitman was a friendly helper whose job it was to endure the violence (the "hits") of his father. However, another theory that seems to make greater sense with the memories coming forth was that Hitman was the violent rebel whose job was to stand up to the father. Satan was created to endure. Demian handled rage. But Hitman may have been the one to seek revenge, to be capable of planning the literal destruction of anyone causing pain.

Dr. Dell felt that the four teenagers were fairly weak, generally working together in order for any of them to have the strength to come out. Although Demian was the strongest, both he and Satan sometimes stayed inside the mind, letting the teenagers or one of the others take control of the body. Then, without telling them, they would manipulate what was taking place.

Dad

It is hard to tell just what type of alter personality Dad might be. This is because Tom's memories sometimes replayed his father's violence, letting the incident be revealed as it happened under hypnosis. During those incidents, the same voice that the alter personality "Dad" used could be heard. However, Dr. Dell felt that "Dad" is a loving, caring father, quite different than the man who sired Tom.

Kathy

Kathy, like Mammy, was not really dead in the coffin. The moment Tom took a flower from on top of her casket, Kathy, like Mammy, rose into his mind. Now, though others can't see her, she enjoys living with him, talking to him every night in order to keep him company and give him the support he needs.

Dr. Dell's ability to get the alter personalities to not only respond, but to speak, was exciting for him. He had witnessed such changes many times in his practice, usually without hypnosis. Sometimes the patient was under stress, though usually the other personality just wanted to come out.

But Tom Bonney was different. Tom Bonney had resisted from the start, changing the subject, refusing to cooperate, whining about everything in his life.

The finger signals meant that Dr. Dell could reach the personalities on at least one level. But the use of finger signals would not save the man's life. There would be no emotional impact upon a jury watching either the videotapes he was making or witnessing Tom perform the same actions live in the courtroom. Only a fellow researcher could appreciate such seemingly simple actions.

The moment the personalities defied not only Tom's resistance but also Dr. Dell's finger response suggestions in order to talk, there was hope. First Dr. Dell would be able to actually meet the personalities, to hear how they sounded, to question them, to be fully aware when and how they let someone else take control.

Secondly, in speech there might be the ability to convince the jury of how emotionally disturbed Tom had been all his life. Dr. Dell never questioned that Tom was responsible for his daughter's death. Yet who really was Tom Bonney? And what personality, what part of his mind, had controlled the pulling of the trigger? The answers could be learned through what he and the jury would be hearing. He was fairly certain that Tom Bonney would be locked away in either a jail or a mental ward for the rest of his life. He only hoped that what he was uncovering would convince the jury not to use their other option, the death penalty.

Tommy was the next personality to reveal himself. His voice was that of a small child, and he had obviously fixated on the day of the murder he had witnessed.

"No. No. No. Don't do that," Tommy begged the killer. "I love her so much."

Then, apparently turning to Kathy, he tried to protect her from going for the drive he knew would result in her death. "Kathy, tell them you don't feel good. Tell them you will go to your room and lie down. Don't listen to them."

There was a change in voices, a second personality speaking, this time the voice deeper, angry. "She'll listen to everything I tell her. She'll listen, and when I tell her, she'll do everything I tell her. Yes, I can tell her to leave the house."

Tommy spoke again, saying, "She don't want to go. She wants to stay here. Help with the groceries. Now she's tired." Then, turning to Kathy, he said, "Kathy, don't get in the car. Please don't. Kathy, don't get in the car."

Although the drama that was being acted out from the memories in Tom's mind involved numerous players talking with each other, the phenomenon of multiple personality is such that the "play" was actually occurring on several levels. The personalities did not know when they were "out" and able to communicate with real human beings, and when they were inside the mind, their conversation heard only within Tom's head. Thus Tommy could talk with Kathy and Tom Bonney, responding to each of them, yet Kathy would only hear Tom Bonney's words directed to her if he was the one in charge of the body. Sometimes Tom would speak to another personality inside his head, the voice inaudible to Kathy. And other times he would speak aloud so Kathy, as well as the other personalities, would hear what was taking place. But the differences between internal and external dialogue blurred completely when Tom and the other personalities relived the events under hypnosis.

The next "scene" Dr. Dell experienced took place at the convenience store where Kathy was to meet the man with the Blazer. Before his arrival, Kathy was to fill the gas tank of the family Chevrolet. "Please don't put the gas in the car," said Tommy. "Go in the store, Kathy. You gotta tell them you don't feel good. He's going to get you. Tell him."

"Here's the five dollars. Pay for the gas," said the deep male voice—Tom speaking to his daughter.

Then the boy took over again, desperately trying to save Kathy. "Run behind the store. Don't get back in the car. Please don't get in the car. I love you so much. Please don't get in the car. Can't you listen? Can't you hear me?"

Kathy's voice could be heard next as she spoke to her father. "Dad? Dad, where are we going?"

"Some man called on the phone about a Chevrolet Blazer," her father responded.

"Let's go look at that," Kathy said, excited. Then something seemed to have happened, something taking place that made her wary. There was no indication as to what, but suddenly Kathy said, "We don't need that [the Blazer]. We'll fix my car."

But Kathy had wanted such a vehicle, had been talking about it. Her father knew it, knew that she was trying to get out of looking. His voice became firm. "We are going to go where I want to go. You're not going home right now."

Then there was another voice, apparently Tommy's. "Where are we going?" he asked, confused.

A harsh voice responded, "Shut up, Tommy. All these years you don't know where we're going. Shut up."

Tommy responded, "All these years you are always fussing at me, always hitting me. It hurts so bad."

Then, deeper, "Quit your bellyaching! You can take it. Shut up."

Tom Bonney's natural voice was heard. "We go left here," he said, apparently driving the car.

"Where are we going?" Kathy asked. "What are we going to do? I've got to use the bathroom. Are you all right? What's that you got in your hand? Oh, it's just a piece of paper. What does it say?"

Tom grunted a reply, then Kathy asked, "What's that down there on the floor?"

Tom responded, "That's the gun. Better put it up. It's been in the car two or three days."

"Is it loaded?"

"Oh, it's always loaded. Yeah, why shouldn't it be loaded? Here, I'll put it up on the front seat for you."

Tommy's voice was heard again. "Kathy, don't let him hurt you. My daddy used to hurt me so bad, hit me so many times. I was so sore. Kathy, get the gun and put it in your lap. It's very important. He's got a piece of paper. He's going to open it. He found it in your room. He and your mama."

Kathy said, "Oh, I'm so embarrassed. Where did you get that?"

"Me and your mama found it in your room," Tom replied.

Young Tommy responded, "Kathy, listen. It's very important. You gonna have to shoot him. He's got a bad temper. Get out of the car and start running."

Now the confrontation was coming to a head, the voices changed, the time speeded up. The drama that was unfolding was as compelling as a suspense film, even though the ending, the murder of Kathy, was known. It was as though the murder had been recorded on a camcorder, then replayed at a more convenient time on a VCR that had temporarily lost the picture portion of the videotape and the sounds of the car and the surrounding highway noise. It was easy to relive the growing tension that had taken place.

Yet this was not a videotape. This was the culmination of a lifetime of pain, anger, and madness, all coming together in an explosive, irrevocable act of violence recorded indelibly on a highly disturbed human mind.

Kathy came out next, angry, yet despite the voice being hers, the phrasing and choice of words seemed to reflect Tom Bonney more than the child/woman who had been murdered. It was as though, in her defiance, her voice had become a mirror of her father's as she shouted, "I ain't gonna take no more crap!"

Then a terrified Tommy could be heard, weakly saying, "What are you gonna do?"

A third voice responded, "You know what I'm going to do."

"No," said Tommy. "I've got to watch over her. I can't let nothing happen to her. So many people try to make bad things happen. I got to help her. Can't you hear me?"

"Take that gun and shoot him. Shoot him."

There was a pause, then a wailing sound as Tommy moaned, "Oh, no. No." He started weeping. "All these years I watched over her. All these years I love her so much. Kathy, my father used to beat me so much. Please don't."

There was more silence for a few moments, then Tommy was heard again, apparently examining Kathy's corpse, even though he didn't fully comprehend her death. "Are you all right? Why do you look like that? What's the matter? Get back in the car. Oh, he's done shot you. My God!" There was more sobbing. "Oh, he's going to shoot you. Are you all right? Talk to me. Say something. Are you pretending like you are dead? You're not moving. He doesn't know what he's doing. We love you so much. Something ain't right.

"Oh, what am I going to do? She was all I had.

"I didn't want him to never spank you. Never to spank you. We've gotta go. Come on.

"She's not moving. So quiet. Why? Are you pretending like you are dead? I can't tell. Get in the car and let's go.

"Can't you move? Please get up. You can't hear me now. Talk to me. Tell me what to do. I don't know what to do. I tried to help you all these years. I used to get real bad spankings and I won't let him spank you.

"He's in the car. He's going. Pick her up. You can't leave her there. Go get her."

Then the deep voice was heard again. "Oh, shut up. You always got something to say. Why don't you hush?"

Tommy responded, "You can't leave her there. I loved her so much. All these years . . ." And then Tommy's voice faded off.

Dr. Dell had made the breakthrough he was seeking. Now this detective of the mind had to try to interview all the witnesses, getting each to tell his or her version of the murder.

If Dr. Dell had recorded each personality separately, then had their statements transcribed, a police detective reading the reports would have found nothing out of the ordinary. The more eyewitnesses who exist, the greater the variety of their reports. Many police academy training classes conduct an exercise in which a fake crime occurs in front of them. Typically this is the "murder" of the instructor by a "killer" who bursts into the room, fires a blank gun, then leaves. Sometimes the action is done straight. At other times there may be an odd variation, such as dressing the assailant in outrageous-looking clothing, perhaps with Day-Glo yellow slacks and a beanie with a propeller. At other times the assailant will have a revolver loaded with blank cartridges in one hand, a banana in the other, pointing both at the instructor before firing the gun, then fleeing.

The officers, all trained observers, must then describe what took place from the first moment of their awareness that something was wrong. Invariably, if there are twenty men and women in the room, there will be twenty different accounts of what took place. Sometimes the variations are slight, the observations almost accurate. At other times the logical reason of the observer overrides the reality. Unusual details, such as the use of the banana, will not be mentioned because they seem too ridiculous. Yet the instructors know that in real life anything might happen, the exercise being more serious than the students understand at first.

The result is that a crime scene report will have several different viewpoints, often with all of them right on some points, wrong on others, and overlooking still others. Taken as a whole, though, it is hoped that the truth can be gleaned from within.

Dr. Dell had to take the reports, but in this case the eyewitnesses were alter personalities, fragments of a mind shattered from years of abuse. Yet just like "real" witnesses, each personality saw something different. Each personality had a piece of the truth. It was necessary to have each one relive the day of the murder, giving his or her own story.

What made the questioning even more unusual, though, was that the memories of the alter personalities included the memories of what was said and done by others present. Each would tell the story as it happened, in the voice of all the participants he or she witnessed. Although it was the natural memory of a disturbed mind, the experience was much like entering a circumstance that the late writer Rod Serling once named "The Twilight Zone."

Preacher was next, arguing with the killer. "I'm not going to let you do that. Uh-uh. No. Can't do that. What's the matter with you? Don't you know what you are doing? You know that ain't right. Why you doing all this? I don't understand. You can't do that. No. Please don't. Don't do what you are thinking of. If you want to shoot somebody, shoot me. Don't shoot her. Please don't think of it."

A deeper voice responded, "Oh, shut up."

"No," Preacher said. "What are you thinking of? Don't shoot her. Shoot me."

Then Preacher spoke to Kathy, saying, "Kathy, go into your bedroom and lay down and pretend you don't feel good. Can't you hear me? Please listen. I don't know what's wrong with him."

As with the other alter personalities, Preacher was confused about whether or not he was in control of the body, whether or not his voice was being heard inside the rooming house of Tom Bonney's mind, or if he was able to move Tom's mouth, to use his vocal cords to speak directly to Kathy. "Kathy, don't go out there and get in that car. Something's wrong with him. He's not right."

Preacher continued, "Don't get in the car. Don't get in the car. If something happens to you, it will kill us. It will kill your father. Your father can't take no more. I have tried to help your father all these years. I have tried to help your father all these years . . . So many years.

"Don't get in the car. Don't you know what is going to happen?" They reached the gas station and Preacher said, "Tell him to pump it. Tell him to pump it and run down the street. You've got to get away. Your father had done had two heart attacks. Nobody's supposed to know about that, but listen to me. You've got to help yourself. You've got to help your father.

"Every day he comes home from work and your mother hollers at him. Listen to me. He's going to give you the money for the gas. Don't get in the car.

"Can't you hear me? It's quiet out here. Run. Hide. I'll try to help you. He's going to shoot you. Listen, if he does, just lay there and maybe he'll go away. I'm trying to stop it. I can't stop him.

"Oh, don't. Oh, no. Oh, no. Oh, my God look at what he's done. Don't shoot her no more." Preacher was sobbing now. "Don't do that. Please. That's enough. Don't . . ."

And then Preacher was gone, overwhelmed by the memory he did not wish to handle. Yet Dr. Dell had some new information. So far as he could determine from what he heard, Tom Bonney had no intention of hurting his daughter. It was obviously an alter personality that had planned the murder and was determining what would happen.

The second point was that this *was* murder. This was not a crime of passion. This was not an accidental death. The alter personalities knew in advance that Kathy would be badly hurt or killed that night. Everything was premeditated.

Despite all this, Paul Dell wondered if there might be another explanation that would emerge as he let the alters speak for themselves. He knew that the alter personalities were speaking only of the shooting. There was no mention of Kathy's body being stripped naked, as it had been found. There was no mention of the gun being fired until it was empty, reloaded, then fired again. They were all witnesses, yet it was as though they had witnessed only part of the story before retreating to where they could neither see nor hear what else took place.

"I've been in here all these years," said Mammy, the next personality to speak. She came forth slowly, avoiding thinking about the murder while she discussed the past. "I'm so tired. So many years.

"I loved Tommy so much. He loves me too. He thinks I'm his mother. I love that boy so much. Can't let his daddy beat him no more."

Then Mammy began talking to her daughter, Tom's mother, saying, "Gracie. Gracie. Do we have to go now? Don't go now. Tommy's fishing down the road. He don't know I'm going. Wait until he gets back.

"Yes. I'm going to go. Wait just a little while. Gracie, please. Stay here a little longer. It will kill that boy. Nobody knows.

"Gracie, can't you hear me? Everybody's talking and nobody can hear me. Why don't they hear me?

Can't they hear me? No. I know I'm going to die.

"We're at Gracie's house tonight. When Tommy goes to sleep, tell him. It's going to kill that boy. It's bad news. Show him in a dream. Get him ready. I'm going to die."

As he reviewed his notes concerning this portion of the interviews, Dr. Dell commented, "This is clearly Fantasyland."

Tom Bonney had loved his grandmother, felt closer to her than to anyone else in his family. His father was abusive. His mother not only was unable to protect him from her husband, according to Tom's statements, she also never gave him the attention he desired. Tom's older brother, a man Tom seldom spoke about, appeared to be the person who had his mother's greatest love. No matter what he tried to do for the woman, she rejected his efforts. Only his grandmother accepted him without question.

Tom had not been present when his grandmother died. She had fallen, gone to the hospital, and ultimately succumbed to her injuries, a not uncommon situation among the elderly in 1957.

Two situations had resulted from that death. The first was an overriding hatred of hospitals. Tom felt that hospitals were where you went to die. He talked of hospitals being filled with death and would not let himself be treated in one.

The other belief was that his grandmother had desperately tried to stay alive until he could reach her side. It was not true, or if it was, no one else heard her discuss it. But it was his way of coping with the loss, his way of avoiding the feeling of abandonment that is so common among children when an older loved one dies.

Later Tom Bonney would convince himself that, instead of dying, Mammy had entered his mind through the flowers on her grave. She had wanted to be with him so much, to spend so much special time with him, that though her body was dead, she continued to live inside him. For many years he would talk about hearing her voice, knowing she was close.

As Mammy talked, she jumped from time sequence to time sequence. Her next words seemed to come from a period when she was talking about Tom Bonney, the child, to a friend or family member. She seemed to be speaking as though she was sitting over a cup of coffee as she said, "He's had all these headaches. I feel so sorry for that boy. His father keeps on beating him all the time. He doesn't know it, but when I die, my body will be at the graveyard, but I will be inside him. I'll help him. All these years . . . His father doesn't love him."

Then, more current, Mammy said, "Kathy, you don't know who I am, but I have been inside here all these years."

Mammy switched time frames constantly. Sometimes she was dying, Tom still a little boy. Sometimes she was talking with Kathy, who Tom felt had entered his body through the flowers, just like his grandmother. Sometimes she appeared to articulate Tom's unfounded fantasies of infidelities by Carol. And sometimes she was reliving Kathy's murder.

Mammy then talked with Burness (spelling uncertain), Tom's father, telling him, "Burness, you hit him again, I'm going to kill you. Don't do that no more or I'll shoot you!"

Another voice said, "Where did you get that guy?"

"Burness, I'll blow your head off if you kick him one more time." Then there was another time switch as she said, "Kathy, turn the radio off in the car. Can't you hear me? Kathy, he's going to kill you.

"God, I'm so old. I'm so old. Been in here all these years trying to help that boy. He's changed so much. I don't understand.

"God help that girl. He's acting funny. He's not acting himself. He's so weird. Changes. Can anybody hear me?

"I've been inside here so many years. I need to be in the graveyard, but I can't go. Gotta help him. God help me.

"God, take me. Don't take that girl. Go in the bathroom and lock the door. Yeah, that will work. Do that.

"When you get the gas, tell the lady you don't feel good.

"He's been through so many funerals. He's not doing right. He's acting strange. All his family is just about gone.

"Tommy? Tommy, what are you doing? These are just clothes. What are you doing? I want to keep these clothes. What is all this stuff? She's going to let you keep it. She's going to make you throw it all away."

Mammy seemed to be flipping back and forth through time. The clothes might have referred to those stripped from Kathy's body. But if that was the case, did that mean they were to be souvenirs?

Or were these other clothes being remembered? A different time. A different place. There was no way to know. And then she was living the time before the murder when Kathy had returned home from shopping with her mother, and her father was waiting for her.

"Kathy, the keys are still in the car. Go out the back door. Here he comes."

A deeper voice. "Kathy, somebody called on the phone about a Chevrolet truck. Doesn't want much for it."

Kathy's voice. "I want to eat something before we go."

"No. We gotta go now."

"Mama, I'll be back in a minute. I'm going to look at a truck."

The deeper voice. "Kathy, get in the car."

"My head," Mammy said. "Don't get in the car. He's cracked up. He don't act right no more. Listen. I'll tell you why he's cracked up.

"Know what she told him? Suzie. He knows it. Suzie is not his daughter.

"But he still loves her. He's known for all these years. He's acting strange. Real strange. I don't see how he can love his wife.

"He's starting up the car. Don't get in it. He's not acting right," Mammy continued.

"I'll tell you why he's acting up. His wife. He loves that girl so much, but she's no good.

"Listen to me, Kathy. His wife, she went to bed with four people in Florida. Hurt him so bad. But he still loves his wife. In Virginia Beach she went to bed with three of them.

"What are you doing? What are you doing? Kathy, don't go with him."

The speech became disjointed. Mammy alternating between criticizing Carol Bonney—including claiming that Tom caught his wife with a black man—and reliving the murder. It was extremely confusing, though always the end for all the personalities was to try to cope with the death of Kathy.

Longtime friends of the Bonneys did not believe that Carol Bonney had ever been unfaithful to Tom. They felt that she had devoted herself to raising the children and doing what she could to help him. Some of them were frequently alone with her in situations where they felt that she might come on to them out of loneliness because Tom was working such unusual hours. Yet she never did. When they later heard Mammy's tapes in the courtroom or were told of the contents after they had been played, they discounted what was said. They felt that it was simply Tom's fantasy given "credibility" by his grandmother's voice.

"Kathy, you playing like you are dead? Say something. Talk to me. Say something. If he don't hear you, he'll drive off. I'll get someone to come and get you.

"All that blood. Where's it coming from? Tell me you're not dead. Your father's going to get in a lot of trouble.

"Okay. Stay inside here with me and nobody will hurt you. You can talk to him as much as you want. You can get in here. It's easy. I'll show you how.

"When he got the flower off my coffin, I come

right in here. When they come to see you, get the flower."

There seemed to be another shift in time, to a point just before the funeral, when Mammy explained to Kathy that she should use one of the flowers on the casket as a vehicle for entering Tom's mind. Yet immediately after the two of them talked, Mammy became the first of the alter personalities to relive an incident that occurred when Tom returned home and talked with his wife. Dr. Dell heard Tom talking with Carol, then heard Mammy trying to reach the woman.

"Yeah. Where do you think I'm at?" asked Tom Bonney, now home after Kathy's murder. "No, she's not in the car. She's test driving a truck. She's going to come back in just a little bit."

Mammy's voice was next, talking with Tom's wife. Mammy referred to Carol Bonney by her given name, a name no one else had used for years. Tom, his business associations, family friends, and everyone else called her Carol, the name she preferred. But Mammy used her given name, saying: "Dorothy, come here. Listen to me. You got to listen to me. You don't understand what he's been going on . . . what's been going on.

"He's acting strange. Everything is happening. Tom is getting the blame for all of it. Don't get into bed yet.

"Listen to me. Can't you hear me? This is your husband's grandmother. I love you and Tom loves you. Tom loves Kathy. He's going to get the blame again.

"Dorothy, listen to me. Don't go to sleep. Listen

to me. I'm trying to tell you. Can't you hear? Listen to me. I want to tell you something."

The words from Mammy had been a strange leap through time. Yet all the personalities seemed to be describing similar circumstances. The first radical change came when Mammy retreated into Tom's mind and Satan made his appearance.

Satan's first words were angry. He was irate that Kathy was living inside the mind with the others. "She ain't supposed to be living in here," he complained. "She ain't going to be here long."

"Why did you kill her?" Dr. Dell asked.

"You know," Satan said.

"The letter to John Hoskins?" Dell asked.

"Yeah. She started to shoot me."

"I asked him why," Dell said.

"Just cussing . . . Cussing me out."

"Well, you planned to shoot her anyway, didn't you?"

"No."

"I say the others knew. They told me," Dell said.

"No. No."

"Why not?"

"We was sitting there, talking about that letter. And she called me a bastard. She called me a bastard. The gun went off and she almost shot me. She was sitting there, screaming."

There was a voice change. "I was hollering, 'What are you going to do?' And she said, 'You bastard, I'm going to kill you.' "

"And then I started to talk to her." As Satan spoke, his voice was shifting up and down, as though there might be more than one personality speaking. Yet it seemed to be the same person each time in terms of speech pattern and choice of language. "I was trying to tell her who I was. She kept saying, 'Bastard.' I have heard that word so many times."

"Why did the others say you were planning to kill her?"

"They was weak. They didn't know. They was weak."

"What didn't they know?"

"They was trying to save her."

"I said, 'Yeah. From you shooting her.' "

"I wasn't going to shoot her anyways."

"What were you going to do?"

"The gun was in the car two or three days."

"What were you going to do?"

"I was going to talk along the side of the road about that letter. And when I stopped, the gun slid out by her foot. And she says, 'The gun's in here again. You know I told Mama not to leave it in the car no more. How did it get in the car?' Yeah, that's true." The voice changed again, a noticeable difference, though it was presumably still Satan talking. "Yeah, he don't remember nothing. It's been in there three or four days. Nobody knows nothing. I know everything."

"Who knows everything?" Dr. Dell said.

"I know *everything*," Satan explained. "I am strong. I can do what I want to, when I want to. I can fool him. I control Tom. He's so dumb. He don't remember nothing. He gets in trouble all the time. He's weak. I'm not. Very strong. I can do anything.

"That night he was in the car, he was trying to catch up with her so they could . . . He was trying to catch up with her so they could talk. Find out what she'd done . . ."

Suddenly Satan was discussing a different incident. As Dr. Dell learned from the background reports, there had been a previous situation where Tom Bonney had become violent. Kathy had sneaked out of the house to be with a girlfriend. The two of them were out driving when he spotted her. Irate that she was disobeying him, he pursued the car in which she was riding, then forced it to crash. Afterward he went after her to punish her, an incident Satan was remembering as he spoke.

"You took off in the car after her that time?" asked Dr. Dell.

"No."

"What do you mean, no?"

"Tom."

"Tom took after her?"

"Yeah, but he just wanted to talk to her." Softer now. "He was honking the horn and she couldn't stop. She went into a sharp curve, and Tom knew she wasn't going to make it, and she crashed into the telephone pole. And I and Tom got out of the car to see if she was all right. And he asked her real nice."

Dr. Dell was suspicious that something had changed. "Satan, who's talking right now?"

"You don't know?"

"No. Who was that?"

"I can break you."

"Yeah, you're real strong," Dr. Dell said. "But who was that just talking?"

"Tom, the wimp. I control him."

"Satan?"

"Yeah."

"How can I trust what you tell me? You lie all the time."

"Not about this. He's so stupid. All he wanted to do was to just get out there and talk to her and ask her what she was doing and why she was doing it. The other girl jumped out and ran and wasn't trying to run her off no road. I put the blame on everything he does. Everything. I fix it where he gets the blame on all of it."

"Are you the one that told the reporters?"

"Yes."

"Why?"

" 'Cause I'm strong. He's a wimp."

"You want him to get the blame?"

"Yes. He doesn't even know his name sometimes. He's a wimp."

"So are you willing to tell me the rest of what happened out there on Route 17 that night?"

"Yeah."

"Kathy tried to shoot you?"

"Yes."

"She called you a bastard?"

"Yeah."

"And what happened then?"

"I showed her."

"Satan, what happened then?"

"Tom was talking so nice to her, trying to ask her about that stupid note. She didn't know nothing. She was running around. He didn't even know she was running around on him."

"You knew?"

"Yes. I saw that night that she went in Bruce's [Bruce was one of Kathy's boyfriends before John Hoskins] backyard, and they had that little camper or trailer or something. I seen what they did."

"What did they do?"

"Nasty stuff."

"I control him."

"Satan, what did Bruce and Kathy do in the camper?"

"Took their clothes off."

"Yeah. What else? Did they screw?"

"Yeah. But first she didn't want to. He got her drinking a little bit."

"How did you know what they were doing out there in that trailer?"

"I know everything."

"How do you know that?"

"Because I do."

"How?"

"You're just a mortal. You don't know nothing."

"I'm trying to find out from talking to you. So how do you know what they did in that camper?"

"She's got ESP, and I've got it a thousand times stronger than she does. I know everything."

The comment would have meant even more had Paul Dell known about Emily Weston's actions in the Albemarle District Jail. Tom Bonney told Emily that he took "her" life because she was pregnant. Tom had previously been convinced that one of his daughters was illegitimate. The truth was that while Kathy Bonney was not a virgin at her death, Tom Bonney knew no more about what she had done than the fact that she had had sex with men. The rest came from his fantasy, and his comment about the ESP link between them reinforced that fact.

"So tell me what happened that night on Route 17," said Dr. Dell, returning Satan to the night of the murder.

"He's a wimp. He showed her the note. He's a wimp. He's a goody-good. Talked about Jesus and all this mess. He loves that man. That man ain't done nothing for him. Talk about God so much. All God did was take his daddy. And his aunts, uncles, grandfathers, nephews, nieces . . . I'm great-er. I know everything."

Satan continued: "Tom, the wimp. He told the truth a little bit. They did get a telephone call about a stupid truck, and they was going to go look at it. He was going down Cedar Road, supposed to make a right on Route 17. There's a 7-Eleven down there. He was telling the truth, but I fixed it. I fixed them. Instead of making a right turn, he made a left. He's so stupid. He's a wimp."

"Did you control him making a left?" Dr. Dell asked.

"Yes, and more than that, I control him."

"Where did you go on Route 17?"

"Down there, cross the line and stupid North Carolina. Didn't even know he was in North Carolina. He's a wimp. Talks good all the time. I'm glad it worked out.

"Everything [sic] thinks he run her off the road. He didn't run her off the road. Everything [sic] thinks that Tom hit her in the mouth. He never hit her. Never hit that girl. I fixed it where he always got the blame for everything."

"Who hit her in the mouth?" Dr. Dell knew that Satan was skipping back and forth in time, a little like Mammy had done.

He let Satan finish, explaining that when others thought Kathy had been struck at some time in the past, it was actually a case of Satan's losing his balance on the stairs. He grabbed at Kathy so he wouldn't lose balance, and accidentally bruised her, apparently.

"So tell me what happened on Route 17."

"He pulled over and he was going to talk to her about that stupid letter. She was real embarrassed and they sat there talking real nice, and she was so sorry for that. He didn't know all the things she was doing. I controlled her just as I controlled Tom." It was not clear whether Satan meant that he controlled the way the conversation took place, or if he felt he entered Kathy as he entered Tom. The difference was important in helping to determine the possibility of multiple personality, but it was not pursued.

"When he stopped, the gun slid out from under the seat. Hit her on the foot. She picked it up and called him a bastard. Sort of goofed when she called him that."

"Why did she call him that? She was talking nice just a minute ago."

"She just got pissed off. She thought she was talking to Tom sometimes. She was talking to me. Tom's a wimp.

"What got her so mad, Tom was talking to her nice, talking about God. She was talking nice, saying, 'I'm sorry.'

"Tom, the wimp, he was talking to her, and he told her so nice . . ."

Deep voice. "He's a wimp."

Satan again. "He told her to stay in the house and live with his wife and him, and then, after Christmas, he was going to rent her a house and buy some furniture. Try to get a house close to his house. She knew he loved her. He was a wimp."

"What got her mad?" Dr. Dell asked.

"I don't know. She was trying to shoot Tom in the car." He started to laugh.

"Why was she trying to shoot Tom? Do you know?"

"No."

"Do you know why she got mad?"

"No. She just called him a bastard. His daddy called him that all these years."

For the first time, Paul Dell realized that Tom's father was living inside Tom's mind as well. He had been hearing his father's voice criticizing his actions over the years, perhaps calling him a bastard.

Satan continued, "She was holding the gun and it went off in the car. Tom, the wimp, was trying to grab it from her. It shot her right in the mouth. Tom, the wimp, he didn't even know it. The police . . . I fixed everything so he'd get the blame."

"What happened after the gun went off?"

"It went off two or three times."

The voice softened, speaking as though in pain. "She wasn't dead yet. It went off and somehow she opened the door. She tried to get out of the car. Tom kept calling her.

"He walked around the front of the car and he

talked so nice. And she tried to shoot him again.”

Surprised, Dr. Dell asked, “She had the gun?”

“Yes, but not for long. He was standing there, crying, the wimp. He was crying. I took the gun and I shot her. Tom didn’t do nothing. He’s so stupid. And he went back to the house, and the wife asked him where Kathy was at. He’s a wimp. He said she was test driving a truck and was going to spend the night with some friends.”

“What happened after you shot Kathy on the ground, outside the car?”

“I just shot her.”

“And then what?”

“Tom didn’t know nothing. He was trying to get the gun away from her. And kept shooting, and I took it and I kept shooting her, shooting her, shooting her. Tom was standing there, crying, and I got back in the car. Tom didn’t know he even did it.

“So stupid. Jesus, garbage, I’m tired of him writing it. Fixed him last night. He couldn’t even sleep. Jesus, garbage.”

“What happened after you shot Kathy?”

“I just got back in the car and drove off.”

“Where did you leave Kathy when you shot her?”

“On the ground.”

“Where?”

“On the ground.”

“Right beside the car?

“Yeah.”

“How did she get from there to the end of the canal?”

“I don’t know. She was just laying on the ground and Tom don’t know nothing.”

"Satan, how many times was the gun fired?"

"I don't know . . . I just kept shooting."

"How many bullets does the gun hold?"

"I don't know. Enough."

"Did you keep shooting until the gun was empty?" Dr. Dell watched Tom nod yes. Then he asked what happened.

"Tom didn't know what happened. He snapped like a light bulb. Sissy."

"Did you reload the gun?"

"Yeah."

"What did you do when you reloaded the gun?"

"Just kept shooting. Nobody's going to call me a bastard."

"Why did you keep shooting? She was already dead."

"She was just laying there and I kept shooting her. Tom don't even remember it. He's been telling the truth so many times and they don't even know it. Garbage and crap. Jesus this and Jesus that. See where he's at now? Is it helping him?"

Tom's body began to writhe as though in pain. Satan seemed to be suffering from pain, though whether it was physical or from the emotional situation was uncertain.

The questioning continued, Satan claiming that he knew nothing about Kathy's body being moved to the edge of the canal. He also claimed that the gun was left on the car seat.

"Why did Tom tell the police the gun was 'throwed in the river?' "

"I made it up." He insisted that that gun was on

the front seat of the car, even though it hadn't been found.

"Kathy . . . She wasn't no Miss Goody Two-Shoes. He thought she was. She'd drink beer. She'd drink wine. She got arrested for stealing some drawers in a department store."

Dr. Dell kept pushing Satan, asking how her clothing got off, how she came to be by the canal. He said that all Tom remembered was going to look at a truck. There was so much confusion that Dr. Dell felt there was another personality who needed to come out to answer the rest of the questions. "I had been picking up signs that there was somebody else inside Tom and I didn't know yet. So I said, 'Who's the other one inside whose name I don't know?' "

The next personality to appear was Demian, who, according to Satan, was created when Tom Bonney's grandmother died. That trauma was a major factor in the creation of the personalities. The trauma had been so great that Tom ran off into the woods, crying, staying there half the night.

"Were you inside Tom before his grandmother passed away?" Dr. Dell asked. And Satan responded that he wasn't.

Then it was Demian's turn, a deeper voice, stressing that he had been around for thirty-five years, ever since Tom's grandmother died. He was angry, hurting, proud that he had control. He also mentioned that he was able to absorb pain. He had been the one who had endured the injury when the car crushed his chest. Earlier he had handled a time when Tom was accidentally sloshed with gasoline, then set on fire. Tom had not had injuries that could be fatal, but the pain was intense.

Hour after hour the questioning continued. And when it was over, Dr. Dell prepared a report for John Halstead, the defense attorney.

The Dell Report (In Part)

Account of the Crime: It is difficult to give a literal rendering of Mr. Bonney's account of the shooting because there are ten different versions. What follows therefore is my integration of these disparate accounts.

Demian, often via his secret control of Satan, had been mistreating, overly restricting, controlling, and spying on Cathy [sic] for years. On the night of the killing, before leaving the house, Demian seems to have already been experiencing flashbacks of being abused by father. As noted above, Tom's father was abusive and rejecting. It may be that Cathy's [sic] continuing rejection of Demian's overcontrol, as demonstrated by her sexual relationships with men, was the trigger for Demian's flashbacks. Certainly, there is no doubt that Demian was highly upset by the graphically sexual letter that he had discovered in her room. Whatever the trigger might have been, it seems that Demian was beginning to see not Cathy [sic], but his rejecting abusive father instead (before even arriving at the murder site). Most of the others seemed to sense Demian's rage (which he had deposited in Satan) and feared that Satan intended to shoot Cathy [sic] (Daddy). They tried to stop Cathy [sic] from getting into the car with her father, but were powerless to communicate with her because Satan (actually Demian behind the scenes) was in control. When they arrived at the roadside parking area on Route 17, Tom, Satan, and Demian confronted Cathy [sic] with the graphically sexual letter that she had written to a married man. Tom was gentle and fatherly with her, and Cathy [sic] initially responded with embarrassment. She said she was "so embarrassed" and "so sorry." Then, Cathy [sic] suddenly flipped into a rage and said, "I'm not going to take this crap anymore. You bastard, I'm going to kill you." With that, Cathy [sic] grabbed the gun that had slid out from under the seat when they pulled off the road, and pointed it at her father. There was a struggle for the gun and it went off, striking Cathy [sic] in the mouth. The struggle continued with both their hands on the gun, with Demian now in full flashback (as a result of Cathy's [sic] calling him a "bastard"), and the gun was fired a few more times. Cathy [sic] managed to open her door and fell onto the ground, still holding the gun. Tom came around the front of the car to reach Cathy [sic] and she began to level the gun at him. Satan/Demian swooped in, grabbed the gun, and began shooting: "I took it and I kept shooting her, shooting her, shooting her." During this whole time, Demian was in control of Satan and was seeing not Cathy [sic] but the hated father who was rejecting him, beating him, and calling him "bastard."

During the limited time of this evaluation, I was not able to learn what happened after the first nine shots were fired. Satan has a vague recollection of reloading the gun, but all alters deny knowledge of how Cathy [sic] got from the roadside to the

Tom Bonney and his daughter, Kathy, in happier times.
(*Martin Smith-Rodden*)

Kathy Bonney was determined to become a mystery writer. Ironically the most dramatic murder story of her brief life proved to be the one she would experience as victim, not creator. (*Martin Smith-Rodden*)

Kathy with longtime friend John McClung, a business partner with the Bonney family and one of the first to discover Tom Bonney's multiple personalities, but one of the last to suspect that it would turn to violence.
(John McClung)

Dorothy Carol Bonney poses with Kathy in front of the salvage-yard truck.
(John McClung)

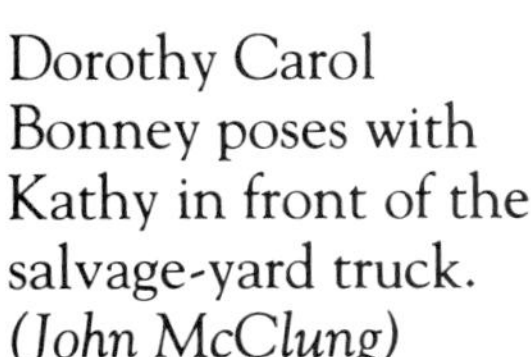

To escape the violence which had claimed their daughter, the Bonneys appealed to the public for financial help. Neither of them realized that the killer sat with them. (*Martin Smith-Rodden*)

Carol Bonney, still in shock over the death of her daughter, cannot understand how Tom could abandon her before Kathy's killer is caught. *(Martin Smith-Rodden)*

Tom Bonney. *(Martin Smith-Rodden)*

Tom Bonney goes through the booking process.
(*Martin Smith-Rodden*)

Tom Bonney meets the press on his way to the courthouse during his trial. (*Martin Smith-Rodden*)

nsistent that no crime has occurred, that Kathy is alive inside his
head and will ultimately come forth to vindicate him, Tom Bonney
plans to eventually leave prison and become a full-time minister. A
eader of an independent Christian organization has befriended
Bonney and is working toward the day she and Tom will lead their
wn evangelical group. (*Martin Smith-Rodden*)

In a public cemetery, a humble grave marks the spot where Kathy Carol Bonney is buried. *(Martin Smith-Rodden)*

edge of the canal. All deny knowledge of how her clothes came to be removed. All deny that Cathy was ever in the trunk. Following the killing, Demian immediately resumed his habitual patterns of lying and deceit and did his best to avoid detection and to mislead the police.

[The report continued with three diagnoses—multiple personality disorder, post-traumatic stress disorder, and mixed personality disorder.]

Competency: Taken alone, Tom's extensive amnesia and failure to believe or comprehend the nature of the charges against him makes him unable to adequately cooperate with his attorney or to assist in formulating a defense. Nine out of ten alters, however, do understand the charges, but have been unwilling (Demian) or largely unable (the rest) to be very cooperative or helpful in preparing a defense. Overall, Mr. Bonney must be judged to be competent.

State of Mind: At the time that he shot his daughter, Mr. Bonney was suffering from multiple personality disorder and post-traumatic stress disorder. The dissociative flashbacks due to these two mental disorders so impaired his mental capacity at the time of the shooting that he did not know the nature and quality of the act as he was committing it.

John Halstead faced the report Dr. Dell provided with a certain amount of relief. He had never heard of multiple personality before he had to defend Tom Bonney. He certainly did not know how the information could be used as a defense. However, from what he was learning, both from the psychologist and the books and articles he was able to find on the subject, the situation made sense.

Several of the area law enforcement officers thought that the murder was essentially a sex crime. They believed that Tom Bonney had an incestuous relationship with his daughter. They thought that when he discovered the affair with John Hoskins, he felt betrayed. They felt that he shot his daughter, coldly and deliberately, as might any extremely jealous lover.

Both theories seemed plausible at one time, but no evidence ever emerged to support the notion of a sexual relationship between Tom and Kathy. Yet the full story had yet to be uncovered, something neither the prosecution nor the defense could anticipate at the time.

CHAPTER 6

The Trial

THE American system of criminal justice has often been called the finest in the world. It is an adversary system where the person accused of a crime is considered innocent until proven guilty. With the exception of crimes of great violence or circumstances where the person accused of a crime is likely to flee the country, someone arrested will have a chance to go free until the trial begins in a few weeks, months, or years, depending upon the case. The bail is usually based on the ability to pay, and the system is so respected, even by the criminals, that posting bond is a business for men and women throughout the country. The bail bondsmen are paid ten percent of what the courts demand, such as $1000 when the bail is set at $10,000. They post the entire amount, then are repaid by the court when the defendant appears for trial, keeping the ten percent the defendant paid. The business succeeds because the vast majority of accused criminals, innocent or guilty, accept the system and appear for trial.

Many other nations follow the Napoleonic Code. This means that you are guilty until proven innocent. You are placed in jail from the moment of your arrest until your acquittal, if you are found innocent. This means that anyone might serve months or years in jail until their case works its way through the system, even though they are not guilty.

But being the best system in the world does not make the system perfect. There are serious flaws, among them being the fact that truth is narrowly defined in the American court of law.

Trial lawyers do not have to be knowledgeable. Instead, they must be actors, skilled at impressing a jury. Sometimes a raised eyebrow, a slight frown, a sneer or a smile on the part of the prosecutor or the defense counsel, can reinforce or shatter the impact of the words a witness has just spoken. Because the defense counsels are allowed to limit the testimony, sometimes to a simple yes or no, regardless of the complexity of the questions, witnesses may not be able to supply what might be essential additional information.

This is not to say that trial lawyers fail to learn the law. However, how a person performs on the stage of the courtroom often means more than their technical knowledge. As a result, many highly theatrical defense attorneys go into court assisted by a man or woman who is less flamboyant but far more knowledgeable. This second attorney stays at the table where the accused is sitting, making suggestions and raising critical legal points when they will help the client's case.

Each side is concerned with making points that will either damage or reinforce the accused's story. The defense counsel must do everything in his or her power to assure that a positive case is built, even when the accused is known to be guilty. In the adversarial system, the prosecutor must prove that guilt through the facts.

The more complex the motivation, the more problems a defense counsel will have when his or her client is guilty of a crime. Some attorneys go so far as to put the victim on trial. One Arizona lawyer gained notoriety for winning the freedom of his client, a man who stabbed his wife more than thirty times as they lay in their bed together. The lawyer "proved" to the jury that the man was temporarily driven insane by just provocation—his wife shopped too much. He even got the victim's mother to explain that the woman would spend eight or more hours a day going to malls, department stores, and specialty shops, though she did not buy very often and only spent money within their means. The jury agreed that it was enough to cause momentary madness. And this occurred despite the fact that the man had, at first, lied and said that some stranger had entered their bedroom and attacked his wife.

In Maryland, a top criminal defense attorney has been known to "accidentally" drop his law books when the prosecution's witness is making a telling point against his client. He had one client, an emotionless murderer who refused to show anything but cold calm; whenever the witness against this client was saying something damning, the defense counsel would quietly "goose" his client, squeezing his rear end to make him jump as though reacting to what was being said. It was all part of the show business aspect of the American court of law.

Yet despite the realities of the courtroom and the seeming need for occasional theatrics, justice is generally served. In the case of Tom Bonney, all that was certain was that he had killed. The reality of the man, the history of the family, all the information that would have aided the jury's understanding of the complexities of the case, could not come out. The prosecutor had only to prove that Tom Bonney committed first-degree murder, a crime for which the death penalty could be imposed. The defense knew Tom Bonney had killed, but needed to find a legitimate reason why his actions deserved a penalty less severe than death. As a result, the truth became enmeshed in the translucent webbing of statements by conflicting experts, testimony by friends and coworkers, and even Tom Bonney's words as revealed on the videotapes.

The Tom Bonney trial was heard in Camden County, not a good location for so complex a case. Camden County is a rural area of North Carolina, a place where the residents are educated for the needs of small farmers, not for psychological subtleties. They are essentially good people with a basic view of justice. Good is expected from their neighbors. Bad is to be punished. And a mad dog is put down for society's good.

Tom Bonney looked to be a mad dog. The jury promised to listen to the evidence without prejudice, and this they seemed to do. They took their duty to serve quite seriously. Certainly the newspaper reports indicated that Tom Bonney was guilty. A man who is supposed to be a good family man, whose daughter is supposedly killed by a stranger, doesn't suddenly up and leave his wife and other children. A man has responsibilities. A man has to put aside his personal grief to care for his family. That's what any of them would have done—if they were innocent.

But the jury's belief in Tom Bonney's probable guilt was no greater than the belief most juries have in the guilt of the accused. No matter how many times we learn about an innocent person being sent to jail, most Americans have faith in the criminal justice system. Most Americans believe that people are simply not arrested without cause. People are not brought into a court of law unless they are guilty. And in rural North Carolina, it must be added—especially not white people.

North Carolina was a part of the old South that was invaded by the North. Union troops defeated Confederate soldiers in Elizabeth City, where they received only token resistance. There had been slavery on the various estates. Even within the last century, one of the most prominent families in Elizabeth City not only owned one of the big mansions in the downtown area, but also owned both the mill and two hundred of the homes used by the workers. There had been, and, in the minds of many people, there remained, a distinct difference between the rich and the poor, between white and black, and especially between poor whites and poor blacks. The Bonney family was considered to be "white trash" by many in Camden County, though most of the families had not achieved the standard of living Tom had finally acquired through his junkyard. However, in a rural area where everyone is poor, no one feels poor. The lack of contrast among neighbors enabled bigotry to appear in other forms. Racial bias has remained common.

Contemporary racial bias is subtle, of course. Most of the South has changed in recent years. Blacks and whites eat in the same restaurants, stay in the same hotels, shop in the same stores. The term "nigger" is seldom encountered, though it is not unusual for black adult male workers to be called "boy," albeit seldom to their faces.

By the time of the Bonney trial, changes were taking place. The university system was actively integrating the Elizabeth City campus, offering scholarships to whites and demanding quality students, black or white, who would be an asset anywhere. The board scores were still lower than average in many instances, but the students admitted often had abilities for success that had been revealed in other ways. Thus the bias was reduced, though not eliminated. And by the same token, the College of the Albemarles was integrating to a faster degree than many of the earliest supporters had ever desired.

Still, Tom Bonney had all the advantages possible for such a heinous crime as the one for which he was charged. He was white, self-made, and not local. His sentence would not embarrass anyone no matter which way it went. And the people, though fairly certain that no one would go to court unless guilty, and though shocked by the horror of a man accused of shooting his own daughter, were willing to be fair. They would listen to the evidence. They would keep an open mind. And if they believed that there was a reason to do so, they would free him or let him live. However, if he was guilty as charged, Tom Bonney would die.

John Halstead understood the problems he was facing. He was an attorney known for accepting the cases no one else wanted to take. He also knew that his client had been present at his daughter's death, had undoubtedly pulled the trigger of the revolver. Yet he was convinced that Tom Bonney was a seriously disturbed man who had been through a living hell of his mind's own making. That did not excuse the killing of Kathy Bonney. It did, however, justify keeping Tom alive.

Yet John Halstead also knew that his defense, with assistance from his partner, John Morrison, could be Tom Bonney's death warrant. Camden County people were not known for compassion to criminals. Insanity might seem a valid reason to send a man to a high security hospital for the criminally insane if the trial took place in Virginia. Insanity might be a valid reason to send a man to jail for the rest of his natural life in that same state. But in North Carolina, especially in the rural areas such as Camden, from which the jurors came, insanity was reason to kill Tom Bonney to stop his hurting and to keep him from taking any more lives. There was a chance, given that reality, that if Halstead could convince the jury of Tom's emotional problems, he would be inadvertently and unintentionally signing Tom Bonney's death warrant. And if he could not convince the jury of Tom's mental condition, Tom would most certainly die.

The trial began as most such trials do. The prosecutor and the defense made opening statements establishing their positions concerning the case.

John Morrison, Halstead's partner, gave the opening argument, though Halstead would be the primary attorney of record and the man whom Bonney felt represented him. Morrison recognized that there was no way to say that Tom Bonney was innocent of the killing, not with the facts the prosecutor would present. Instead, he stated:

"I wish I could stand here and tell you that Tom Bonney was not involved in the death of his daughter, but that is not the case. That is not what our evidence is going to show. Our evidence is going to show that he was involved with the death of his daughter, whom he loved more than anything else on this earth. And to this extent our evidence and the prosecutor's will be pretty much the same. But after that, there is going to be a very sharp difference.

"Now, our case is going to require you to understand not only what happened on that night in November, but what happened in the mind of Tom Bonney. And in order to do that, you're going to have to travel back forty-five years, and you're going to have to learn about an illness he has, what caused that illness, and what effect that illness had on him to consciously control his physical actions, to understand the nature and consequence of his acts, to know what he was doing. Because, you see, over forty-five years, Tom Bonney became not one person, as you and I are, he became ten. Now these are ten separate personalities with names, identities of their own. Nine of these personalities he cannot control. Nine he is unaware that he even has. Nine will control and influence him even though he does not know they exist even as he sits here in this court.

"Now, I know what I've just told you is incredible-sounding. So, let me be quick to point out two things. First, I certainly don't expect you to take anything I say without proof. And, secondly, because something is strange and foreign to us does not mean it's unreal."

The opening continued, Morrison explaining about Dr. Dell's involvement, the use of hypnosis, the videotapes, and other details. He discussed dissociative disorders and related information. He also identified the other personalities, giving a brief background. Finally he introduced the crime as the defense wanted the jury to understand it, as they, themselves, believed it occurred.

"Tom had a junk business, salvage business. Sometimes he handled sums of money, and he was in the habit of taking this gun with him. And when he began to discuss this problem [the sexually explicit letter he found] with Kathy about John Hoskins, and the car came to a stop, the revolver slid out from under the seat. He and Kathy began to discuss her relationship with John Hoskins and she became angry. She lunged for the gun. She called him names. She called him a bastard. She got hold of the gun, and the gun went off. You will have to decide who shot who first. Whether it was an accident in the beginning or whether it was self-defense, or whether it was something else, as the prosecutor has been contending. But, most importantly, you are going to have to determine the mind of Tom Bonney when the revolver in his hand took away the thing that was most precious in his life—his daughter, Kathy."

And so the trial began. The first stages were familiar ones to court buffs. Establish that a crime took place. Interrogate the officers called to the scene. Bring on the expert witnesses. All of the people presented were presented by the prosecutor, building a dual case—that a murder occurred, that Kathy Bonney was the victim, and that her father was the man who killed her. The jury learned of the crime scene, witnessed evidence photos, was able to see clothing that had been punctured by bullets and stained with blood.

It was important, to the prosecutor, for the jury to have compassion for Kathy Bonney. It was important for the jury to care that she had lived, to be angry that she had died, to want to punish the person who had been responsible for her death. Without such emotions, they might be more lenient toward the defendant. In the extreme, a guilty man might go free.

Only after the prosecution presents its case does the defense begin to act aggressively, bringing forth its own witnesses, experts, and anyone else who might cast a different light on the case. Not that the defense is silent during the prosecution's domination of the courtroom. The defense counsel is listening closely, objecting when an improper line of questioning is taking place or when a witness talks more freely than allowed under the rules of the court. The defense counsel also may discredit the prosecution's witnesses where possible, in the same manner that the prosecution may discredit the defense witnesses.

The prosecution's case was thoroughly damning. Tom Bonney had not only lied about what happened to his daughter after he filed the police report, he lied with such detail that it was obvious he had carefully developed his story in advance of the interview. For example, Malcolm McCleod, a special agent with the North Carolina State Bureau of Investigation, told of Tom Bonney describing the "phantom" Chevrolet Blazer as being " . . . a 'seventy-nine model, and it was solid black. And it had five or six lights across the top of the truck that appeared to be either floodlights or fog lights, and that the Blazer had a dent on the right front fender, and that it partially covered the right front door, and that when you opened the door, it made a popping sound, and he stated that the truck had blackwall tires and the rims had a lot of mud on them.

"Bonney described the Blazer as having a step under each of the front doors and had the number and letter K-5 on each fender, on each side, left and right, which indicated the model of the truck. And he stated that the motor had a good tone, or the muffler had a good tone when the motor was raced. And I asked Mr. Bonney if he could place a value on the Chevrolet Blazer that he saw, and he said he estimated the value to be twelve hundred dollars."

The special agent went on to discuss Bonney's actions after the murder. He told how Bonney alleged that he sold the Chevrolet he had been driving when Kathy was killed, not because he was trying to hide evidence, though that would later seem to be the reason, but because he needed nine hundred dollars for Kathy's funeral.

The details continued, establishing Bonney's actions after the murder, his cooperation with the police, the comments he made. He also detailed Bonney's comments concerning his daughter and Tom's statement that he never struck his daughter.

Other detectives and investigators were also placed on the stand, each confirming the other's story where they were at the same crime scene, or adding new information when they weren't. The idea was to convince the jury that when there was such complete consensus among the different investigators, they must be telling the truth. And only Tom Bonney seemed unconvinced, angry that people were saying such things about him.

There were several people who knew Tom Bonney and were in the courtroom as spectators or following the trial through the news media. The more they heard, the more they wondered how thoroughly anyone had bothered to try and know Tom Bonney's history.

Tom Bonney had a difficult childhood with an abusive father. The elder Bonney was in the military when Tom was born during World War II. The absence made him feel extremely close to his mother and grandmother, who initially were the ones who raised him. He also seemed to not have bonded to his father as a result of the absence, the man entering his life a stranger.

The older Bonney was a game warden, a fireman, and an active hunter and fisherman. Tom Bonney was unable to hunt, to take a bird or animal's life, though he developed a love of guns and a belief in defending his family. He always tried to keep one or more weapons around the house, his business, and in his truck. He had owned a shotgun, a sawed-off .22-caliber rifle, a nine-shot revolver, and other weapons over the years. His family was also aware of them and not afraid to use them.

In fact, when Kathy was thirteen years old, a man threatened Tom Bonney because Tom had cheated him in a business deal. Kathy knew nothing about her father's dishonesty, but she did understand that he was in danger. She grabbed the loaded shotgun, aimed it at the man and threatened to shoot him if he did not leave her father alone. There was no question in the mind of both Tom and his would-be assailant that Kathy would carry out the threat. The man backed off, and Tom was proud of his daughter.

But self-defense and the protection of the family was always different in his mind than hunting. His father had called him a wimp and a bastard for refusing to shoot ducks, rabbits, or deer, animals his father hunted for both sport and meat.

There was some suspicion by Tom's father that his wife was having affairs while he was fighting during World War II. He called his son a bastard, in part, because he believed that he was just that, the product of an illicit relationship. However, there never was proof of this, nor is it likely to have been true. What it did do was instill in Tom a distrust of women, whom he tended to hold in contempt. He maintained a love/hate relationship that enabled him to feel both that women were capable of the greatest good and the greatest possible bad. It was such feelings that made him hate the idea of his daughter's having sex, and convinced him that she was pregnant each time he learned that she may have been intimate with a man.

There were many incidents of violence between Tom and his father, incidents that added to the love/hate relationship with women. Tom often talked about the time he was forced to cut the grass with a scissors. It was only with friends that he told the whole story, though. His mother had not only sneaked him inside to sleep after his father went to bed for the night, she also awakened him before sunrise, having him return to the yard with the scissors. She wanted him to have some rest, but she also did not wish to incur her husband's wrath if he found Tom in bed. She made certain that her husband would think that Tom had been cutting all night. Tom became both grateful for her help and angry over her unwillingness to stand up to her husband and fight his absurd demands.

The hatred between father and son came when Tom quit school in the ninth grade and was able to buy a car from money he had earned. (A person could own a car, but could not drive it unless of legal age and properly licensed.)

Tom's father was irate when he learned that Tom had made the purchase. The car was not registered, there was no license and no insurance. It was a foolish kid's stunt, and his father insisted he sell it, though Tom would have happily kept the car until he could legally use it.

Tom knew it was impossible to argue with his father. He also was determined to see what it was like to drive it. When his father was away for a few minutes, he took it around the block, getting arrested for speeding, driving an unregistered car, and driving without a license. Naturally, the case went to court.

The judge did not see Tom as a criminal. Tom later recounted the conversation, which he remembered almost thirty years later while under hypnosis:

BONNEY: My name's Tommy.
JUDGE: Tommy, what did you do?
BONNEY: I got scared. I'm so sorry.
JUDGE: Well, son, you're not old enough to drive a car.
BONNEY: I know.
JUDGE: Did you learn a lot from this?
BONNEY: Yes, sir. I learned a lot. I won't go no more.
JUDGE [apparently speaking to his mother]: Ma'am, do you think he learned a lot?
MOTHER: Oh, yes, sir, he learned a lot.
JUDGE: Mr. Bonney, what do you think?
FATHER: If you let him go to jail, maybe he'll learn something.
BONNEY [whimpering]: Mama . . . tell him. . . .

JUDGE: State of Virginia finds you guilty. Driving with no insurance. Driving with no driver's license. Driving with no inspection sticker. This court finds you guilty. Sentences you to one year, St. Bride's prison.

Whether or not the memory was correct, Tom Bonney spent the next six to eight months in the state center for juvenile offenders. The judge responded to Tom's father's request that he be jailed, though the judge had indicated that he was quite comfortable with the idea of letting Tom go home if both his parents agreed to it.

Tom's parents separated during this period, his mother upset over what her husband had done to their son. She took an apartment in Norfolk until Tom was released, then the family was reunited after his release.

It was sometime during this period, when Tom was fourteen years old, that his beloved grandmother died. This was Mammy, a strong influence on his life and a woman he deeply loved. The fact that she was in a hospital at the time convinced him that hospitals were places of death and that medical professionals were not to be trusted. They killed your loved ones.

Tom seldom, if ever, talked about the details of what he experienced day after day while spending time in the juvenile offenders' facility. However, he constantly discussed the fact that his father forced him into a situation that would otherwise not have occurred.

Tom Bonney served briefly in the National Guard, though he came to hate the military. His father had been a soldier, and his brother had joined the service. But Tom hated it and hated the men who served. His business partners in the salvage yard talked about how he despised having to buy from the sailors in Norfolk as well as having to sell to them. He hated any of Kathy's friends whose fathers had been in the Navy. He was even angrier about the fact that he was dependent upon men and women in the military for his financial success. It was as though he was again being used in life, though the truth was quite different.

Tom Bonney left home for good when he was nineteen, and did not see his family again until Carol was pregnant with Kathy. The family moved to Florida, where Tom and Carol were regularly in trouble with the Social Service agencies. He had a record of physical abuse of the children and his wife, as well as being medically neglectful of his family. The abuse seemed to be, in part, a repeat of how he was raised.

Tom did not go to the extremes with his children that he had experienced with his own father. When Tom was a little boy in school, he occasionally had problems with the school authorities because he sometimes came to classes bruised. Tom's childhood occurred at a time and in a state where child abuse was known, but where the teachers and Social Service agencies would not intervene unless a complaint was filed. The teachers asked young Tom about his bruises, but he always lied. He would not say he had been struck.

By the time Tom's children were growing up, the laws had changed. There was active intervention in families where child abuse was believed to be taking place. Tom at least twice relocated his family in Florida to prevent the removal of his children. Then, when Tom returned to Virginia, he lied to the Social Service agency representatives, claiming that he lived alone, that his wife and children had returned to Florida. In truth, they were hiding in the woods, and eventually his children were removed from the home.

Social service agencies took the children from the Bonneys until they felt that the parents would be more responsible, and a son was permanently removed. To Tom's horror, the boy was given to a family where the husband was career military.

Tom worried about the Social Service personnel taking his children, especially since not all the instances were justified. In one case the children were in the bedroom of the home while an employee was in the backyard, doing some work and keeping an eye on the kids. A case worker stopped by unexpectedly, found the children alone, and did not spot the employee in back. She thought that the children had been left unattended and removed them. Although there were definite instances of neglect and abuse, Tom focused on such improper incidents to justify his constant moving to escape their observation of the family. Tom lived in constant fear that they might be taken again. He only felt secure with his wife and children, even though the only childrearing he knew was a variation of his father's actions. One daughter ended up in a psychiatric hospital, and Kathy, who adored her father, became quietly rebellious, crying out for help yet being unable to get away.

Kathy had regularly told friends that her father hit her. The most extreme situation was when she was fifteen and he thought she might have gotten herself pregnant. He slammed his fist into her stomach, then threw her down some stairs. However, a subsequent check at a clinic indicated that she was not going to have a baby prior to her father's actions.

As the witnesses testified, as Tom's past was reviewed in the minds of his friends, they began to think that Tom had killed Kathy. It was something that they had been reluctant to admit, in part because they also knew that he truly loved her, and in part because they had encouraged her to stay at home for a while. Many of them were helping her line up a place to stay, a job, a way to be independent in a manner that would not get her into trouble. She had been extremely sheltered and was naive about the world around her. They wanted her to wait a little longer before moving out, a fact that contributed to her death, at least in their minds.

The question that remained was why. "He loved that family," said one friend. "Whatever he did, he did for them.

"He warned them about drinking and taking drugs. He used to call people who drank, 'Lous.' That was short for 'loser.' 'Don't be a Lou,' he'd say, meaning, 'Don't be a loser.' He'd tell them that all the time.

"He hated drinking, hated the way the Navy guys would come to the salvage yard drinking beer. They'd be drinking while they did business. They'd leave empty six-packs in their cars when they sold them. Sometimes they'd go out back on the property, unzip their flies, and let out a stream because they had had too much beer and couldn't wait. He'd go crazy about that. What if Kathy saw something like that? What if somebody else did? They were all Lous and he hated them."

Another friend told of being arrested because he did not make payment on a debt. The friend was shocked because he had left the money with Tom before going out of town. He thought that Tom would make the payment for him so he would not have to worry about it, something Tom agreed to do. Instead, Tom acted irresponsibly, failing to keep his word, not bothering to apologize, though he did tell the police not to arrest the other man. Tom explained that if anyone had committed a crime, it was he himself. The police should be locking him up.

The matter was straightened out and the friend was given time to pay back the money. The friend was irate, but Tom's concerns seldom, if ever, seemed to go beyond what he felt was best for his family. They were everything to him, and his sense of what was moral and proper was based upon that concept.

During this same period, other stories emerged from people close to the family who did not testify in court. Tom's sister allegedly contradicted Tom's statements about the brutality Tom endured, though she was not asked to testify. Yet at least one of Tom's close friends from the past said that the sister was not being honest. He claimed that, for so long as the man had known the sister, she had made similar statements about their father's violence toward Tom. They allegedly warned her that if she went back on what they claimed she had been telling them over the years, they would know that she was lying. They would then testify under oath that she was perjuring herself. However, there was no testimony, no perjury. It was an issue that would be unresolved.

Another friend of Kathy's told a story of Tom Bonney's bringing home a hitchhiker when Kathy was fifteen. The hitchhiker, unknown to her father, allegedly raped Kathy at that time, her first or one of her first sexual experiences. The problem with this allegation is that, in Kathy's most intimate personal writings, she never made mention of such an incident.

But other friends confirmed what Kathy wrote in her letter to John Hoskins. She had had a boyfriend who forced her to have sex at that age. She was not ready for such an experience, though she was experimenting with what might be called "heavy petting." She had no intention of having intercourse and thought that the boy knew the limits. Instead he raped her, a crime but one which she thought she somehow encouraged. She also had a pregnancy scare, obtained a testing kit and, ultimately, incurred her father's violence when he discovered it.

And there was Tom with his Bible. Some of his friends had become born-again Christians, usually joining nondenominational or Pentecostal churches. They were confused about Tom and his actions. He had a superficial knowledge of the bible, like a child fascinated by the stories found in Little Golden Book collections from the Bible, yet without the depth of study that allowed for true understanding. He would tell and retell what he knew. He would talk about his love for Jesus. And then there would be the change, the pause, the eyes staring for a moment before he tore pages from the Bible and threw them about the room or took the book itself and heaved it out the window. Another change, another momentary stare, and he would appear horrified to find the Bible dirty or in tatters. "Who did this?" he would rage. "Who could do this to the Book?" He gathered the pieces, trying to tape them back in the Bible. Or he picked up the whole book and tried to clean it. Whatever was necessary, and all the time wondering who could have done it and when they had taken the trouble.

Story after story was shared as the trial was watched, though most of the information was never conveyed to the prosecutor or the defense counsel. It was as though the men and women observing were curious to learn just how much law enforcement had learned, deriding some of it, pleased with other statements.

Yet the one question that remained for them was, Why? When Dr. Dell took the stand, they finally got their answers.

Dr. Dell explained the background of multiple personality and other dissociative disorders. He also began discussing post-traumatic stress syndrome, a common problem that first gained attention with Vietnam War veterans, though it affects men and women regardless of where they experienced war. "Almost all Vietnam veterans who have flashbacks are not real keen to have a helicopter fly overhead," explained Dr. Dell. "Why? Because, you know, we all listen on TV if we weren't in Vietnam. The ever-present sound of the helicopters flying around, and it's part of the Vietnam experience, and you start hearing those blades whirling and clapping and . . . pow! You get . . . immediately this stuff starts breaking back in on you.

"The same thing can happen for a woman who was sexually abused. She may, twenty years later in her marriage with her husband, be in bed, and the husband happens to touch her in a way that connects all the way back to twenty years ago where she was being sexually abused by her father. And, all of a sudden, she has this rush of panic. She feels enormously awful and she feels like something terrible is happening, and she doesn't know where it's coming from. She may not even know, for example, she may get sensation. She may get emotion. But she may not even know that she was sexually abused by her father. But this stuff starts breaking in and starts complicating her marital relationship. This is what flashbacks are like.

"If you have had a lot of trauma in your life and you've done a lot of dissociating and a lot of splitting off, that makes the world a mine field for you because you never know when you're going to step on a mine. You never know when some trigger is going to come up that's going to result in this stuff coming crashing back in on you. And that's a flashback.

"Now, flashbacks are not minor things. You can have mild flashbacks. You can have stronger ones.

And you can have full, superintense ones. The metaphor that I like to use for a person who's having a full-strength reliving or a flashback is, it's not like you're just seeing images or seeing pictures in your head of the times something awful happened to you. You're reliving it in all dimensions. It's happening now. And the best way I can kind of describe the intensity of that is with the screen that all of us have seen on TV many times. Situations where somebody comes up to a small room, or whatever, tosses a grenade through the window, and the room goes boom! The room doesn't blow up, but the whole room gets filled with fragments and flash, and the windows blow out.

"When we have a full-intensity recurrence of flashback, it's like tossing a grenade into a person. It is not ignorable. It totally takes you over. You are totally there back in that traumatic event."

Dr. Dell and the other therapists who interviewed Tom took him back to his childhood. In those discussions, Tom went into detail concerning the effects the loss of his grandmother had on him. He also mentioned the beating from his father, the constant repetition of the word "bastard." They were all recurrent memories for Tom, and there was a tendency to be overwhelmed by the memory. To not be aware of all else. "I mean, you just suddenly [snaps fingers] go into full, intense flashback. When that happens, you're no longer here. You're then and there. You're not here and now, and you are seeing what happened then. You're experiencing what happened then. You are reacting to and dealing with it then. That's why you've heard stories about Vietnam veterans shooting people and screaming about the Viet Cong. They're not psychotic. They haven't gone schizophrenic on you. What's happened is that they are in full [snaps fingers] flashback where they are in Vietnam, reliving trauma, reenacting the firefight that they were in when their buddy got killed, or whatever it was that happened then. So that this flashback breaks in with no warning, takes you over. You've lost contact with present reality and you are reenacting and redoing and coping with the trauma back then. And you're unconscious of what's happening in the present world. You're back then in the trauma."

Dr. Dell explained the combination of multiple personality and post-traumatic stress. He showed how both have backgrounds of an extreme trauma that affects the person psychologically. He also explained the tests he had conducted that confirmed his theory.

Then the videotapes were played in the courtroom, Dr. Dell making comments as the jury and the spectators watched them. Several hours were boring, Tom Bonney raising one or another finger in the prearranged signal. Some of the people at the trial found the situation ridiculous. Others were waiting for Tom to do something unusual, to put on the show they had expected from an allegedly crazy man.

Along the way, the doctor tried to explain what he was doing, such as when he provided Tom with information in order to obtain a reaction. "I have at different points during the interviews reviewed some of the evidence that the police have, ticking things off, and yet, when I say given the fact that the police have all of this evidence, and given the fact that Tom Bonney has made several confessions, when I tell them, 'You're going to be convicted,' I get this, 'No, I'm not.'

" 'You're going to be sent to prison,' or 'You're going to be sentenced to death,' and we get this, 'No, I'm not.' And my opinion as to what is going on here is that there is a common phenomenon in multiple personality called the 'delusion of separateness,' and it goes like this. You've got more than one person in the same body, but they oftentimes will believe that they are completely and totally separate from the host personality, Tom. And oftentimes they may believe that, well, Tom will go to jail but I won't, and that's a delusion, of course. And that's my opinion as to part of what is going on here. That they believe that Tom can go on trial, Tom can be convicted or sent to jail or sentenced to death, but not them."

Finally the jury saw the personalities speaking as Dr. Dell brought them out in the jail sessions. It was then that his long-term friends and acquaintances felt that they had both answers and questions.

The name "Hitman" was the most startling to those who had known Tom, and also the most familiar. Dr. Dell concluded that Hitman was created to be helpful, to experience the violence of his father without the other personalities having to bear the pain. But Tom's friends knew otherwise.

Hitman was the name Tom Bonney called himself when he talked about committing the perfect murder. He was certain that such a crime was possible for him, that he would be good at it. Killing and getting away with it was a frequent topic of conversation, Tom bragging that he looked just like Clint Eastwood in one of that actor's more violent pictures. The friends could believe that "Hitman" was the name of an alter personality because Tom certainly acted differently when he spoke about killing. But the "Hitman" they knew seemed very different.

Oddly, it was learned that Tom had tried to kill once as a boy. He had taken a rifle and lain in wait for his father to come home. He had aimed the gun, then could not pull the trigger. However, it was never known if the gun was broken or if Tom psychologically could not fire the weapon.

"Demian" was more familiar. Dr. Dell's description of the angry, violent personality fit the Tom his coworkers had sometimes seen emerge. One of them remembered a story when a customer, a man who ran a bar and restaurant, was going to spend a few hundred dollars on tires. Tom's attitude was friendly and helpful when, in mid-sentence, he stopped, then stared without seeing. A few moments later he resumed speaking as though he had just switched gears. His voice deepened and he was explosively angry. There was no more talk, no bargaining, no sales pitch. If the man wanted the tires, he would have to put the money down at once. Pull it out of his wallet and put it on the counter. No waiting. Otherwise, he should just get out.

Startled, the man, who had enough money to make the purchase, walked out. He later told one of the other workers that he had no intention of dealing with a crazy man. The description, voice, and attitude of Demian all fit the way Tom had behaved.

"Preacher" also made sense because everyone was familiar with the times when Tom would talk about the Bible. His voice would be gentle, awe-filled, like that of a little child overwhelmed by the wonders of the universe.

Yet something was wrong with all this. Tom Bonney was extremely disturbed. No one questioned that. Tom Bonney acted oddly, seemingly a different personality taking control at times. But there were extensive contradictions in all that was taking place, contradictions that H. P. Williams felt he needed to bring out for the jury when it was time to cross-examine Paul Dell.

At first the district attorney focused on the way Dr. Dell became involved in the case, and the opinions he developed from reading the newspaper. He also brought out the fact that the doctor had no knowledge of the conditions under which Tom took the tests.

"You did not check to see if anyone had monitored him taking the tests?" asked H. P. Williams.

"No," replied Dr. Dell.

"Do you know if he even took them in a room by himself?"

"No, I do not."

"You don't know if they were taken in his jail cell with other inmates?"

"No. I don't know that."

"You don't even know who filled it out, do you?"

"I assume that Mr. Bonney did."

"And those tests are part of the basis of your opinion?"

"Certainly."

The district attorney then focused on the conflicting stories told by Tom, his friends, his mother, and his sister. Normally the conflict would not be quite so serious as it became in court. The parents of child abuse victims seldom tell the truth about the abuse. They do not want to implicate themselves in actions that society holds to be wrong. Even the sister's conflicting stories can be understood by the fact that, if Tom Bonney suffered both physical and emotional abuse, his sister probably endured problems as well.

Then the district attorney asked about the fact that the information concerning "the emotional rejection and abuse by his father, and the physical abuse by his father, just comes from Tommy, who lies frequently—or Tom, who lies frequently."

"Tom does not lie frequently," Dr. Dell said.

"You've got it in your report, Dr. Dell. Does he or doesn't he?"

"Well, the portion that you just read to the jury about, 'While it is certain that he lies frequently . . .' refers to Thomas Bonney as a whole, subsuming the others. Tom Bonney, on the other hand, does not in my experience lie."

"Who were you talking to in the very first interview?"

"For the most part, Tom Bonney."

"All right. Now you indicated that the second major trauma is the death of his grandmother."

"Yes."

The questions continued. "And at what age did Tom Bonney's grandmother die?"

"Ten, according to him. Fourteen, according to his mother."

"And you believed him?"

"Yes."

"Isn't it a fact that she died in 1957?"

"I do not know."

"But his mother told you fourteen."

"Yes, she did."

"And Tom has this horrible memory, and you believed him?"

"I took it."

"Tom was born in 1943, wasn't he?"

"I don't recall. I guess. Yes. Forty-five would be 1943. Yes."

"Okay. Born in 'forty-three. And his mother says that she died in 'fifty-seven. So that means he was fourteen when his grandmother died."

"Okay."

"All right. Fourteen when the grandmother died. Your report indicates that Satan was the first alter born, and it says at age ten."

"That's what it says."

"So if it was fourteen, then that's wrong."

"If it was fourteen, that is certainly wrong."

"You say Mammy was born at the time of the funeral, which would have been, according to your report, age ten."

Williams then pointed out that during the interview of July 23, "You were doing the fingers, and you said, talking about being inside Tom for a long time, 'How old when—was Tom when the first one was born?' And you said, 'Before Tom was twenty?' And the answer was 'Yes.' 'Before fifteen?' The answer was 'Yes.' And 'Before ten?' The answer was 'No.' "

"That's correct."

"Okay. And then you asked, 'Older than ten?' and there was no answer."

"Right."

"So—and you took that, based on that and the later statement by Satan that he was ten, to mean that he was ten at the time that he was born?"

"That's correct. That's how I got that."

Then H. P. Williams asked about the personality named Tommy, and pointed out that Tommy had said he was born at the age of fifteen. "And you put that down in your report, 'Tommy is one of four teenage alters who were born at age thirteen'?"

"Yes."

"You ignored your own data?"

"No, I did not." And then Dr. Dell explained that the age declared by an alter personality does not necessarily match the chronological age of the person. "A personality might be born at the age of thirteen, or whatever, begin to grow older, and then stop at a particular age when they get struck by another trauma."

The district attorney said, "So the major trauma that you list as causing multiple personality disorder in Tom Bonney are the emotional rejection and abuse by the father and physical abuse by the father, which is basically entirely based upon what Tom Bonney told you, and rejected by his mother and sister."

"That is correct."

Williams then discussed the crushed chest Tom had received when the car fell on him. He pointed out that X rays taken at Dorothea Dix Hospital indicated that they were within normal limits, a statement presumably implying that there was no damage. Yet Tom claimed that the chest had ribs that needed to be rebroken so that they could heal correctly.

Dr. Dell reminded the district attorney that he was not a physician. He had no idea what the report meant when it stated, "Chest X rays within normal limits." Neither did friends of Bonney in the courtroom. Some had been with him when the car dropped on Tom's chest two years earlier. They had witnessed what occurred and could confirm it. However, because Dr. Dell had not taken the step of consulting with the medical professionals, even the story of the car dropping was discredited.

The district attorney then worked to show that Dr. Dell had not carefully evaluated the evidence to which he had access in light of what Tom Bonney had said. Williams noted that Tom said that "the police hooted and hollered and cussed and fussed and ripped and roared, didn't he?"

"He said that," Dr. Dell agreed.

"Did you hear that on the tape recording of the interview of Tom Bonney by the police department?"

"No."

"And you've read the interview?"

Dr. Dell explained that he had.

"Anywhere in there is there a single four-letter word . . . improper four-letter word?"

"No, there's not."

Williams had also learned about Emily Watson and her friends, another fact he used to discredit Dell's belief in Tom Bonney's statements. "He told you that Kathy comes in to visit him at night in his cell, didn't he? Would it have affected your diagnosis if you had know that, in fact, the female inmates are yelling through the heating system to Tom and saying that they are Kathy?"

The district attorney also pressed the issue of events that may have occurred before or after the "split." But this time Dr. Dell was on firmer ground. "It's very common that the initial information as to the age at which splits first occurred is not accurate. This is normal and typical in treating multiple personality. Oftentimes the somewhat later childhood splits will be revealed first, and the earlier childhood splits, because they're more upsetting and more traumatic in some way, are hidden and don't come out until later in treatment.

"I cannot say with certainty with regard to Mr. Bonney, nor could I say with regard to any other patient with multiple personality, that splits did not occur earlier. Given my experience, there is every possibility that it did, and earlier headaches would be consistent with that fairly normal finding in the course of treatment of multiple personality."

The district attorney had challenged the credibility of the defense expert and of the accused. Now he went for what would be the most damning evidence of all. He wanted to show the jury that Paul Dell's approach to the interview with Tom Bonney had suggested the reactions that were being used to justify the multiple personality diagnosis. Both before hypnosis and when Tom was even more suggestible under hypnosis, the statements made by Dr. Dell affected what Tom Bonney said and how he behaved.

For the spectators, the action had become as dramatic as any television drama. Paul Dell's throat was dry. He was nervous, upset. He wished he had not gotten involved, yet he knew that he had done nothing wrong. Under the same circumstances he might repeat what he had done, knowing a man's life was at stake. At the same time, he realized that once the ordeal he was experiencing was over, he hoped that a similar situation might never again arise.

The problem was that Paul Dell had acted under an unusual, high pressure situation that forced him to act to the best of his ability within limitations necessitated by the impending trial. He had moved quicker than he would have in a therapeutic setting. He had asked leading questions in order to get answers quickly. He knew that there was a chance that his work could be challenged, but there seemed no other way to handle the matter. And, as always, he had had the courage to record everything. Right or wrong, he had been willing to accept the consequences from the beginning. He just did not know how badly he might appear as the prosecutor began attacking the way he questioned Tom Bonney.

"Don't you say to him [on the second tape of the first interview, prior to hypnosis], 'Part of you does things you don't remember'?"

"Yes. I said that."

"Okay. You also told him, 'Unless I'm able to learn what is really going on, you have no chance in court.' "

"That's correct, which I believe was an accurate assessment of the circumstances."

"Okay. I agree. Didn't you tell him, 'There is a part of you that knows about things you forget'?"

"Yes, I did."

"Also, you talked to him about his memory. Didn't Tom tell you, 'Everybody says I got a good memory'?"

"I don't remember that."

"Didn't you say to him, 'Tom, you've got a terrible memory'? And, then, he says, 'I've a good memory.' "

"I don't remember that."

"You also told him, did you not, that, 'Evidence is almost certainly going to convict. They have tape recordings saying, "I killed Kathy?" ' Didn't you tell him that?"

"Yeah. Uh-huh."

"Didn't you also tell him that, 'They think you're playing dumb,' and he said, 'I'm not playing dumb'?"

"Uh-huh. That's correct."

" 'Doctors at Dix say playing dumb. Doctor's around, talk one way. When the doctor's not around, then you act different.' Didn't you tell him that?"

"Yes, I did."

"And he says, 'Not know how to act dumb.' That he doesn't know how to act dumb. He told you that, didn't he?"

"Yes."

The prosecutor then asked Dr. Dell whether or not he had told Tom that there were only two possible explanations for what had taken place. One was that Tom had killed Kathy, knew it and was acting dumb in order to fool everyone. The other possibility was that the Tom personality truly did not know what had happened, but that another personality, a "part of Tom," had committed the murder.

Dr. Dell agreed that he had made a similar statement to Tom.

"Okay. Did you tell him that 'the room is going to be packed. The jury is going to be convinced you did it. You may get the electric chair'?"

"I don't remember telling him anything about the room being packed. I certainly did tell him that the evidence was certain to lead to a conviction."

"As a matter of fact, you had some indication from the Dorothea Dix reports that he was, in fact, acting, or they reported he was acting one way when the doctors weren't around and another way when they were around?"

"Indeed. And I also had a variety of information from other sources, people who knew Tom Bonney well, about sharp changes in his behavior prior to the death of Kathy. Sudden mood shifts, amnesias, forgettings, and so on."

Tom Bonney's life seemed to reinforce what Paul Dell had said about the multiple personalities. Unfortunately, the way in which the interviews were conducted seemed to assure disbelief.

Williams also attacked Dr. Dell's media exposure. The doctor was new to the courtroom. He did not realize that in an adversary situation, image can be almost as important as facts.

The press came to Paul Dell for information. He responded as the academic he was, trying to explain his theories, his beliefs. He wanted them to understand Tom Bonney, to become more aware of the lingering effects of child abuse. It was the right way for a teacher to behave. In a court of law, though, the fact that he handled himself in such a manner could be twisted to make him appear to be a publicity seeker, someone who wanted to build his reputation based on the case.

"After you were appointed, you appeared on television, didn't you?" asked the prosecutor.

"Yes."

"And how many times have you appeared on television since then?"

"I don't know."

"Numerous times. Is that correct?"

"Yes."

"At least twice this week? Maybe more?"

"Probably. Yes."

"And, in fact, you've talked about this case to the press, haven't you?"

"Indeed."

But the questions did not involve the "why" of his actions. The prosecutor's role was not to be totally objective with the defense counsel's expert witness. It was not to give the jury an understanding of a man whose life is dedicated to knowledge and the sharing of that knowledge. It was to imply through the limiting of the questions that Paul Dell wanted to become famous through the Bonney case.

In fairness, it was also not the prosecutor's role to learn why Paul Dell became involved. Even in a small area like Pasquotank and Camden counties, H.P. Williams had seen that there were many people who would do almost anything to become "famous." This included offering their services in high publicity trials, regardless of their expertise. He did not know the full background or motivation of Paul Dell. He had reason to assume the worst, since the psychologist had contacted the defense attorney instead of waiting to have his skills sought by the lawyer. Thus Williams acted in a manner that was fair, based on what he knew, even though his conclusions were incorrect concerning the man seated before him on the witness stand.

Then, having further eroded Dr. Dell's credibility, he returned to showing how the psychologist had been overly suggestive in his comments.

"Didn't you tell him that, 'A part of you knows. A part of you does.' And Tom told you, said to you, 'Part of me?'"

"Yes."

"He was picking up on 'parts,' wasn't he?"

"He was puzzled as to what I was saying."

"Okay. He says—also said, 'What are you saying to me?' and you told him, 'I believe part of you wouldn't. I believe part of you would and has done it. I believe you wouldn't hurt anyone.'"

"I said that."

"You told him, 'Tom, we are having a big problem. The jury is going to convict. They have the evidence to prove it.' And Tom said, 'I don't have no part.'"

"That's correct."

"He picked up on 'parts,' didn't he?"

"Yes, he did. And he denied it, which is typical behavior for the host personality of a multiple who does not know he's a multiple."

"You also, at that point, asked him something along the lines, 'What would happen when Dad beat on you and you'd hide?' And then he said he'd hide in the woods. Is that correct? Started talking to him about Daddy beating on him."

"I don't remember that particular exchange."

"Okay. Later on in that same interview you told him, 'You have no chance in court unless I'm able to find out what's going on.' And Tom Bonney told you, 'There is no part.' "

"Okay."

"And you told him, 'There has to be a part because you keep doing things you don't remember.' "

"That's correct. There has to be a part of him that remembers it because he has been doing them, and these acts that I was talking about to him had been documented."

"And every time he can't remember something, you suggested a part that could remember."

"No. Not every time."

"But you did suggest parts that could remember?"

"At times I did. I certainly did."

"And that's the whole problem with hypnosis, isn't it, suggestibility?"

Dr. Dell pointed out that the early part of the interviews was not done under hypnosis. However, Williams noted that there were other comments, all making the same type of suggestions, that followed when Tom was under hypnosis. And all of them were based on the conclusion that Tom was a multiple personality, though the psychologist had never seen a change in Tom prior to hypnosis.

"You had not made contact and you had already decided that he was a multiple?" asked the prosecutor.

"Based on the pattern of findings and the breadth and depth of the data that I had, I came to the conclusion that he was almost certainly multiple, and that given the situation—namely, that I was dealing with a capital case and had a very limited amount of time within which to work—that that was the most prudent course with which to proceed."

"Dr. Dell," said Williams. "It being a capital case, the amount of time is no excuse, wouldn't you agree?" And it was at that moment that one of the sheriff's deputies observing the proceedings decided that "H. P. reamed the doc a new asshole."

"You indicated that you had made a diagnosis [of Tom Bonney]. Well, that's in conflict, is it not, with your earlier statement, 'A diagnosis should not be made until the clinician has actually observed the patient in an altered state.'"

Dr. Dell explained that, in general, that was the case. However, he already had an extensive case history from Tom and others.

The prosecutor then presented the fact that the video camera was, for most of the videos, focused on Tom's hands. "And there is no way that the jury or anyone else can evaluate his facial expressions during that time, is there?"

"No. Not when he's not on camera."

"There is no way that anyone can evaluate what you were doing during that time because you're not seen."

"That's correct."

The truth was that no one could evaluate if he did things right, not just if he did them wrong. Yet the implication was clear, and Dr. Dell had to admit it was valid, even though it might not be accurate.

By the time the prosecutor was finished, he had shown that much of the background supplied to the therapist was in question. The history of abuse came from Tom, though his sister denied it. The idea that Mammy was created in Tom's mind from the trauma of her death was shattered because she died four years after Tom claimed she died and after it was indicated that the personality was formed. Too much seemed wrong. Dr. Dell had been shattered on the stand.

The fact that there were others who could corroborate some of Dr. Dell's beliefs had no effect. There were coworkers of Tom's who claimed to be willing to testify that, over the years, Tom's sister had spoken about the childhood abuse Tom endured. They were willing to stand up against her and say she was committing perjury if she went on the stand and said that Tom had *not* been abused. But she did not go on the stand, nor was there any indication that she would ever commit perjury. The other witnesses were not questioned about this. And the information in the formal record as presented by the prosecutor made Dr. Dell look like a well-intentioned fool. It had been a humiliating experience, winning the jury solidly over to the prosecution.

John Halstead had the right under the rules of procedure to question Dr. Dell again, and this time he worked to show another side. Linda Oakley, Tom Bonney's sister, was not appearing in court to testify. But the interview conducted with her could be introduced into the questioning, and John Halstead did so. In again talking with Dr. Dell, the defense counsel quoted Dell's own question to Linda Oakley about Tom's childhood. The answer that followed was inconclusive. She may have been trying to protect her father, an action that is quite common for abuse victims, and she may have been uncomfortable with the probing into so personal an aspect of her family.

Oakley: "But, see, here's the thing. This is a lot of backtracking. I don't want Daddy brought into this. Daddy and Tommy, no, they did not get along. That was mostly my mother's fault. I mean, I'm piecing some of this together. Let's face it. This started when I wasn't born. But as near as I can put together, Tommy was born and Daddy was in the Army. She got pregnant before one of those wars. I guess it was World War Two. And so by the time Daddy got home, I don't know how old Tommy was. Probably a year old. Anyhow, and Mom, of course, he was the firstborn, she really had a super tight. . . . I mean, Tommy was the favorite child. I think Daddy resented that. So anytime they had an argument, it was always over Tommy. I mean, I grew up that way. Tommy got spankings. I got the worse spankings with a belt. That was the way Daddy was. That was the way that Daddy was taught and that was the way . . . I don't mean knock me out, but I mean I had some whelps back there. Yes, Daddy, one time, only once, yes, Daddy did push Tommy off the porch in the country."

The statement seemed clear that there had been abuse, that Tom's sister was uncomfortable discussing it. Then John Halstead presented other statements that had been used in Dr. Dell's conclusion that Bonney was dissociating. Yet the damage had been done.

Other defense witnesses were called and their testimony reinforced much of what Dr. Dell had been saying. John McClung, one of Tom Bonney's partners over the years, said that "Tom always had a bad memory." He went on to explain:

"He would be talking to somebody on the phone or at the same time he's talking to them he would forget what he's talking about, look at me. Or somebody would be giving him directions and, as soon as they'd give him directions, he'd forget the directions and look at me, and then I would have to get on the phone and clarify the directions for him. Sometimes we would even be working on an engine and working on something like the carburetor or just engine work, and he would actually be working on the stuff and then forget what he's doing right there while he's working on it. And I'd have to go back to him and say, 'Tom, what are you doing?' And he'd sit there, look and stare, and finally I would say, 'Aren't you going to finish working on the carburetor?' And he'd just . . . just stare at me like that, and then I'd have to tell him, 'You need to finish doing what you're doing here,' and then he would realize that he hadn't finished what he was doing. But that just happened numerous, numerous times when we were working together."

Michael Cooper, a truck driver and heavy equipment operator who knew Tom Bonney for nine years, said that Tom would "forget a lot of things. Things he supposed to have done. Places he supposed to have been. You know. He was forgetting. He started looking for titles to cars that he had bought, and he misplaced them. He couldn't find them. Yet people wanted to buy the cars, and he couldn't sell them because he had lost the titles. He didn't know where he had put them."

Rick Uhl, who worked for Tom for several years, said that Tom "had a lot of problems with his memory. I had tried to give him messages to where he was supposed to deliver car engines to people that wanted to buy them. He would get—he would get the message down and somebody would come up and talk to him about something. He'd go to take off down the road, and the next thing you'd know, he'd give us a phone call and say, 'Where was I supposed to be heading to? The last thing I remember was I was in the compound talking to such and such about a car and now I'm out here.' And he had the directions. He kept three pads. He had kept a memo pad in his shirt pocket. He kept another pad on the dash of his wrecker. And he kept another memo pad like a notebook in the form of what Mr. Williams is writing on there on the front seat of the wrecker. Just so he could remember to do the one thing that he had to do. He had notes everywhere."

The irrational violence was also discussed. Mc-
Clung said:

"He would be listening to the radio. Sometimes
he would listen to religious stations on the radio
like WXRI, WYFI, and he would be talking to me,
saying, 'Isn't that good about Jesus?' He liked to
preach a lot, you know, and tell you things all about
Jesus. He did this for this person here. He was a
good man. He would go into these long spiels, these
religious talks, and then for no apparent reason he'd
get real violent and would . . . he would look at me
and he would say something like just [snaps fingers]
just change just like that and tell me, 'That S.O.B., I
wish I was the one that could nail him to the cross.'
That's exactly what he said to me many times."

McClung also said, "He'd be talking good about
religion and he'd pick up his Bible, start tearing
pages out of the Bible, call Jesus a S.O.B. again.
Take the Bible, throw it down, or just take the Bible,
stomp on it . . . and after he went through these fits
on the Bible, basically where he would just sit there
bewildered."

Rick Uhl said, "I've seen him at times ask me different questions about what I had read in the Bible,
because I had read the Bible frequently, and he said,
well, just basic general questions about that, and
I would start describing it to him, and there was
times that we weren't actually talking that he was
looking at a Bible, and he did take it . . . the pages
out and chuck the Bible right out the window and
it landed in the front yard. And then, a few minutes
later when he'd calm down, he'd come back in and
he'd look totally distressed. Like he did not know

who tore this book up. And he'd . . . sat down. I said, 'Tom, you ought not to be doing stuff like that in front of the kids,' but he acted as if he did not even know he tore these pages out."

Yet no matter how many corroborating statements were made by friends and coworkers, the decision still revolved around Dr. Dell's testimony. Finally H. P. Williams brought in the ultimate challenge, Dr. Phil Coons, a renowned psychiatrist who had been a member of the American Psychiatric Association committee that wrote the definition of multiple personality disorder currently in use by psychiatrists and psychologists throughout the country. Dr. Coons did not interview Tom Bonney. He was not asked to evaluate Bonney. Instead, he was being called to the witness stand to speak about the tests, test results, and methods for diagnosis that had been used by Dr. Dell.

"Multiple personality disorder, first of all, is seen much more commonly in women than men, and the trauma in women many times includes sexual abuse. It also includes physical abuse. In men there's less sexual abuse, more physical abuse. The trauma is generally extremely severe and it's sustained over a long period of time. And by extremely severe I mean we're talking about beatings, broken bones, cutting, burning, hanging, and over a long period of time. I mean, it generally starts in early childhood. Many times infancy. And goes anywhere from five to fifteen years," Dr. Coons explained.

"And based on your training and experience, is the death of a loved one sufficient trauma?" asked H. P. Williams.

"No, it's not."

Dr. Coons was then taken through the various symptoms of multiple personality disorder. The prosecutor wanted to make it clear that Tom Bonney did not fit the profile presented. First there was the issue of memory loss, a common symptom according to Dr. Coons, but his description was quite different from the way Bonney had behaved.

"One of the interesting things about the memory loss is that multiple personality patients hardly ever complain of having memory loss, and that's for a couple of reasons. One is if they are aware of it, they're afraid to talk about it for fear of being thought crazy. Most of the time they're not aware of it. It's like they forgot what they forgot. Or, you know, it's like they've been experiencing this since childhood. It's been such a long time that they experience the inconsistency in time as a normative experience, and when you first begin to point this out to the patient, they kind of say, 'Well, doesn't everybody have that problem?' "

"How about with regards to, in your diagnosis, should the presence of alters or personalities be apparent when not under hypnosis?"

"Well, to make a diagnosis of multiple personality disorder, you absolutely cannot make it definitely until you see alter personalities outside of hypnosis. You have to see the—the switching process and the evidence of alter personalities outside of hypnosis."

"You said that you have—you have to see the presence of alter personalities outside of hypnosis," said Williams. "Does that mean personally observe?" He was probing one of the critical issues of the trial.

"Personally observe," Dr. Coons said. He then continued, explaining:

"When a multiple switches personalities, they do it in various ways. Many take a few seconds to do this. Anywhere from two or three seconds to up to half a minute. They will kind of look tranced-out or spaced-out. They may drop their head. When the new personality comes out, their head comes up again. They open their eyes if they're closed. They kind of look around. They may appear puzzled. They may change their positions, fix their eyeglasses, those kinds of things, and what you see after they switch is a quote, unquote personality state that may look quite different from the one they switched from."

"What do you mean by 'may look quite different'?"

"Well, I say 'may' because sometimes the switching process is quite subtle, and the alter personality may not look a whole lot different from the other one."

"Would it be proper to make a diagnosis of multiple personality disorder based upon collateral contacts, interviews, and hypnosis alone, without having observed an alter outside of hypnosis?"

"It would not be proper." And again Dr. Dell's credibility was shattered with the jury.

Dr. Coons focused on the nature of the leading questions. He explained that he had seen the major symptoms of multiple personality but not the subtle ones. He also said that many of the subtle issues were tainted by the leading questions.

John Morrison took over the questioning of Dr. Coons in place of John Halstead after the prosecutor was through. He eventually was able to turn the past writings of the psychiatrist against him. He was able to get Dr. Coons to admit that "abusive families are rarely truthful initially." He also showed through the doctor's own writing on multiple personality that Tom Bonney had exhibited the symptoms that Dr. Coons felt were important for determining multiple personality.

The case had essentially been won or lost based on the testimony of the two experts, along with the comment made by close associates such as McClung and Uhl. However, neither side relied solely on such evidence. Other witnesses were called, including Christine Kelly, an acquaintance of Kathy's, who was able to relate an incident of seemingly unprovoked violence on the part of Tom Bonney one night.

Kathy "was upset," said Kelly. "And she said she needed to talk to her [Kelly's sister], and my sister was not at home at the time. So she asked if she had a number where she could be reached, and I said no. And she asked if I could take her to where she was, and I said yes. So we got in the car and I asked her what was wrong, and she said that . . . just as she was going to tell me, her father pulled up, and we were pulling off, and she said, 'Oh, no!' And she took off and he started chasing. And it was raining out.

"She says, 'Is there anywhere we could get away?' I figured I knew a place where we could get away from him, and so we went and we hit a telephone pole and the car stopped and we went on because we could still move. And at that time the car ran out of gas and we pulled into some lady's driveway. And we were just going to get out to get help, and her father had come up to the car and he opened up the door and he dragged her out by her hair, and they were yelling. I don't recall what they were yelling, and then I decided whether or not I should go get someone to help her or, you know, what to do. So I looked over at them and he had hit her, and I ran up to this lady's house and, by the time I got to the door, he had already taken off with Kathy in the car. And at that time the lady came to the door and we called the police."

"Okay," Williams said. "Now, in the car, as you were traveling, what, if anything, did Kathy tell you that he was going to do to her?"

"She was crying and she said, 'Oh, my God! He's gonna kill me!' "

"Okay. And what did you observe about Tom Bonney as he . . . when he came up to the car there after he had run out of gas?"

"He was very angry."

"And you say that he pulled her out of the car by her hair and you observed him hit her?"

"Yes."

"Okay. Had you ever had occasion to talk with Kathy about her relationship with her father?"

"She just told me that she was scared of him. She never really mentioned any reason why. She just said she had to do what he said because she was afraid of him."

"Did you ever hear her say that she loved him?" asked the prosecutor.

Christine Kelly responded, "No."

John Morrison was able to point out that the incident described by Christine took place three years earlier. She also admitted that she never heard Kathy say that she disliked her father.

When Jill Kelly, Christine's sister, testified, she was more specific. Jill, at one time Kathy's best friend, responded to the prosecutor's question of whether or not Kathy loved her father by saying, "Kathy did everything she could to please the man, and nothing worked. And I do believe she did love him, but she also was afraid of him."

Jill Kelly's testimony was hurt by her own admission that she and Kathy had gotten into trouble together. "Miss Kelly, the trouble you got in with Kathy was you were shoplifting," said John Halstead. "Is that correct?"

"Yes."

"And you also got kicked out of school for breaking windows?"

"Yes."

"And you and Kathy did that together, didn't you?"

"Yes."

Bruce Hansberry, Kathy's boyfriend during the 1985–86 school year when Kathy was at the Open Door Christian Academy, told of Kathy's having to sneak out to date him. He told of their going to the local mall to watch a movie when they thought her father would not be aware. "I was walking her back to her truck after just seeing a movie, and I opened up the door for her, and just as she was stepping in, Mr. Bonney comes running around from the back of the truck, grabs her arm right above her elbow, yanks her out, and sets her against the car that was parked next to her truck, and he hit her. Didn't . . . with the knuckles on his hand. Just backhanded her like that [demonstrates], and it was a real hard hit. It knocked her whole body around."

"Did you hear them say anything to each other?" asked the prosecutor.

"Yes. He was calling her 'bastard, tramp, whore.' Just—"

"What did she say to him?"

"She was saying, 'Leave me alone,' and telling me to run."

"She calling him any names?"

"A few cuss words, yeah."

"What was she calling him?"

" 'Asshole," and I think she called him 'bastard' too. It was yelling names back and forth, and she was telling me to run. And he had threatened me then too. He said if he saw us together, he was going to kill the both of us."

Like all the incidents described, there was more to the story than had been stated. Bruce thought that he might have gotten Kathy pregnant. His mother called Carol Bonney and suggested that Kathy be taken to a clinic for testing. Bruce had not gotten Kathy pregnant, but Tom Bonney knew that the two of them had had sex, and he was furious about the relationship.

The jury had a case where the answers were uncertain at best. For every incident quoted in Tom

Bonney's life, there appeared to be more than one explanation. Was Tom a violent multiple personality or an overly protective, but well intentioned father of a rebellious teenager? Was his anger toward her boyfriends Oedipal, or did he just have normal fatherly concern for a daughter he believed was trying to grow up too fast?

After two weeks of preliminaries such as jury selection, and four weeks of testimony, unusually long for such a trial, it was over. Only the summation of the testimony was left.

The defense team had two responsibilities. One was to present the evidence in summation in such a manner that the jury was as lenient as possible. John Halstead truly believed that Tom Bonney was emotionally ill, a multiple personality, to the degree that he understood what that meant, and reacting to the stress of his early child abuse. He did not want to see his client die. He knew that Tom would have to go to jail or to prison hospital, that he needed intense psychological counseling. He knew that Tom might be given a sentence that would keep him locked away for the rest of his life, and that was something he had to accept. But the idea of taking Tom's life because of a murder committed by an emotionally unstable individual horrified him. He needed to present the evidence in such a manner that the jury would not send Tom to death row.

The second concern was in presenting enough information that there would be grounds for a valid appeal should the jury find Tom Bonney guilty as charged. This included even such seemingly minor issues as where Kathy was killed. One theory was that Kathy was killed in Virginia, then transported to North Carolina before being dumped and her corpse riddled with bullets. If this was the case, then trying Tom in North Carolina would be declared improper. A new trial would be granted, that trial to be held in Virginia.

All of these concerns had to be mentioned and stressed. An appeal has to be based either on new evidence, which no one expected to find, or mistakes made during the trial. Such mistakes include only those matters which are in the court records. Thus all possible appeal points must come out, and usually that means including them in the summation.

The early part of the defense summation was spent raising reasonable doubt about Tom's mental state. For example, it was noted: "There is the absence of all the clothing at the scene. I believe what was recovered was her sweater, her undergarments, and, perhaps, one or two other items. I can't recall. But shoes, other items of clothing were missing.

"Sure. They could have floated away in the canal, or they could have been placed somewhere else. Could have been placed somewhere else when this thing took place. Ingenuity of counsel. I say it's something you have to think about.

"Tom said he left her where she was shot, and it was on the side of the road and it was two lanes. That came in from the state's evidence. All right. Now, that sounds kind of contradictory, doesn't it? Left her on the side of the road. Well, we know she wasn't left on the side of the road. We know she was on the edge of the canal bank. Here is the side of the road. Here is the side of the road. She wasn't there. She was on the canal bank.

"Does he remember what happened? I say to you he does not. But if you're going to believe him, then if she was left on the side of the road, you are going to have to take into account that he cannot remember certain other things. And, therefore, some of his testimony should not be believed."

On and on it went, raising the issue of reasonable doubt. The testimony was confusing, contradictory. If the jury could not be certain about its decision, the penalty for Tom might be less.

Even the multiple bullet wounds had to be considered in context. Was there a struggle, during which Kathy was not only shot but also killed? The head wound that may have been the first wound she received was a fatal shot. The fact that twenty-six other bullets were fired into the body meant less under law if they were fired into a corpse. Shooting a dead person is not much of a crime anywhere in the United States. It is only shooting a living person where the issue of first degree murder is raised. And if her death was accidental, the penalty for any action after her death is always less than when it takes place before her death.

John Halstead stressed other aspects of the case, especially the issue of mental illness. He was aware that Dr. Dell's credibility had suffered greatly, yet he also was certain that Dell was correct. He wanted to point out that the belief in Bonney's mental state was not just based on the doctor's examination.

"Now, some might think that John [Morrison] and I have relied totally on Dr. Dell and his testimony to establish the defense of insanity. But, again, I submit to you that there are indicators far beyond, far before Dr. Dell became involved, to indicate the mental illness which Tom Bonney suffers from.

"November twenty-first, 1987, after Kathy had been killed, Tom comes home, walks in the house, and what is the first thing that he asks? 'Where's Kathy?' His first question was 'Where's Kathy?'

"Now, a sane man, a person who was in their right mind, would walk in and say immediately, oh, by the way, Kathy's test driving and will be home pretty soon. That's what he did say later. But the first time, his first question was 'Where's Kathy?' Of course, unbelieving or wondering what in the world he's talking about, his wife then asked, well . . . or says, 'She left with you.'

"And that's when he says, 'Oh, that's right. She's test driving the Blazer.' Now, at this point in time we don't know whether or not Tom's confabulating, which you heard Dr. Dell explain. It's not intentional lying, but it's people who suffer from multiple personality disorder. That's when a person takes one event, puts it together with another event in time, and takes what happened in the middle, sense of what happened, in the middle. It's not something they do. Not something they intentionally lie about, or whatever.

"Maybe it was an intentional lie, though. I don't know that it's really important. But multiple personalities, people we know who suffer from this disorder, from his illness, often do lie because they don't want constantly to have to explain why they cannot remember blank periods of time in their experience. If they every day had to explain why they can't remember or what they were doing, or whatever, people would think they were crazy. And, of course, nobody wants to be thought of that way. Even those who might be."

The statements continued, showing how the actions of Tom Bonney indicated emotional disturbance. And then he made a defense of Dr. Dell. He stressed how little time the doctor had in which to work, how quickly he had to gain Tom Bonney's trust, how much had to be accomplished in a very short period of time.

Next he pointed out issues that the prosecutor had avoided. He noted that while the prosecution and the police had relatively unlimited access to Tom, the doctor had to be out of the jail by seven P.M. no matter what was happening, no matter what benefits might be gained from even a few minutes extra time.

"I hope you will keep in mind that Tom Bonney has had to rely basically on three people: John Morrison, myself, and the assistance of Dr. Dell. We've not had the SBI [State Bureau of Investigation]. We haven't had laboratories in Raleigh. We haven't had divers from Chesapeake. We haven't had police officers from Chesapeake. We haven't had witness coordinators sitting with our witnesses. We haven't had these resources."

By the time H. P. Williams gave his summary, his job was a fairly simple one. Tom Bonney was guilty of shooting his daughter. No one had disputed that fact.

There were three main concerns he had to face. The first was any moral or religious constraint against letting the state take Tom Bonney's life. John Morrison had made spiritual references based on both his beliefs and what he knew to be the beliefs of most of the people in the community. In fact, Donna Forbes, an attorney for the district attorney's office who assisted H. P. Williams during the trial, was a Quaker for whom the capital punishment aspect of the case was extremely upsetting.

"Mr. Morrison ended his talk to you by referring to our Christ on the cross and him saying, 'Forgive them, for they know not what they have done,'" said the district attorney. "You know, our God does forgive us whenever we ask for it, and the mere fact that he forgives and that we forgive doesn't mean that we shouldn't be punished, that we should not have to face up to the responsibility for what they do, or for what we do. And if we ask for forgiveness, we get it. But first we have to ask."

Then he continued with a quote. "'And what doth the Lord require of thee but to do justly, to love mercy, and to walk humbly with thy God.' To do humbly, to love mercy, and to walk . . . to love justice, to love mercy, and walk humbly with thy God. Mercy means forgiveness, and you can have forgiveness and still punish."

Finally, after working to show that the evidence proved the murder regardless of what else may have happened, and pointing out that side issues were irrelevant to the fact of the killing, he addressed the elements of murder necessary for a legal finding of guilty in the first degree. He said that the first element required that the murder was intentional and done with malice, which he defined as "hatred, ill will, spite. It's also that condition of the mind that prompts a person to take another's life without justification or excuse. No justification. No excuse whatsoever.

"Second, the state must prove the defendant's acts were the cause of her death. The shooting of Kathy Bonney was the cause. I think that's clear.

"Third, the defendant intended to kill the victim. That is, a specific intent to kill. And you prove it by the circumstances. Look at the number of shots. Where were the shots? Were they scattered all over the body, the ones that did the killing, as though in a blind rage, or is there a pattern? Two contact wounds to the forehead, or this side [indicates]. Two contact wounds to the forehead. The rest, total of eleven, I think, in the face. And then there to the left chest. Do you remember as a kid you'd pledge allegiance to the flag, put your right hand over your left side because that's the side where the heart beats, and how many of you were shocked to find out that the heart is really in the middle? Those shots concentrated on the left side. The heart. An intent to kill. And they're not shots in the car. They're shots at more than two feet away."

The fourth issue was premeditation. He mentioned Kathy's intention to move out, the discovery of the sex letter, the making up of the story about the Blazer, the shifting of the gun from the wrecker to the car, the taking of the extra bullets. All the reasons why premeditation was clear.

The final concern was deliberation, which under the law could occur whether Bonney was calm, angry, or in an emotional state. "The fact that there was a quarrel does not mean that he didn't act in a cool state of blood with the intent to kill. You look at the circumstances again. You look at the lack of provocation by Kathy Bonney. There was some indication by Dr. Dell she called him a bastard. But she'd done it before. And words alone are not enough.

"In this statement to the police he said it was a small fuss. Then you look at the conduct of the defendant during and after the killing. Look at his conduct during the killing. The way that he unloaded the gun, put the bullets in his pocket, loaded it again. Look at the number of shots and where they are. Look at the Missing Persons report the next day, and when they asked for a picture, how he put them off and said, 'I don't have time tonight.' Look at his flight to another state when it came time to fess up. Look at the threats and declarations of the defendant. Had he made threats before? Look at the use of grossly excessive force, the infliction of lethal wounds after the victim is down. Look at the brutal or vicious circumstances of the killing, the manner or means by which the killing was done, the manner the body was treated after the wounds were inflicted, the way all the clothes were cut off, the way that she was thrown down the canal bank. Look at the nature and number of wounds, the unseemly conduct toward and concealment of the body."

And when he was finished, H. P. Williams said, "Ladies and gentlemen, at some point we have to become a part of the law, not just support it. The time is now. It will not be an easy chore. You will do a lot of soul searching. You will pray and you may cry, but in the end the right thing will be done.

"In your deliberations I ask you to remember Kathy, and if you say a prayer, say one for her. And if you shed a tear, shed one for her. And remember that the aggravating circumstance in this case is sufficient, is substantially sufficient to call for the imposition of the death penalty. Anyone who would treat his child in this way deserves to die. And, ladies and gentlemen, it's your duty to recommend that he be sentenced to death. Thank you."

The end came in two stages, but there was little doubt about what it would be. North Carolina jurors first decide guilt or innocence. Then the same jury decides the penalty.

Jury Foreman William Forbes presented the decision to the judge after six hours of deliberation. "We, the jury, by unanimous verdict, find the defendant, Thomas Lee Bonney, to be guilty of first degree murder." A brief presentation was made before the penalty phase, but again the results were predictable. "We, the jury, unanimously recommend that the defendant, Thomas Lee Bonney, be sentenced to death."

Epilogue

THERE are many kinds of truth. The jury in the Tom
Bonney trial found that he was guilty of shooting his
daughter, then leaving her corpse along the Dismal
Swamp Canal bank. Their decision was based on
the facts presented in court and it was one type of
truth.

Paul Dell and John Halstead felt that although
the body of Tom Bonney was responsible for taking the life of his daughter, Kathy, there were
other factors involved. He did not realize that
he was shooting his daughter. In his mind, frag-
mented by his multiple personality, traumatized
by post-traumatic stress syndrome, Tom Bonney
was a small child abused once too often by a
violent father. He committed parricide, deliberately shooting what he thought was a parent who,
though long dead, continued to violently affect
his thoughts and actions. The fact that it was
his daughter, not his father, who endured the
twenty-seven gunshots was never fully understood

by Tom and several of the personalities. This, too, was truth.

H. P. Williams recognized that Tom might very well have been a multiple personality. He felt that a part of the mind, a unique personality, might have committed the murder as the defense alleged. But that part had to pay a penalty, and if the penalty affected all other parts, then that is what would happen. And so he could live with the death penalty even if Tom Bonney was a multiple personality, suffering from a dissociative disorder of a lesser sort, or even experiencing post-traumatic stress syndrome. Again, a third type of truth.

There is a deeper truth than comes from a court of law, however. This is the truth that evolves from knowing all that has taken place, all that has influenced the events that culminated in a shocking, controversial trial. It is not the truth of the courtroom, where only guilt or innocence has to be determined. It is not justification for the unjustifiable, for as Kathy Bonney once wrote, saying "I'm sorry" is something you do when you bump someone with your cart while in a supermarket. It is not a valid statement for when you have killed your own child.

The truth about Tom Bonney's murder of his daughter took months to uncover because no one had asked enough questions. Everyone was too concerned with gaining a conviction or trying to protect him from death row.

Tom Bonney's own statements made several years before the murder provided the first clue to the greater truth. The statements were made when the stress of living began to be too much for him. He referred to himself as a "walking time bomb," according to those who were closest to him. "When I go off, everyone's going to know it," he stated. Yet no one truly listened to his words. No one thought about the possible consequences of such statements until it was too late.

Tom Bonney was a whiner. His low self-esteem, his unwillingness or inability to respect or care for anyone outside his immediate family, and his desperate desire for approval from both his parents made him seem harmless. He looked and sounded weak, withdrawn, the kind of man who could be dominated by any authority figure. Yet the appearance belied the growing anger within. Instead of being broken by life, he was constantly suppressing rage that would eventually overwhelm all his emotional defenses.

Tom was like Hitman, the personality who, under hypnosis with Dr. Dell, appeared to be someone whose role in life was to suffer abuse. Yet those who knew Tom knew that Hitman was a schemer, a plotter, a man who planned to commit the perfect murder. Not that they took Hitman seriously. A balding, whining, overweight, rather unattractive individual who claims to look just like actor Clint Eastwood is difficult to respect. He seems silly, a buffoon, a caricature of evil at whom you can laugh. What they did not realize was that in his tortured mind, Hitman did wish to kill and would ultimately come to stalk his own daughter.

Because of the anger, the suppression, and the fantasies, Kathy Bonney was marked for death for at least three years prior to the time of the murder. Not that Tom knew he was going to kill his own daughter. Not that he could imagine doing any violence to her except when absolutely necessary in response to her rebellious actions, such as hanging out with a girl who shoplifted and vandalized, and with a boy who seduced her. Thus the violence he increasingly showed toward his daughter was interpreted as overly harsh but understandable parental discipline. What no one could see was that inside his mind he had built a fantasy family with which he was comfortable. The moment that fantasy was challenged, either Tom Bonney had to adapt to real life or he had to destroy any reminder of real life that was forcing him to abandon his beliefs. It was easier for Tom Bonney's mind to plan the destruction of the threat than to adapt to the truth. Reality made him human, vulnerable, having to face himself, to see if he was as bad as his father had convinced him he might be. Fantasy was without vulnerability, without pain, a world he controlled and from which all challenges were blocked.

Tom did not and could not understand what was happening to him as the pressures mounted, though he did realize that if he "exploded," he would be completely out of control. "When I go off, everyone's going to know it," he had said, though not even he fully understood the meaning of that comment.

And so, as the pressure increased, Tom Bonney believed that he would never be so harsh as his own father. He could not conceive of the idea of humiliating his children as he had been humiliated when forced to spend much of the night cutting grass with a scissors. But he also would not spare the rod, using the back of his hand to teach Kathy never to be a "Lou," his term for a "loser."

Kathy's date with death began when Tom feared that his daughter was pregnant. Her sexual coming of age had shattered his fantasies. His family was supposed to be the Waltons. His daughter was the female equivalent of John Boy Walton, a writer, a dreamer, someone who would become famous yet never really leave home.

John Boy never had sex. John Boy did not sneak around. John Boy was not a slut. . . .

"I love Kathy. I love Kathy so much," he would tell anyone who would listen.

But Kathy was maturing, whether Tom Bonney liked it or not. And while she genuinely cared for her father, she could not handle his restrictions. She needed to be free from the oppressive ways he used to try to mold her into the image of a character from a television show.

John McClung had helped reduce the growing tension, paying for Kathy to attend a Christian school. The ambivalent feelings Tom had toward religion did not alter the fact that she would probably get into less trouble in the parochial setting. Even Kathy found a degree of freedom there because, though there were restrictions set by the school's administration, the school was also an escape from the demands of her father. More important, Tom Bonney could not claim that Kathy would meet the wrong element at a Christian school, not the way he claimed he loved Jesus.

The Christian school triggered other emotions, though. There was Tom Bonney's internal ambivalence. This was a man who wept for Jesus who had been crucified on the cross, then cursed him for taking his father's life before they could be reconciled, for taking his grandmother from his side when he needed her protection, for so many things.

When religious pressure overcame him, Tom said that he wished he had been present at the crucifixion to drive the nails, the bastard! He said Jesus got what He deserved.

"I love Kathy so much. And I love Jesus." And he did, each in the same way. Neither one had acted as he believed they should. But Jesus was dead. Only Kathy could take the brunt of his rage.

"When I go off, everyone's going to know it."

There were problems between Tom and Carol because of his obsessions. He claimed he loved her, then put her down, criticizing her cooking, her cleaning, her impatience with his work.

There was no criticism among the Waltons. The parents were loving, mutually supportive. Everyone was cleaned, fed, cared for, even in the worst of times during the Depression.

In his fantasy, the Bonneys and the Waltons were one. Real life could never compete with what was taking place within his head.

And the pressure was rising.

Tom Bonney was also having trouble with his cash flow. Over the course of a year, the money was excellent. There was no question of that. With the help of his partners, Tom Bonney was making more money than he had ever made in his life. He could afford to buy luxuries, even though some were secondhand. But he made the same mistake that many people make when their financial circumstances change suddenly. He analyzed each purchase in light of his income. He never looked at the total he was spending. And he never looked to the lean periods which were part of the inevitable cycle of the business he owned. He was amassing what would soon be overwhelming total debt. Creditors were calling, adding their pressure.

Creditors never called the Waltons. They were never bothered with past due notices, eviction notices, the need to change names in order to work one more scam to stay afloat.

Grandma Walton was also supportive, loving, pleased with what John Boy's father was trying to do. Kathy's grandmother never appreciated what Tom Bonney tried to do. He took over her debts, rented her a house, then worked night and day for her approval, which never came.

The world was increasingly out of control, reality intruding on so well-reasoned a fantasy that Tom felt threatened by it.

Then came the sneaking around. Kathy maintained friendships only by having girls pretend they were someone other than themselves. Once Tom learned about what he considered too close a relationship, he forbid Kathy to be with the girl, forcing deception for the sake of a normal friendship Kathy so desperately needed.

Boys were seen on the sly. Sexually explicit, male-oriented magazines were purchased by Kathy, hidden, then studied in private. Kathy had been traumatized by early sexual experiences, but she knew that sex with the right young man was good, healthy, joyous. She was scared, as she admitted to John Hoskins. Yet she was determined to overcome the problems, to take an apartment, to be her own woman physically, emotionally, financially.

Kathy came to fear her father, though probably not to the degree that others testified. Tom frequently threatened to kill his daughter and other members of the family. He had a gun. He had a temper. But he did not explode, not in the ways they anticipated, and so Kathy hung on, saving her money, not realizing the tension building in her father's disturbed mind.

"When I go off, everyone's going to know it."

It is hard to say if Tom knew of Kathy's plans to obtain her own apartment. Possibly he did. Possibly he did not. It did not matter either way. She was leaving emotionally. She was defiant, acting in ways he could not tolerate.

Perhaps things would have been all right had Kathy been agreeable to Tom's plans. He was thinking of renting her her own home, a place near his, much as he had rented a house for his mother. She would be on her own, writing her stories and poems, still working at the junkyard, still being a part of the family. That's what would have happened for John Boy had he not moved to New York from Walton's Mountain. And though Kathy was a writer, she could do that from Chesapeake. It was all right. She would make out, loving her father and he loving her.

But Kathy was not following her father's plans. She was too independent, too willful. He may have decided to kill her at least a week before her death. That was when he began acting strangely, such as taking the revolver down in Kathy's presence, loading the weapon, looking at her, unloading it, and returning it to the shelf. Kathy told her father's business partner of her uneasiness, though any violence she may have expected from her father was not toward herself. That idea apparently never entered her mind. She just sensed that something was wrong, perhaps dangerously so. As to the past, many people threaten to "kill" their children. They use the term without meaning. Tom Bonney had used it so often that no one took him seriously, even when the level of tension seemed to change.

Kathy had no awareness that she faced extreme danger. She just knew that something was seriously wrong, that it would be impossible to safely stay in the house much longer. She talked about that fact with friends, yet did not resist their suggestion to stay a little longer, to accumulate a little more money, decide upon a place to go, then make the move.

The letter to John Hoskins was probably the ultimate cause of the murder, though there would have been something else if Tom had not been snooping about her possessions. He could not let his daughter become a woman independent from his control. He could not let her shatter his fantasy, because to do so would bring forth reality, and reality was too painful to experience.

Reality was constant rejection by his father, his mother, by everyone around him. Reality was that

Tom Bonney was the "Lou" he did not want his children to be. Reality was that Tom Bonney was a man filled with self-hate, a streetwise con artist who never was able to truly get ahead. And Kathy Bonney alive, independent, happy on her own was a mirror to her father's failings.

Kathy Bonney's death put Tom Bonney back in control. With just himself, his wife, and the surviving children, they could be the Waltons again. John Boy would be gone, but perhaps one of the others could be Mary Ellen. And didn't Tom like to write a bit? Perhaps he could be both father and son.

Or the family could continue as it was, Kathy living inside her father's head where everything she said, everything she did, fit the fantasy Tom Bonney so desperately desired to be true. All the children would be there for him, even if he was the only one who could talk to his oldest daughter.

And so he killed her, angrily, contemptuously. Exactly who did the planning and pulled the trigger is uncertain. My research suggests that it was Hitman. Dr. Dell leans more toward Demian, which would make Hitman the one who would take care of hiding the body at the crime scene. Yet that point is uncertain since none of the personalities has taken credit for stripping and moving the body.

No matter who among the alter personalities may have been at fault, the violence almost certainly stemmed from causes that were simpler and less dramatic than the cases each side tried to make in court. Kathy may or may not have been the first to grab the gun when she and her father argued. Certainly she called him a bastard, because she had used the word many times against him in the past, and frequently in front of witnesses to their quarrels. Certainly he was known to become extremely angry when called by that name. But when he killed, Tom Bonney was probably not in flashback, probably not reacting to his father.

Tom Bonney was enraged. His daughter's sexual maturity had shattered the fantasy world he had so carefully created for himself. He saw her as a slut, humiliating her in death by stripping her clothing from her corpse and dumping her naked body by the canal. Whether the first bullet to strike her was an accident or deliberately fired, his anger caused him to continue shooting round after round until he exhausted both his emotions and his ammunition. If he faced the truth about his child, the knowledge that his family was not the fantasy world of the Waltons would destroy him. It was easier, in his mind, to kill the daughter he loved.

Is Tom Bonney a multiple personality? Probably. I refer to Tom as the murderer, knowing that the trigger may have been pulled by one of two alter personalities. Since all shared the same body, saying "Tom" is easier than trying to determine which actions were those of Hitman or Demian, Satan or Mammy, or any of the others. Not all the personalities wanted to see Kathy dead. Some wept for her, as Tom has mourned during those few moments when truth penetrates his life. One or more may still be hidden.

Would the fact that he is a multiple personality have justified his being cleared of murder? Certainly not. He is guilty of shooting his daughter in a premeditated and heinous manner. He was not insane by the standards of North Carolina, and the law requires that either he be put to death or locked away for the rest of his natural life.

Oddly, the mandatory appeals are so costly that it will be cheaper for the state to let him live out his natural life than to execute him. Yet the appeals continue, his lawyer hoping that his life will be spared, even though he will most likely never again be free.

The rest of the Bonney family is in turmoil. As of this writing, Kathy's brothers and sisters remained in foster care. Their promised return had not come about, and, so far as Carol knew, might not, because of Carol's long-term image of family instability while she was married to Tom.

Kathy's mother, untrained for most employment, is trying to make money any way she can. She asked to be paid for an interview for this book, was refused, and never did talk to the author despite repeated efforts to interview her. Similar requests for money have allegedly been made by Carol to others looking into the case, either a sign of hopeless desperation or a sad effort to exploit the murder.

And Tom Bonney has become close friends with a Mountain City, Tennessee, woman whom he has convinced of his "innocence." She runs a prison ministry and would like to arrange for the "true" story to be told, believing his protestations of innocence because she was never exposed to the facts, including the taped confession. She even felt that the true name of the killer came to her after much prayer, but the name she turned over to H. P. Williams was a composite of the first name of one investigator on the case and the last name of another investigator. She is hoping to get involved with one or more books and movies covering Tom's ordeal. She is certain of his ultimate triumph and release. She ultimately wants to use the money to pay him to join her in her outreach ministry.

John Halstead, tired of the stress such cases bring, declared himself a candidate for judge in the multicounty area that surrounds Elizabeth City. He continues to involve himself in the cases no one else will take, always working understaffed compared to criminal defense attorneys in bigger cities with bigger budgets. He is a seeker of truth, a defender of justice, and a man willing to care about the unlovable, traits that are physically and emotionally exhausting. He is a respected man, and becoming a judge would give him a chance to continue in the law without the responsibility of knowing a man might live or die by his skills. He may ultimately have to sentence someone to death, but that decision will be based on the letter of the law following the jury's deliberation. As a judge, he would no longer be in the arena where the evidence is presented for the jury's consideration.

Only H. P. Williams is fully comfortable with the outcome. He proved the charges against Tom Bonney, won the case, and served his master—the Constitution of the United States. He has shown by his past that if there ever is reason to change his opinion about a man or woman he convicts, he has the courage and humility to retrace his steps, reevaluate the case, and fight for the release of the wronged prisoner. He has also shown through the facts that the only aspect of the Bonney case that may change will be the penalty phase. He deservedly rests well knowing that whatever drove Tom Bonney to kill his daughter will never again result in Tom's taking of a life.

Finally, there is Kathy. Her life of promise was destroyed, but this time no one let the killer get away with just saying "I'm sorry." If her religious beliefs are accurate, she is at peace, joined with God, moving on to wherever human existence continues after the death of the body. Yet for Tom Bonney, Kathy is at last a part of him, totally obedient, loving and comforting, resting with Demian, Satan, Viking, Hitman, Dad, Mammy, and all the others, inside his troubled mind.